DUCHESS BY DESIGN

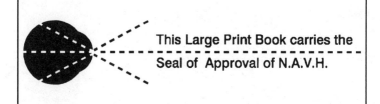

This Large Print Book carries the
Seal of Approval of N.A.V.H.

THE GILDED AGE GIRLS CLUB

DUCHESS BY DESIGN

MAYA RODALE

THORNDIKE PRESS
A part of Gale, a Cengage Company

Farmington Hills, Mich • San Francisco • New York • Waterville, Maine
Meriden, Conn • Mason, Ohio • Chicago

LIBRARY OF CONGRESS CIP DATA ON FILE.
CATALOGUING IN PUBLICATION FOR THIS BOOK
IS AVAILABLE FROM THE LIBRARY OF CONGRESS

ISBN-13: 978-1-4328-6091-2 (hardcover)

Published in 2019 by arrangement with Avon Books, an imprint of HarperCollins Publishers

Printed in the United States of America
1 2 3 4 5 6 7 23 22 21 20 19

*To everyone who has
taken a chance on me*

PROLOGUE

London, 1895
White's Club
St James's Street

His Grace, Brandon Alexander Fiennes, the Duke of Kingston, had the good fortune to inherit a prestigious title, exceedingly good looks, and an impressive though impoverished estate. One might think this was enough, but in an ever-changing world, it was not. He also required a fortune. And for that, he needed a woman.

"The dukedom is broke." Kingston — for he was Kingston now — confided in his friend and cousin, Freddie, Lord Hewitt. They were in White's, where generations of noblemen before them had drank, smoked, gambled, and lamented the sort of problems that only the most privileged men in the world had the luxury to suffer.

"You only just inherited and already you've lost everything?" Freddie replied with a quirk of his brow. He *would* make light of this situation. "And here I thought you were the responsible one of us."

"Not that it's any great comparison."

Freddie flashed that grin, the one designed to undo any manner of trouble. It would not work now. Not with a matter this grave. Kingston didn't even know why he'd brought it up to Freddie — lighthearted, featherbrained Freddie — except that they weren't just friends or family. They were both, thick as thieves, and had been ever since they'd toddled out of the nursery to charm the cook into serving them extra biscuits with tea.

Kingston's utterly irresponsible, wastrel of a parent had gone on to the other side and left his son and heir with a prestigious title, a few cash-strapped estates, some crushing debts, and female dependents. It wasn't just expected that Kingston would be the one to save them all; people were counting on it.

"It really is unfortunate," Freddie said, punctuating the remark with a dramatic pause before he leaned in. That grin again. "Did you see what I did there? Unfortunate. Literally without fortune. Like you."

Kingston shook his head.

"Eton and Oxford were wasted on you."

"Glad to see you still have your sense of

humor while your ancestral lands are on the chopping block," Freddie carried on. "But I imagine a thousand acres of prime Berkshire farmland ought to go for a good sum. What will you do with the proceeds?"

Kingston wasn't so sure about proceeds. If the lands were sold for any decent amount of money, it was so they might be developed or mined. Farming wasn't exactly a profitable venture these days. Those lush rolling hills his ancestors had claimed — gone. Those thick forests where generations of Kingstons had hunted and haunted — gone. The feeling that these lands were their birthright and would last forever — cruelly wrenched away.

"I imagine the lot of it will go toward fixing the roof at Lyon House."

Hewitt gave a low whistle. "That's a lot of roof."

"It's a lot of house."

"Ever think of selling and settling into something more cozy?"

"Like Buckingham Palace? The damn thing is entailed. My choices are to keep it in good repair or keep it in disrepair."

The upkeep on old castles and crumbling manor houses was not cheap. There was no money left over for investments, improvements, or anything other than the most essential repairs, so that the infernal draft never got fixed. At any of the houses. Plural.

There wasn't enough for his sisters' dowries, modern girls who had ideas about marrying for love. There wasn't enough to keep his mother, the duchess, in the style to which she was accustomed. It did not help that his mother's style was best described as wildly extravagant and always *au courant.* Lord save him from dressmakers and their bills. Lord save him from women with intentions to be leaders of fashion.

"What about torching the lot of it and collecting insurance money?"

"Besides the fact that it is dishonorable and illegal? Freddie, the house is made of stone that has survived *actual wars.* I doubt *your* attempts at arson will be its undoing."

"Have I mentioned that I am so glad to have been born a second son and thus never to have to make such decisions?"

"I think we're all glad of that fact."

"There is one glaringly obvious solution to your problem."

"Of course — something countless generations of men such as myself have done when in dire straits." Kingston took a bracing sip of whiskey before he said the words aloud. It was one thing to think them, privately in the confines of one's study when reviewing the tragic account books. It was another to admit it aloud.

"You'll have to follow my example, for once. You'll have to marry an heiress," Freddie said. "As I have done."

"A marriage of convenience."

"The stuff love stories are made of."

"Be still my beating heart."

"Being grossly unsuited for the clergy, army, or any employment — and one who has recently become wed to an heiress myself — I can well advise you on this plan," Freddie said. "There is only one obstacle. All the other peers — and their daughters — are as broke as you."

"I'm sure someone is still doing well," Kingston said. "Huntley invested in the railroads. We'd all mocked him then — my father especially — but who is laughing now?"

"Huntley is, all the way to the Bank of England. He doesn't have any daughters though," Freddie said. "The problem is that heiresses are not exactly thick on the ground in England these days. And the ones that are here know that blokes just want their money. Makes things dashed hard for a mere second son. That's why I had to travel abroad to find my heiress."

"Good thing I'm a duke. Will trade ancient

11

and prestigious title for cold hard cash. A love story for the ages."

"Aye, you just have to walk in and announce yourself, don't you? Well, as long as you're not keen to wed someone who you'll want to cozy up to in that drafty old house, that plan should work out fine for you. Because let me tell you about the girls who are out this season who come with money . . ."

Freddie told him about the girls who were out this season who came with money. He listed their names, described their personalities, appearances, etc. The list was not long. The options were not appealing, which posed the question: how much of himself was he willing to sacrifice to preserve his way of life and protect the women in his family from any hardship?

He'd always been the responsible one.

He'd been born knowing the right thing — the noble thing — to do and he'd been born with the fortitude to do it.

"If you really want to wed a wealthy bride, there's only one way to go about it." Freddie downed the last of his drink, leaned forward dramatically, and said: "You will have to go to America."

CHAPTER ONE

Manhattan's dollar princesses ought to pinch their cheeks and don their finest: the Duke of Kingston is enroute to New York City in search of his future duchess.
— *The New York World*

New York City, 1895
The Fifth Avenue Hotel

A chance encounter with the duke was only the second most interesting thing to happen to Miss Adeline Black that afternoon, but that was life in New York City for you. One never knew whom one might meet, what good fortune or disaster might befall you, or when you will crash into the town's most eligible bachelor in the lobby of the Fifth Avenue Hotel.

Tuesday. That's when.

Tuesday, precisely seven minutes before two o'clock in the afternoon.

This meant that she had precisely seven

13

minutes to make her way through the vast hall of the Fifth Avenue Hotel on her way to the suite of rooms of Miss Harriet Burnett. Adeline didn't know her from Adam, but she knew an opportunity to change her life and make her dreams come true when it requested a two-o'clock appointment.

She could not be late.

But this lobby was an absolute crush. The great hall was full of everything a hotel guest could want — from tickets to tea — and it was packed with the city's wealthiest and most prestigious guests. They strutted their stuff, showed off their finery, made deals, and traded gossip in the luscious surroundings of the city's most exclusive and opulent hotel.

And they got in her way.

These out-of-towners walked slowly in front of her, delaying her progress to the elevator, to Miss Burnett's rooms on the top floor, to her future.

For the occasion, Adeline wore her best ensemble: a plum-colored walking dress paired with a crisp white shirtwaist bearing a cascade of delicate little ruffles from her throat to her waist. The cropped jacket was darling, edged in gold cord and tailored to show off her narrow waist. A simple matching hat was perched perfectly on her dark

14

hair. On her feet were French-style heels like *ladies* wore, though hers were purchased from a pushcart downtown for the astronomical sum of a week's wages. But they were worth it.

They pinched her toes, but they were *so* worth it.

Adeline darted to the left to avoid a trio of Wall Street types in three-piece suits lumbering toward her with no regard for the people in their path. She spun to the right to dodge a pair of ladies, deep in conversation as they walked. She had too much momentum going to stop herself when a man stepped into her path and turned toward her.

And so she crashed into his firm, muscled chest. Firm, muscled arms enveloped her. She took a deep breath of evergreen-scented soap and clean linen and man. She noted the feel of exceptionally fine cashmere wool against her cheek.

Adeline stilled. And, in all honesty, she savored the moment. It was not every day that a seamstress found herself in a gentleman's arms, at least in such a respectable fashion.

Well, on Tuesdays.

Except, apparently, on Tuesdays.

Adeline took a step and tilted her head

back to look at the gentleman with whom she collided.

He *felt* like he'd be handsome and the truth did not disappoint. He had the kind of good looks a woman just wanted to stare at all day, all night, and then again at the breakfast table. Forever.

There was something about that well-groomed dark brown hair. Something about those deep blue eyes and the faint lines at the corners. Something about that firm, sensuous mouth cocked into a seductive half smile.

"Well, hello." His voice was low, his accent distinctly British. Her heart fluttered. "Are you all right, miss?"

She was more than all right.

"Besides being left breathless, I think I am just fine." She flashed him a flirtatious smile because he was a handsome fellow and she was in the mood to seize opportunities today. "And yourself? Have you recovered from your display of heroics?"

"Oh, I don't know that I would call catching you heroic. Any decent gentleman would try to catch a pretty girl when she was falling."

Adeline smiled at him the unfeigned way of a girl just complimented by a handsome man and leaned in close to say, "Don't look now, but everyone is watching us. You'll be the talk of the town by supper."

"You're assuming I'm not the talk of the town already."

"Ah, you're a confident one. You'll fit right in. Welcome to New York."

As a dedicated reader of *The New York World,* particularly the gossip columns in said paper, Adeline had a hunch about just who this handsome stranger was.

He would more than fit in; this man was poised to conquer the Four Hundred and the rest of New York society. It wasn't just his good looks or his fine suit of clothes, either. He wore his wealth and power effortlessly. It simply radiated from him. All these New York new moneymen dressed the part in fancy wool coats and satin waistcoats; they built veritable palaces along Fifth Avenue, they dropped cash and coin on diamond-studded trinkets and every imaginable, outlandish entertainment. But none of them managed to radiate power and authority as this man did, dressed plainly but excellently.

She had an eye for fashion; she knew these things.

She wanted to breathe it in. Bottle it. Sell it at the counters at Goodwin's Emporium on the Ladies' Mile. She'd make a fortune.

That was the New Yorker in her. Everything was for sale.

Adeline glanced at the large clock towering over the lobby hall and saw the time was five minutes before two o'clock. If she kept her wits together and remembered her priorities, if she didn't allow herself to get distracted from her one true purpose by a man, there would be just enough time for her to get there without rushing and arriving gasping for breath.

"Thank you for the heroics. Lovely to make the acquaintance with your chest, if not the rest of you. If you'll excuse me, I have an appointment."

She gave him another wide smile and continued on her way toward the elevator. To the top floor. To the chamber of Miss Harriet Burnett. To her best shot at the future she'd always dreamed of.

Oh, but she could not resist a glance over her shoulder; there stood the most eligible bachelor in town in the middle of the Fifth Avenue Hotel lobby, smiling, with his gaze fixed on her bustle as she walked away.

Brandon Alexander Fiennes, the duke of Kingston, was definitely not in London anymore. In fact, New York City was something else entirely. The crowds of people pulsed and surged around him; everyone in this town seemed to be in a mad dash to get someplace, to meet someone, to do something. Right now, no, yesterday! It was exhilarating and exhausting all at once.

The pace was nothing like that of England, where one had a sense of centuries stretching into the past and presumably forward, too.

Though Kingston hadn't time to waste in finding his bride, he had expected to spend a month or two in the city enduring rounds of soirees and introductions before finding someone suitable, which is to say someone rich, respectable, and keen to trade her fortune for his prestigious title. To say nothing of a girl who felt like perfection in his arms, who had a sparkle in her eye that enchanted him and who had a sway of her hips that captivated him.

He'd only just arrived and already he'd met a girl, quite possibly *the* girl.

How very New York.

He watched the sway of her hips, mesmerized.

She was headed in the direction of the elevator banks. As luck would have it, so was he.

"So we meet again," he said, coming to stand beside her as she waited for the elevator carriage to arrive. "What a small world."

"Well hello again." She smiled. "You're not following me, are you?"

Kingston would feel like the worst sort of rogue were it not for the sparkle in her dark eyes and the amused upturn of her lips. She was flirting with him. There was something between them and she felt it, too.

"No, of course not. That would be unseemly. I'm returning to my rooms to lie down. Such a display of heroics takes a lot out of a man. I fear I might need some tender ministrations to help me regain my strength."

"I hope you're not propositioning me," she said in a way that made him very much think about propositioning her. She shook her head and lamented, "Here I thought you had potential."

"I'm afraid I'm too much of a gentleman to proposition a woman. Especially when we've only just met."

"Too much of a gentleman?" She raised her eyebrow and gave a little laugh. "I haven't heard that one before. As it happens, I'm quite busy."

And not that kind of woman. She didn't need to say the words for them to be understood. And in truth, he never thought she was. Her attire and manners were as fine as any society woman of the Haute Ton or Four Hundred. That she was waiting for the elevators to her rooms in the Fifth Avenue Hotel indicated that she was a woman of a certain wealth. She had the potential to be suitable.

Those lips, though. He wanted to kiss them. Here. Now.

"I must confess that I find you enchanting."

"Of course you do." She rolled her eyes heavenward, but her lips reluctantly curved up in a small quirk of an *indulgent* smile that made his heart stop for a moment. Then it struck him: they were flirting but she wasn't *falling* for him. She was *politely* flirting with him.

Well, that was a first.

A novelty.

He was a duke. One easy on the eyes, if empty in the pockets. And women fell for him, hard and fast. It took nothing more than his seductive smile, a wink, a charming quip, a hint of a kiss, a promise of pleasure. But that was with English girls.

Perhaps this girl didn't know who he was. Perhaps she was well aware and not impressed. Not for the first time since arriving in New York did Kingston feel his entire equilibrium rocked.

"I've only just arrived and already I can see that New York City girls are different than the ones in London."

"Oh, you haven't seen anything yet."

With a ping of the bell, the elevator arrived and the uniformed attendant silently rolled the doors open. Kingston and the girl stepped into the plush, velvet-tufted carriage. They were, alas, not alone; the attendant was there to do his job of operating the elevator while doing his best to be invisible in the small, confined space. He performed spectacularly.

The doors had been shut but a moment when she asked, "Well, I suppose I should ask, what brings you to New York?"

Kingston gave her the honest answer. "I'm here to get married."

"Congratulations!" But her smile quickly faded. "Well, I *suppose* congratulations are in order. Does your bride know that you are ensconced in elevators with a woman you find enchanting?"

"Oh, it's too soon for felicitations," Kingston replied.

"Have you not yet proposed?"

"Not exactly. I have only just arrived in New York City. My ship docked just last night."

"Ah, I suppose it's too soon for you to

have met the right woman."

"I don't know that I'd say that . . ."

Their eyes met. His heart pounded. Actually pounded in his chest.

"You'll have to stay a few more days in the city, at least, to meet someone," she told him matter-of-factly and apparently oblivious to his inner turmoil. Because he found her enchanting and she was merely flirting with him as something to do on a Tuesday afternoon. This was not a situation with which he had ever been confronted; a woman who didn't let it be known that he would only have to say the word and she would be his.

"And what if I have met her already?"

She smiled and replied, "Something tells me that I don't think you'll have much trouble finding a wife."

"Because you'll say yes if I ask?" He gave her his most winning smile. The one that made all the girls swoon. That was the moment that the elevator bell chimed, indicating they had arrived at their floor. The attendant opened the door and she stepped out into the corridor.

"It was lovely to meet you," she said.

And then she said, "Goodbye."

And then she was gone.

"The pleasure is all mine," he murmured

as he watched her hips sway as she bustled down the hall and knocked on the door to the suite adjoining his. Fancy that: less than four and twenty hours in America and he was already half in love with the girl next door.

CHAPTER TWO

Heiresses come to Manhattan from all over the country to shop the Ladies' Mile, stroll through Central Park, seek the favor of Mrs. Astor and buy themselves an English aristocratic title.
— *The New York World*

Never mind the duke — *this* is what Adeline had come for. At precisely two o'clock she rapped confidently on the heavy oak door, and a mere moment later, a maid opened it to reveal an opulent set of rooms with large windows overlooking the greenery of Madison Square Park.

"Good day. I'm Miss Black, from the dressmaker's shop. Madame Chalfont has sprained her ankle and won't be able to attend, so I have come to do the fitting instead," Adeline explained.

Adeline was a seamstress by trade, with grand ambitions to be a dressmaker. Ambitions that were *not* encouraged by Madame Chalfont, for whom she worked, though she certainly capitalized on her skills. Adeline had a gift with a needle and thread, a deft hand when it came to cutting expensive fabric perfectly, and a gift for creating dresses that fit a woman's body.

She was supposed to cut and fit in service of Madame Chalfont's vision of fashion and womanhood — not her own. More than once she'd vexed everyone by attempting to alter the designs to suit her taste, which required her fellow seamstresses to rework the gowns and strip away all her inventiveness.

Adeline had passionate dreams of one day opening a shop of her own and creating incomparable dresses for incomparable women. She talked about it all the time with her friends, Rose and Rachel, and anyone else who would listen. At the very least, she longed to see a gown of her own imagination brought to life and worn in high society.

This personal, solo fitting with Miss Burnett was her big chance to persuade a client to adopt *Adeline's* designs, not Madame Chalfont's. While her employer would never listen to Adeline's suggestions, a client's demands were another matter entirely.

It was her best option for seeing her work out in the world, and then who knows what might come of it? Perhaps more orders and more clients, and dress by dress, she'd establish herself as *the* dressmaker for the Four Hundred.

It was probably the *only* option for a girl from the tenements of the Lower East Side.

Adeline was shown to a lady's bedroom where a rich assortment of silks, satins, and cotton gowns had been set out for the fitting, having been delivered earlier. Everything was ready, except for the lady herself.

She wasn't sure what to expect from Miss Harriet Burnett.

She'd been a darling of Manhattan society — until she wasn't. It was the stuff of lore and legend: she had refused the aged, unwanted suitor her father had chosen for her and had been cast out of the family's home for saying no. Rumor had it that she had supported herself as a hack writer for the newspapers; other reports suggested that she'd engaged in more nefarious work. But now her parents had passed and Miss Burnett was an heiress, intent upon making a return to society.

Hence, the new wardrobe.

"Hello, I'm Miss Burnett. This is my companion and friend, Miss Ava Lumley."

Miss Burnett was a statuesque beauty with fair hair, a complexion that would complement a variety of colors and a figure that could carry off more ambitious designs. Miss Lumley was a full-figured brunette and loveliness personified.

"You must be the dressmaker," Miss Burnett said, with an approving glance at Adeline's customized shirtwaist. "The girl with the needle, thread, and silks and satins who will help me take the town by storm. Let me tell you my particular problem: I need gowns that will look like I'm trying to land a husband but which will not actually land me a husband."

The silence that followed let it be known that neither woman was inclined to marriage.

"That is a lot to ask from a dress, Harriet," Miss Lumley said after a moment. She shrugged and dropped into a plush chair. "It is just a dress."

"A dress is never just a dress," Adeline replied. "At its simplest, a dress is merely a garment to keep one modestly covered and protected from the elements. But a dress is also magic: it can make a woman feel bold and confident so she might indeed take the world by storm, as more women ought to do, in my opinion. It can be her armor

28

protecting her from prying eyes or would-be husbands, or the protection she needs to go forth and battle the world. Such is the power of a good dress."

Neither woman had a reply to that.

The silence was excruciating. It had all been going so well until she had to go and say too much. Her mother had always emitted indulgent sighs when Adeline went on about the life-changing magic of a stylish dress, or the transformative power of well-constructed unmentionables, or the necessity of the right accessories.

"Well, we never learned about that at Oberlin," Miss Lumley said, finally.

Ah, so they were college girls.

Then Miss Burnett quipped, "Well, aren't you something else?"

Feeling emboldened, Adeline tilted her chin up. "Not yet, ma'am. But I hope to be soon."

"For the first time, I find myself looking forward to a fitting," Miss Burnett replied. "Here are the dresses that the shop delivered earlier."

Her maid helped her into the first gown and Adeline stood back to appraise the fit and style. The gown was a frothy but fashionable concoction of dark green silk with large puffed shoulders and narrow sleeves, a tapered waist and a full skirt. It was all fine enough, but it was nothing that would declare the wearer to be a woman to be reckoned with. This was a dress that said *Respectable Matron in Training* and didn't seem to suit its intended wearer at all.

"I don't know how I am supposed to do anything with these ridiculous sleeves," Miss Burnett remarked. "And I can hardly draw a decent breath."

"I don't think you are supposed to, dear," Miss Lumley answered.

"Breathe or do anything?"

"A lady of leisure should do as little as possible — just enough breathing and activity to get by," Miss Lumley replied and Adeline was intrigued by the touch of sarcasm in her voice and the smirk on Miss Burnett's lips.

"We both know that I do not aspire to being a lady of leisure." Turning to Adeline, Miss Burnett said, "At college, where I met Miss Lumley, we dressed simply and functionally so we could focus on matters of the mind. And now I have grand plans. And I need to be able to draw a breath."

Adeline was curious about these grand plans that did not include marriage. Whatever they were, she wanted to provide the wardrobe.

"If we move this seam slightly and shrink the puff of the sleeve, that should give you more ease of movement," Adeline replied, which was her way of saying *I understand you.* "If we add a few discreet pleats to the skirt, you'll be able to take greater strides while still maintaining this season's fashion."

"Hang fashion. I should like to breathe and move my arms."

Sensing that Miss Burnett was open to her ideas, Adeline dared to go further and suggest the scandalous design element that she'd been incorporating into her own gowns — one that Madame Chalfont was vehemently opposed to.

"We could also add a small pocket."

"A pocket!" Miss Burnett gushed. "Now you're talking."

"Won't it ruin the line of the dress?" Miss Lumley asked.

"With these voluminous skirts? I should think not," Adeline answered.

"And, as I said before, *hang fashion.* Especially if it means I can have a pocket," Miss Burnett said. "If such a thing is possible, I don't know why Madame Chalfont didn't design them thusly to begin with."

Adeline elected not to say anything. It was one thing to subvert her employer's designs

31

that would bear her name. It was quite another to speak ill of her. But Miss Burnett was no dummy.

"Ah. I see. You have previously made these suggestions and they have been disregarded. I wonder if she sees you as competition. Women can be their own worst enemies sometimes."

"Madame Chalfont has a very firm artistic vision," Adeline said diplomatically. "She is very traditional. It is her shop."

Her employer did not care for anything new or potentially scandalous and suggestive, like a too-low bodice, a too-short skirt, or a pocket. Mention bloomers or the new cycling costumes, and she hovered on the verge of hysterics.

She was vigilant about her own reputation and those of her seamstresses, given that certain people were always worried that a female-helmed dressmaking establishment was actually a front for more negotiable and *affectionate* services.

"But you have vision as well," Miss Burnett replied. "And you understand a woman's body and that despite society's dictates, you understand that it is capable of more than lounging on a settee."

"I have an abiding love of fashion and pretty dresses, but I don't see why a woman should sacrifice comfort and mobility to be fashionable," Adeline replied, pinning a seam that would need to be adjusted. "A great dress should make a woman feel as if she could go out and conquer the world because she looks and feels good."

"I couldn't agree more. I will require a full wardrobe — evening gowns, day dresses, riding dresses, undergarments and the like. I will order them all from Madame Chalfont — but *only* if the gowns incorporate your ideas. Money talks, does it not?"

Adeline's only thought was *Tuesdays*. That was when luck and pluck and good fortune conspire to give a girl a chance at her dreams. And a duke had nothing to do with it.

CHAPTER THREE

Attention Ladies: His Grace, the Duke of Kingston is in town! Though he has only just arrived, he has already been spotted in an intimate conversation with a mysterious woman in the lobby of the Fifth Avenue Hotel. And that's not all . . .

— *Town Topics*

The next day
Madame Chalfont's Shop
34 West Fifteenth Street

When Adeline happily bustled into work at Madame Chalfont's the following morning, she found her fellow seamstresses immersed in the newest edition of that oh-so popular scandal sheet, *Town Topics.* Wealthy society women read it for gossip about their peers (and themselves), while girls like Rose and Rachel read it for a window into a glamorous upper-class existence.

Adeline was known to read it for the dress

descriptions, much to the despair of her friends who were far more intrigued about what some-one had done and with whom, rather than what they were wearing while they did it.

Rose Freeman glanced up when Adeline entered the shop, her big brown eyes sparkling and her voice trembling in excitement. She had a talent for embroidering designs that made a regular gown into something unique and special. She was also an avid reader of dime novels and a hopeless romantic. "Oh, did you hear, Adeline? The duke has arrived. He was spotted in the lobby of the Fifth Avenue Hotel."

Adeline had suspected as much.

"Where else would you spot a duke in New York?" Rachel asked, raising one brow. "Other than Mrs. Astor's ballroom or the Metropolitan Club?"

In other words, exclusive enclaves of the upper class that none of them would ever grace with their presence.

"Though he is a duke, he is also technically a tourist," Rose pointed out while carefully stitching tiny seed pearls to the train of an evening gown. "So he might visit a museum, or venture to St. Mark's Place, or stroll through Central Park. One might catch a glimpse of him there."

"What else does the paper say about the duke?" Adeline asked tentatively. She had her suspicions that the man she'd collided with yesterday was His Grace, the Duke of Kingston, whose impending visit the papers had been reporting on for days. But this new report just about confirmed it.

"By all accounts he is tall, dark, and exceedingly handsome," Rose said. "The most eligible bachelor in town."

"You don't say," Rachel Abrams said dryly. She was not known among her friends, or anyone, for her romantic streak, but she had a way with a scissors and satin that was incomparable. Cutting expensive fabrics was a high-stakes endeavor and she was a master.

"I bet he's made all the women swoon already. I bet he's a millionaire," Rose replied dreamily.

"I bet he's not," Rachel replied, crushing hopes and dreams of young girls every-where, particularly those in the immediate vicinity. "Everyone knows these titled gen-tlemen only come to New York so they might snare an heiress."

Rachel was right.

One of New York City's finest exports was the "dollar princesses," those heiresses to fortunes made from railroads, shipping, mining, real estate, and oil who were snapped up by England's increasingly impoverished landed aristocracy. The Duke of Kingston was not the first, and unlikely to be the last, aristocrat who traveled to the "former colonies" for a wealthy bride with her new money to save his old estate.

And that was why Adeline had laughed off the duke's flirtations the day before. Despite their collision and instant connection, she was not the woman he had traveled across an ocean to find.

Far, far from it.

The only *something* that could happen would be a dalliance at best and quite possibly her downfall. She had seen firsthand how a man's empty promises and kisses could ruin a girl's prospects by either distracting her from her real dreams, wrecking her reputation, or both. Adeline had seen enough to know that relying on a man was no assurance of security at all; her mother's three husbands had demonstrated that. She had long ago vowed that she would never surrender to temptation, nor would she ever allow herself to rely on a man.

Not that she met many tempting men.

Except for yesterday afternoon in the lobby of the Fifth Avenue Hotel. At precisely seven minutes before two o'clock.

But absolutely nothing would happen between her and the duke, even if locking eyes with him gave her a zing of pleasure and their snappy banter had her pulse sparkling and racing with the thrill of such an instant and powerful connection.

Even if he managed to find her (which he would never do because he did not even know her name) and even if he deigned to pursue a courtship (which he would never do because she was a working-class girl), nothing would come of it.

Adeline put the matter of the duke firmly out of her mind.

Or tried to.

Rose still had that newspaper, was still drinking in every inch of ink about this mythical romantic hero who had sailed across an ocean and landed on the city's shores.

Rachel was less starry-eyed about the whole business. "What good is a duke without money anyway?"

"It does ruin the fantasy. Just a little," Rose admitted.

"Ah yes, the fantasy of the working-class girl swept off her feet by the handsome millionaire bachelor before she quits her job and they settle into blissful domesticity," Adeline said, summarizing the plot of nearly every novel the girls brought into the shop. They read them on their brief lunch breaks and traded them around until the cheap paperbacks disintegrated but the dream remained.

"A girl can dream." Rachel and Rose said this at the same time, one with more heart than the other.

"It sounds like he already set his eyes on a girl," Rose said, a devilish smile playing on her lips as she read more of the story. "It says here he was seen in 'intimate conversation with a well-dressed mystery woman' in the lobby. They were then spotted taking the elevator *together.* Alone."

"I'm sure they weren't actually alone," Adeline remarked to the interest of no one. "There was probably an attendant operating the elevator."

Rose carried on: "She is described as a woman with dark hair and doe eyes, wearing a rather fetching plum-colored skirt and matching jacket open over a delicately ruffled shirtwaist."

"Well now, doesn't that sound like someone we know?" Rachel asked. Two pairs of eyes fixed their attentions on Adeline, who suddenly became very interested in examining some stitches on the sleeve of a lemon-yellow jacquard jacket.

"Someone we know who happened to be at the Fifth Avenue Hotel just yesterday afternoon? Who just happened to have spent last week sewing delicate ruffles onto her best shirtwaist?"

"It must be a coincidence," Adeline said, trying to deflect their questions and attention. There was no point in discussing her encounter with the duke; it was the sort of fun, flirtatious, and insignificant amusement a girl had here and there in the city. A moment's delight before it was forgotten entirely. Forever.

But Rose and Rachel were still staring expectantly for the full, delectable story. Oh, they leaned in close, eyes wide. Waiting.

"Who did these stitches, by the way?" Adeline wondered. "They are far too loose."

"Never mind the stitches!" Rose huffed.

"It was you, wasn't it?" Rachel said, grinning now. "You were the dark-haired and doe-eyed woman who had captured the duke's attentions and has thus made every single woman in New York City jealous of you before breakfast. You saw him when you were there for the fitting with Miss Burnett. I knew it!"

Rose didn't even wait for confirmation, she just sighed mightily. "Oh, Ada, what's he like?"

He was like a fantasy come to life. He was handsome and self-possessed. There was something intensely erotic about the way he looked at her: like *she* was his living, breathing, fantasy and he wanted to know her and to touch her to make sure she was real. He looked at her with those piercing blue eyes like *she* might save *him*. Just being near him made her want to pull him off to some secluded spot where they might occupy themselves by *saving* each other.

But she didn't want to give her friends fodder for further discussion. Or to herself for further fantasies.

"His jacket was very well made," Adeline replied. "It was a fine cashmere wool, expertly tailored. Saville Row, probably."

"Of course one would expect a duke to display excellent tailoring of his clothes," Rachel remarked.

"Who cares about clothes and stitches!?" Rose threw up her hands in despair. It had to be agony for her to possess enough romantic feeling for all three of them.

"The better question is why she was close enough to know such details," Rachel pointed out. "Must have been a very inattentive elevator attendant."

Again, her friends gave her The Look.

It was The Look of a friend who *knows*

there is a story and that they will not cease until they are privy to every last dramatic, romantic detail. Their workday was a good ten hours long at least — not only did that make diversion necessary, it meant that Rose and Rachel were prepared to wait her out. It wasn't often that any of them had even a mildly romantic encounter worth gossiping about, and now Adeline had an encounter that made the newspapers. She could hem and haw and comment on stitches all she liked, but they wouldn't stop badgering her about the duke until she told them everything.

Everything.

Adeline paused, dramatically.

Then, with a flash of her impish smile, began: "It was seven minutes before two o'clock, when I was due at Miss Burnett's rooms on the top floor of the Fifth Avenue Hotel."

Adeline related everything: the accidental collision with the duke's wide, well-muscled chest clad in the finest cashmere wool. How his ducal hands clasped her arms after he had, in a manner of speaking, nearly swept her off her feet.

She told them about the way his presence took up all the air and space inside the elevator, leaving her light-headed, but she still managed some flirtatious banter. Yes, she told Rose, he took her breath away. She told her friends how he spoke of marriage, when they had only just met.

Rose had that dreamy, faraway look in her eyes and even Rachel's usual stoic expression softened into a smile. Adeline was happy to provide this little escape, this little fantasy, but . . .

"But nothing will come of it, of course. We never even exchanged names."

That was the exact moment that a young man in a uniform from the Fifth Avenue Hotel entered the shop.

Bellmen from the Fifth Avenue Hotel were not the usual clientele of Madame Chalfont's Dressmaking Establishment.

His presence generated a burst of excited chatter among all the ladies, who paused in their sewing and ironing. Even Madame Chalfont herself was intrigued. She stepped away from her work to approach the man who dared to enter her shop.

"I have a letter for Miss Adeline Black," he declared.

"It's most likely from Miss Burnett, perhaps about her dress order," Adeline explained to her curious colleagues. Yesterday, she had returned from the fitting of the first few dresses with orders for a dozen more. Madame Chalfont was so pleased she actually smiled — though it quickly faded when she read Miss Burnett's stipulation that they be customized by Adeline. She did seem to feel competitive with regard to her younger trainee.

Madame Chalfont frowned and clapped her hands and barked out, "Back to work, ladies," in her distinctly Midwestern accent — not her feigned French accent — which happened when she was vexed.

Rose and Rachel leaned far over Adeline's shoulders so they could read the letter.

"It's from the duke, isn't it?"

"Don't be ridiculous."

"Well, let's have a look."

> To the enchanting girl from the elevator —

Her friends sighed. In spite of herself, Adeline smiled, then frowned, curious as to how he had found her. But he was a high-and-mighty duke, so he must have ways that a girl like her would know nothing about.

"It's definitely from the duke," Rose said.

"Or the elevator attendant," Adeline suggested and everyone ignored her.

"They already have pet names for each other," Rachel muttered.

"I'm swooning," Rose said, placing her hands on the worktable. "Actually swooning."

"Shall I stop reading and fetch the smelling salts?"

"No!"

As I have only just arrived in town, I must see all the sights Manhattan has to offer. Would you do me the honor of joining me for a walk in Central Park?

— Kingston

"You are definitely free that day," Rose said.

"He didn't specify a day," Rachel pointed out.

"She will make herself free. It's a duke! A handsome duke!"

"I'll tell him no, of course," Adeline said.

"What?"

"Why?!"

"We have a massive dress order to attend to, for one thing," Adeline said. "Nearly two dozen dresses for Miss Burnett. She wants them immediately."

"We'll get them done; we always do," Rachel said.

"You absolutely will get them done," Madame Chalfont interrupted. "And you

45

will start now instead of standing idle and chattering about the untoward attentions of a man. He'll never be interested in you for anything decent, Miss Black, and any hint of an illicit liaison will ruin you in this business. Mark my words, a woman's good reputation, once lost, is gone forever — and all her good opportunities go with it. The world thinks little enough of dressmakers as it is — no man is worth the risk."

Her word being final, she walked away with the expectation that the excited chatter would cease and the sewing would resume and all thoughts of handsome dukes would simply vanish. But practical matters could not compare.

"What we don't always do is walk in the park with a handsome duke," Rose continued in a whisper. "On behalf of all of us you must go. For the sisterhood, Adeline. For *us*. For all the girls who dream of something like this and never get the opportunity."

That was a difficult plea to resist. Adeline thought of all the girls dreaming for chance encounters with dashing strangers and romantic walks in the park with handsome dukes and eligible bachelors. What was wrong with a little romance to brighten up their hardworking day-to-day existence? It was madness — a wonderful, glorious madness — that this opportunity should fall into her lap. Any one of these girls would seize it without a moment's hesitation. In fact, any one of them would have already sent a reply saying, *Yes, Duke, just say when and where.*

But Adeline did not want the distraction.

She wanted to make dresses. She wanted to make dresses according to *her* vision. In fact, she had an idea about that green silk for Miss Burnett that she was eager to get started on.

But then Adeline glanced down at the newspaper Rose held in her long, tapered fingers. Words jumped out at her. *A rather fetching plum-colored walking dress with a tailored matching jacket. Delicately ruffled shirtwaist.* That was her dress described in print and read by all the women of high society.

All at once, the idea occurred to her.

"It could be good advertising. *Free* advertising. I could wear one of my own creations and on the duke's arm, I'll be sure to attract attention and perhaps have my dress written up in the newspapers. Again. Perhaps that will lead to my own shop."

There was a collective groan from the other girls. They were all well aware of Adeline's dreams and plans. How many times had one of them been assigned to "correct" her inventive work that went against Madame Chalfont's vision and wishes? Too many. But this was taking her single-minded determination too far.

"Romance, Adeline. *Romance!*" Rose exclaimed.

"Romance is a dirty trick and you know it," Adeline replied. "No good comes from romance. It's just silly notions that lead a girl to make ridiculous decisions."

Just like her mother. Just like a thousand women before her.

"It's just a walk in the park, Adeline," Rachel pointed out.

"There is no such thing as *just* a walk in the park with a duke."

CHAPTER FOUR

Must host house party for the girls at
Lyon House to find husbands. Stop.
When will the roof be repaired? Stop.
Girls will want the new style of walking
dresses. Stop.
— Telegram from Her Grace,
the Duchess of Kingston

The next day, Sunday afternoon
Central Park
Kingston strolled toward the corner of
Fifty-ninth Street and Fifth Avenue, toward
one of the entrances to the already famed
and fabled Central Park. Massive, ornate
mansions lined the streets leading up to it.
Though his traditional male British pride
would never allow him to say such a thing
aloud, he privately thought that such palatial
homes would put many an English house to
shame.

Not Lyon House, though. That ancient

and massive heap of limestone in Buckinghamshire was at least twice as large and ornate as any of these, and it was surrounded by thousands of lush, rolling acres of farmland, steeped in history, and any number of royal heads had slept under its roof. But unfortunately, it was without modern amenities such as running water — unless one counted the leak from the roof after the rain.

Which one did not.

But — Kingston's heart started to quicken its rhythm in his chest as he considered it — if he were to apply one of these Fifth Avenue fortunes to his own holdings, he'd have his family's ancestral estate up and working again. He could stop the damage that time had wrought. He could restore Lyon House to all its former glory, a home befitting a man of his position.

He'd be The Duke Who Saved Them All.

With a renewed sense of purpose, Kingston approached the entrance to the park and waited for her, that charming and enchanting girl from the elevator who just happened to be residing in the suite of rooms next to his. Damn, but he loved the convenience of falling for the heiress next door.

After making some discreet inquiries with

the hotel staff, Kingston had learned that the woman who occupied the suite of rooms adjacent to his was Miss Harriet Burnett. It was intimated that she had something of a scandalous past — which he could certainly overlook, considering his circumstances and their instant connection — but she had recently come into a great fortune. Her stay at the hotel was temporary while her town-house was being renovated and redecorated.

Kingston had never given much thought to marriage until recently, when it became necessary that he marry quickly and richly. Thus, he had never given much consideration to marrying for love. Until yesterday. Now the idea that he could marry to his heart and purse's desire was irresistible — to say nothing of the woman herself — and it seemed impossible that he should settle for anything less.

He'd be The Duke Who Had It All.

He quickly caught sight of her, thanks to the eye-catching sky-blue walking suit that she wore. It stood out among all the other women's Sunday finest on parade. He was no fan of fashion and thus lacked the appropriate words to describe the ensemble — he did tend to tune out his mother when she chattered away about frocks and such — but even he noticed such finely made attire that seemed to hug and caress, to shape and show off her figure. He instinctively recognized the confident, self-assured way she moved in this suit as belonging to one who could, say, reign over a ballroom.

Like a duchess.

"Why, hello."

"Hello to you, too."

Their eyes locked. For a moment he had no other thoughts than *you're pretty* and *I found you.* She was lovelier than he had remembered, which was really something, because his thoughts had strayed to her often. He had lingered over the way her lips had turned up, the glimmer in her eyes when she had teased him. His thoughts had strayed to kissing her.

The full force of this infatuation hit him all of a sudden. It damn near took his breath away.

Kingston smiled. She smiled. And the woman standing beside her cleared her throat pointedly.

Then his gaze moved from his heiress to the tall and beautiful dark-skinned woman who was smiling pointedly as she waited for an introduction.

"This is my" — his heiress began to explain.

"Chaperone," the other woman cut in

with a smile. She extended her hand and he shook it. "I'm Miss Rose Freeman. I couldn't let my friend scandalize everyone by enjoying a walk in the park alone with a —"

"Gentleman," his enchanting girl cut in, making Kingston wonder if she hadn't been about to say *duke.* He couldn't blame her if she, too, had made discreet inquiries or read the newspapers. He'd glimpsed the headlines that seemed to have followed him from London to New York. But whether her ignorance of his position was genuine or feigned, he appreciated the opportunity to not be The Duke and to just be . . . himself.

"Don't mind me," Miss Freeman said, waving off any possible concerns. "I shall just blend into the background and you'll never know I'm here. Go, enjoy your romantic walk in the park."

"Rose . . ."

"Of course a lady ought to have a chaperone on an occasion such as this. I am glad to have your company, Miss Freeman. You shall keep us from wandering off into dens of iniquity."

"Oh, I can't imagine you'll find those this far uptown," Rose replied with a laugh.

"Shall we be off?" He offered his arm to the girl, quite possibly The One, and they set off for a walk in the park on a lovely spring day. Trees were bursting with blossoms and fresh green leaves. Squirrels dashed to and fro. The air was full of birdsong and sunshine.

In London, it would be raining.

In London, he'd be ensconced in his study, consumed with account books and dismal meetings with secretaries and solicitors. Freddie had been right about coming to New York for a bride; a walk in the park with a pretty potential wife was a far more pleasurable method of attempting to save his estate than, say, meeting with mining companies or railroad executives.

Yes, marrying a woman of wealth was definitely the way to go; there was a reason it had been tradition for centuries, and who was he, the fifth duke of Kingston, to defy the done thing? But Miss Burnett offered something he had never even dreamed of: the possibility of a bride he could love. A wife he would *want* to spend his nights and morning-afters with.

"So this is Central Park," he began, silently admitting to himself that it was a remarkable park that *all* manner of New Yorkers seemed to be enjoying — the obviously wealthy shared the same paths with those who were clearly less fortunate and everyone in between. The people seemed to have come from all over the country and all over the world; the range of humanity was notable, intriguing, and nothing like, say, White's or Parliament.

"Magnificent, isn't it? New York City has everything a girl could possibly want," she replied. "Shops, entertainments, magic. And parks like this, for when one wants a bit of greenery."

He chuckled at *a bit of greenery*. "You are quite enamored of the city."

"How can one not love New York?" She opened her arms wide. "The buildings are breathtaking; there are so many interesting people and ever so much to do. It's never dull."

"I certainly find it . . . enchanting." Kingston paused to gaze down into her pretty brown eyes. Yes, he could gaze into those eyes for a lifetime. "I hope to see more of it."

By *it,* he meant her.

Behind her, Miss Freeman heaved a dreamy sigh.

"Tell me, how does New York compare to London?" his enchanting girl asked. "I've never been to England."

"I must admit weather here is far superior. In the few days since my arrival, it hasn't rained once, which my mother and sisters would enjoy. They often lament about how the weather ruins their gowns."

"Given all the care and consideration a woman puts into her dress, it must be dreadful to be cooped up inside unable to show oneself or to risk wrecking a carefully constructed ensemble."

"One would think the solution is to be less invested in one's attire and appearance."

"I would think a more reasonable solution would be to move where it rained less," she replied breezily.

"More reasonable to move?" He was shocked. Horrified. Aghast. "Women put far too much stock into fashion," he replied tartly, thinking of the tradesmen's bills for ostrich feathers, rare furs, custom gowns from Paris that arrived regularly. Astronomical sums for things that must be worn precisely once and then never seen again. He had the distinct sensation of his heart sinking and taking his hopes for this woman down with it.

Good God, not another fashion-mad female. Lord save him from the dress obsessed.

"Said by someone who misunderstands the power of elegant dress and how it is often a woman's sole means of control and communication," she retorted.

Kingston found himself shocked, again. Somewhat horrified. Slightly aghast. Never had he met a woman who contradicted him so early in their acquaintance and who dared to confront his ignorance. No English girl would ever dare to. The title, you see. Was it arousing or enraging? He couldn't read the quickening of his heart or the constriction in his lungs. He couldn't be sure, but he knew he could not quit her just yet.

"I pay the tradesmen's bills and cannot imagine why anyone needs dozens of hats decorated in the plumage of dead birds and more dresses than anyone could wear in a week."

"For whom are you purchasing these hats, might I ask?"

"My mother. My two sisters. I hate to deny them anything, even if I think it's silly."

"How positively noble of you."

"You are not impressed."

"I am one of those women who finds fashion singularly interesting and empowering to womankind."

Yes, another fashion-obsessed female. One who might even lecture him.

Those lips, though. He wanted to kiss

57

them. His pulse quickened when she smiled at him. Maybe he could just listen to what she had to say.

So he said, "Convince me."

She gave him a smile that said *challenge accepted.*

"It's simple. Women are raised to be seen and not heard; why, it's still scandalous for a woman to speak publicly. So we make ourselves heard with our clothes. We wear full skirts to take up space in the world that wants us to be shut away in drawing rooms and kitchens. We wear bright colors to remind mankind that we exist. For example."

"An interesting perspective I had not considered. It does have a ring of logic to it," he conceded. "But what is the message that a dead bird on a hat is trying to convey?"

"That one feels trapped and powerless in their existence."

This was a novel interpretation of the fashion obsession of Her Grace, the Duchess of Kingston. It was an obsession that threatened to bankrupt the already dwindling estate. He feared it all reflected poorly upon him and his father. It was a theory that probably merited more consideration at a later date when he was not walking arm in arm with an enchanting and confounding woman who might be the answer to his prayers — or who might make things infinitely worse.

Her passion for fashion complicated things. Was she perfect for him or would she only be more trouble? It was too soon to tell but the yearning to explore more was undeniable. He was not in the habit of denying his yearnings.

"After all this discussion of fashion, I hope I haven't compromised your sense of masculinity," she teased.

"I assure you, my sense of masculinity is just fine."

"I daresay it is as well," she murmured.

The pathway was now winding toward a tunnel which promised a cool, dark, and private respite from the sunshine and the crowds. In this little secluded spot in an otherwise crowded city, there was nothing to distract them. And, oddly, no one to see.

Miss Freeman, chaperone extraordinaire, had conveniently made herself scarce by lagging behind a few steps and developing a sudden interest in the foliage.

Kingston offered a prayer of gratitude for romantically inclined chaperones.

Especially when this enchanting girl seemed as keen for *something* as he was.

Her gaze had locked with his. Her lips parted.

Was it too soon to kiss her?

Yes, they had only just met. She might or might not be perfect. A short acquaintance had never stopped him from stealing a kiss from a willing woman before. He may not know how to read a dress, but he knew desire in a woman's eyes. He knew what it did to him.

A look like that made a man think of kisses and wedded bliss.

It was a look so captivating that he almost missed the swarm of bicyclists rushing toward them. Without thinking he grabbed her around the waist and tugged her close against him, out of the way of those dangerous riders.

She clasped the lapels of his jacket. Her lips were just inches from his.

The throng of humans on bicycles flew past with their wheels whirring, buzzing and generating a gust of wind in their wake. He didn't move an inch. Not at all. She clung to him and he didn't exactly let go.

He stood tall above her, acutely aware that her breasts occasionally brushed against his chest, achingly aware just an inch would close the distance between his arousal and her skirts. He held her, his hand hot and possessive on her waist.

Kingston flirted with the possibility of kissing her.

He came so close he could taste it.

A slow, sweet kiss was just there between them, ripe for the plucking. Something stopped him, though. It was a deep, instinctive sense that once his lips touched hers it would be impossible to stop. When he kissed this woman, he was going to kiss her so thoroughly and completely that they would require all night and the morning, too. They would require privacy.

He was a duke. A gentleman of honor, breeding, and refinement. He did not debauch and ravish women during an afternoon stroll in the park.

But he thought about it.

And so he took a reluctant step away from this enchanting, bewitching woman.

They resumed their stroll, following the meandering path until it deposited them on a grand promenade. It didn't escape his notice that people stared at them. He was accustomed to being the subject of attention and he hid behind an air of reserved indifference.

The woman on his arm bore up well under the scrutiny. She kept her head held high, her shoulders back, all to show off her costume to its best effect to the admiring eyes of those in the vicinity.

Yes, he could definitely see her taking London by storm.

"So you have come to New York to find a bride," she started. "Most come here to seek fame and fortune."

"Those things are not necessarily mutually exclusive," he replied carefully. Kingston was hesitant to reveal himself as a duke just yet — she didn't seem to know, and he was enjoying this sense of getting to know each other before titles and fortunes got involved.

"On that point, I must agree. I've read enough dime novels to know that fame, fortune, and matrimony go hand in hand."

"My usual reading material consists of parliamentary reports. I'm not familiar with dime novels."

"They are thrilling novels of adventure for ladies — the dime novels, not parliamentary reports — featuring a girl who is definitely impoverished and probably an orphan, and who encounters every possible obstacle before discovering she's really an heiress and then marrying a millionaire to boot. You know, as one does."

"I love dime novels," Miss Freeman said, cutting into the conversation. "I must have read a hundred."

"At least," her friend confirmed.

"This is what ladies prefer to read?"

"Yes, and you had better watch out," Miss Freeman said. "You look and sound like a character from one. Not that I have been eavesdropping while I've been diligently chaperoning. Mostly."

"It's true," Miss Burnett replied. "You're tall, dark, and handsome, and prone to displays of heroics . . ."

She stopped short of making a direct reference to his wealth — or lack of — and he did not correct her. But God, he hated that it was a delicate subject. He didn't think he needed a fortune of his own to win her, or nearly any woman, but a man ought to be able to provide. Keep a woman in feathered hats and the first stare of fashion. At least.

"I suppose ladies read such books as they don't have such adventures in real life," he remarked.

"Oh, we have plenty of adventures — at least until the wedding," said Miss Freeman.

"*If* there is a wedding," Miss Burnett added.

"If? Do you mean to suggest you might not marry?" He was shocked. Slightly horrified. Somewhat aghast.

Falling for a woman who did not wish to

wed was not in accordance with his plans. Kingston hadn't even considered that a woman wouldn't want to wed him or wed at all. He could not discern if this girl on his arm was a distraction and complication or the one. He just knew he didn't feel *finished* with her. She confounded him and that intrigued him.

"You needn't sound so surprised," she said. "It's 1895. Times are changing."

"Yes, but this is holy matrimony. It is what people do."

She shrugged — shrugged! — at a centuries-old institution and he found himself actually feeling . . . old-fashioned and stodgy. Missish, even. Which was decidedly *not* how he — or most women — saw himself. He was young, virile, powerful. The stuff of women's dreams.

"The marriages I have seen are not happy ones," she continued with the faraway look of one who was remembering something. "The woman does twice as much work and relinquishes control over her money and, as such, her security."

Kingston wanted to protest this, but he knew that reason or facts were not on his side. His duchess would be consumed with the management of the households, plural, and he would need her funds at his disposal.

He could make all the promises in the world about providing for her after his death, but they would just be promises or special provisions. And so, without being able to make an argument with logic or reason, he relied on another age-old point:

"But what of children?"

"Lovely little creatures, but they are not the be-all and end-all of a woman's existence." Then she tilted her head thoughtfully. "Much as they try to be."

"I see the suffragettes are making inroads here, too," Kingston said with some chagrin. "They make a man's job harder. Now a bloke must convince a woman to marry at all, not just marry him."

It was just his luck. Impoverished duke must choose between marriage of love or fortune but quickly finds a woman who possesses a fortune and whom he could quite easily love and for whom he definitely lusted.

And she didn't want to marry. At all.

Maybe he should tell her that he was a duke. Once upon a time, that would have been enough. That, and the fact that he had a full head of hair, all of his teeth, never mind that he knew how to please a woman. He'd be more than happy to show her.

"We've only just met and here you are

with the marriage proposals again," she said with a laugh.

"I didn't mean —"

"I'm teasing you, English."

She glanced up at him, laughter still dancing in her eyes, her lips still upturned in a smile, and he thought it was going to be impossible *not* to love her. No one ever teased him. No one certainly ever teased him about something as serious as marriage.

It went without saying that he'd never, *ever* anticipated having to do more than stand about and let it be known that he was a duke and to take his pick from the throngs of women vying to be his duchess. He'd never imagined having to *try.* But just one walk in the park with the shocking and intriguing Miss Burnett, and he was ready to dart into Broadway traffic for her. He was shocked. Exhilarated. Aroused by the challenge.

Behind him Miss Freeman sighed again and he wanted to reply, *I know, I know!* But men did not issue heartfelt sighs, even if that's what they felt on the inside.

He concluded that if this girl, his enchanting elevator girl, could afford to make light of the matrimonial attentions of a duke, she must be very rich indeed. Between the flirting and the fortune, this girl was definitely duchess material. Kingston couldn't believe his luck. Now he just had to woo her . . .

CHAPTER FIVE

Ostrich feathers are all the rage. Stop.
You know Clara and I hate to be
unfashionable. Stop.
— Telegram from Her Grace,
the Duchess of Kingston

A few days later

No one was anyone in Manhattan until they had been feted by Mrs. Astor — *the* Mrs. Astor with the ballroom that could fit the infamous Four Hundred, otherwise known as the four hundred best, most important people in society. For the duke of Kingston, she hosted an intimate, exclusive, and outrageously opulent dinner to introduce him to four hundred of her closest friends.

And so began his grand tour of the ballrooms of Fifth Avenue mansions and Park Avenue palaces. With Freddie and his wife Marian as his guides — for they had relocated from London to New York at her insistence, to be nearer to her own family — Kingston embarked on a whirlwind tour of meeting everyone and anyone who might make a suitable duchess. His days and nights were a swarm of eligible women.

Tonight he made his way through a pack of pretty young women at a soirée hosted by Mrs. Fish, one of the town's renowned hostesses.

"Have you met Miss Gould and her sisters yet?" Freddie inquired and performed the introductions.

"I don't think I've had the pleasure," Kingston said as he kissed the outstretched hand of a stunning raven-haired beauty. Her shorter sister pushed her aside and stepped forward with a coy smile.

"How do you do, Your Grace? We are so eager to make your acquaintance. The previous dukes we've met have been so . . ."

Don't say poor.

"Old."

"Stodgy."

"But a young duke . . ."

The Gould sisters closed around him and Kingston feared he might be devoured alive. It wouldn't be the worst way to go. These American girls were so . . . bold. Centuries of British reserve and good breeding made him initially resistant to their frank overtures. The novelty of such forward women was intriguing, he had to admit, but it didn't compare to the playful, teasing wit of Miss Burnett.

Thus far, of all the women he had met, not one compared to her.

"Tell me more about your silver collection," he said to one heiress. She proceeded to do so, at length. A lady with fiery red hair was very committed to public sanitations works — a noble endeavor he wasn't keen to discuss over dinner. But at least they conversed, even if it was somewhat one-sided. Another woman he met was too shy to say multisyllabic words, and he feared it was because he intimidated her too much. With others he managed perfectly pleasant conversations but soon found himself exhausted from the sustained effort.

It wasn't hard to imagine years stretching out before him — of polite, silent breakfasts and cold, awkward nights — should he marry one of these women.

Everywhere he went, from ballroom to street to back again, he kept his eyes wide open for the enchanting girl from the elevator. The more women he was introduced to who did not compare, the more he wanted *her.*

So where the devil was she?

How hard was it to find the heiress next door?

"Let me introduce you to Miss Penny-packer, Cousin. Her family first made their money in cotton, and now their business is shipping."

And so Kingston was introduced to Miss Pennypacker. And Miss Watson, of a railroad fortune. Dozens and dozens of women were delighted to make his acquaintance. They were honored and pleased and eager to show him the city.

And then, finally, there she was. Freddie said the name he'd been aching to hear for days.

"Duke, I want to introduce you to Miss Burnett," Freddie said, pulling Kingston away from one conversation to engage him in another.

Miss Burnett.

Kingston paused before he turned around. Should he pretend not to know her, so that they might be allowed to claim a proper introduction and perfectly respectable relationship? More to the point, *could* he pretend not to know her? Already his heart was racing and for the first time in his life, he understood what people meant when they spoke of feeling butterflies in their stomachs.

71

Finally, he turned.

His heart sank. The butterflies died off all at once.

A tall, fair-haired woman with gray eyes extended her hand. "How do you do, Your Grace?"

"Miss Burnett?"

"The one and only."

"But you're the second one I've met this week."

"Is that so?" She smiled at him and her eyes sparkled prettily. He did not understand.

"Is Burnett a common name in America?"

"Well, it's not Smith or Jones, but it certainly isn't as rare as, say, DeMilla Featherbottom."

Kingston smiled tightly. He had the feeling that she was, to put it indelicately, taking the piss. But unwed women of marriageable age, richly attired in formal gowns and idling in gilded ballrooms did not take the piss of an English duke who had been declared the most eligible bachelor on the whole island of Manhattan.

He thought of the *other* Miss Burnett.

She also teased.

But this felt different.

He hadn't stopped thinking of the other Miss Burnett. Not wanting to seem overeager, he had forced himself to cool his heels and exercise some restraint. And so it was only this afternoon that he had penned another invitation and left it with the hotel staff to deliver.

"How are you enjoying the city thus far?" she asked him. "I trust you are taking time to explore the city and finding enchanting company to join you."

Enchanting. She had to use that word.

"As a matter of fact, I have."

"Central Park?"

"How did you guess?"

"It was either that or the Ladies' Mile," she joked.

"I'm not exactly the type to enjoy women's shops."

"That's what they all say." She smiled again. Teasing. Eyes sparkling. He couldn't shake the feeling that she was finding amusement at his expense. He didn't entirely mind; it was preferable to conversing with women who couldn't resist subtle innuendos or blatant suggestions.

Before he could say more, a woman with flushed cheeks pushed through the crowds and came to stop at Miss Burnett's side. "Ah, there you are, Harriet!"

"Harriet?" Kingston echoed.

"I've been looking everywhere for you.

This ballroom is a crush."

"I've been having a lovely conversation with the duke."

"Miss Harriet Burnett?" the duke questioned.

"Yes. That's me. Like I said, the one and only." She gestured to the pink-cheeked woman beside her. "May I present my companion, Miss Lumley."

"How do you do," Miss Lumley said perfunctorily. This woman had no time for the attentions of a duke; she turned to her friend. "Listen, Harriet, there's someone I really must introduce you. Mrs. Belmont. She's awaiting her carriage now."

"Oh! We must go at once."

"Wait —" he called out.

Questions. He had questions. To start: how many Harriet Burnetts were there in this city?

"Did you bring the calling cards?" Miss Lumley asked. Then Miss Burnett curiously reached into the folds of her gown to find them. "Yes, yes I have some." And only then did she remember the duke — *a duke!* — standing there, desperately wanting her attention and utterly speechless as so many questions fought to be the first ones expressed. "Your Grace, it was lovely to meet you. If you'll excuse me."

And like that, she was gone.

Save for a letter that fluttered from her pocket to the parquet floor. He picked it up and recognized the stationery of the Fifth Avenue Hotel. He recognized the name upon the letter — Miss Harriet Burnett. He also recognized the handwriting. It was his own.

CHAPTER SIX

The duke has been making the rounds of all the best Fifth Avenue ballrooms but no particular heiress seems to have caught his eye — yet.
— *The New York World*

The next morning
The Fifth Avenue Hotel
This. *This* is why a walk in the park was not just a walk in the park when a duke was involved. Especially a tall, dark-haired, blue-eyed duke who was prone to heroics and dashing moments of romance. To say nothing of tantalizing near kisses that made a girl forget sense and reason.

Because here she was at the Fifth Avenue Hotel for another fitting with Miss Burnett, an unprecedented professional success, and all she could think about was the duke.

They had almost kissed.

She could not stop thinking about what

might have been.

Too bad about daylight, public spaces, a sense of courtship, romance, and decency. Such was a thought that had actually crossed her mind more than once ever since her afternoon walk with the duke, when in fact she should be offering a prayer of thanks for daylight, public spaces, a sense of courtship, romance, decency.

Reason and decency had prevailed.

She had not kissed the duke. Or he had not kissed her. Their lips had not met.

And so, she had not excessively risked her reputation, her heart, or her future on a man who would never marry her for reasons of wealth, class, and expectations.

Which was fine, because she wouldn't marry him anyway.

She had no wish to wed anyone at all, especially a man who did not hold women's fashion in much esteem. How could she ever share her hopes and dreams with him, knowing he'd declare them frivolous? If they wed, he would likely insist she give up her dressmaking dreams. She could not. She *would* not.

Adeline knocked on the door.

To be specific, she knocked on the door to Miss Burnett's suite of rooms. This time Adeline would do a final fitting for a variety of day dresses, riding outfits, evening gowns, and other ensembles, all of which she had customized. This might have been just a dress fitting for her client, but for Adeline it was a chance to finally see one of her own creations modeled by someone other than herself and her friends.

In that sense, it would be momentous.

While she rapped at the door to Miss Burnett's, she eyed the door to the adjacent suite of rooms. The duke was in there, probably. Being lordly and ducal and whatever men did when they didn't have a care in the world.

The duke, not *her* duke, as Rose insisted on calling him. Of course, they hadn't seen or heard from him after that walk in the park, which Rose had crashed under the pretense of being her chaperone.

She hadn't expected to hear another word from him, honestly.

A man like Kingston must have a lot to keep his days and nights occupied. He probably had dozens upon dozens of eligible potential brides to meet, for example. He could not spend his precious minutes with a poor seamstress.

She just hadn't expected to feel forlorn about it. The world had returned to rights and she had the opportunity of a lifetime right in front of her. There was no reason for her to feel miffed that a man had pursued her and then disappeared.

But she had liked him.

She spoke freely to him and he seemed interested in what she had to say, even if he disagreed with it. She had almost kissed him and a small part of her regretted that they hadn't seized the moment — scandal be damned — for a long, deep kiss.

A maid opened the door, putting an end to Adeline's thoughts of kisses and handsome British men next door, and showed her into Miss Burnett's bedchamber, where Miss Burnett was writing a letter, and her friend, Miss Lumley, was sitting on the settee, reading. A small side table nearby was loaded with delicacies — a bowl of fresh grapes, a plate of pastries, a delicate silver teapot with a china cup.

"The dresses arrived from the shop this morning, ma'am," the maid said. "I'll go ready the first one."

"Hopefully they should fit, save for a few final adjustments I can do on the spot."

"Splendid." Harriet smiled. "I have an afternoon tea that I do want to wear something fetching for."

"Oh, the ladies of the club will be so jealous," Miss Lumley said. "You'll spend all your time talking about your new dresses — when there are real problems in the world!"

"One might say that for half of humankind those problems include wearing gowns without pockets," Miss Burnett replied to her friend. "A woman wears seven pounds' worth of dress and hasn't a spot to put anything! We need rational dress. Shorter skirts. Looser corsets. More pockets. Then we shall take over the world."

"But how will you catch a duke, dressed thusly?" Miss Lumley teased.

Miss Burnett rolled her eyes. "Oh, the duke!"

She turned to Adeline, whose every nerve had started thrumming at the mention of him. "Everyone in society is obsessed with the duke. All the young ladies hope to be his duchess."

That — that clenching feeling around Adeline's heart, like a big fat fist squeezing a little rag doll — was why she should not entertain any thoughts of the duke. At all. Whatsoever. It would lead only to heartache.

"But as I said," Miss Burnett continued with a lingering glance in the direction of Miss Lumley. "I'm not inclined toward marriage."

Adeline murmured her agreement. A maid helped Miss Burnett into the first gown and

Adeline stood back, appraising the fit. She would have to take the hem up another half inch. They proceeded to try on and make slight alterations to the remainder of the gowns. Time flew by, and the ladies' idle chatter eventually returned to the subject of His Grace, the Duke of Kingston.

"Speaking of the duke, what do you think of him, Miss Black?" Miss Burnett asked. "Did you enjoy your walk in the park with him?"

For a moment, Adeline was terribly confused.

"How did you know about that?"

"He sent a letter to my rooms, but I quickly realized it was not intended for me. I didn't recall enchanting anyone in the elevator. I assumed he meant it for you and so I sent it along to the shop."

"I wondered how he found me," Adeline said as awareness dawned. "He caused quite a stir with my fellow seamstresses."

"Dukes tend to do that."

"Why did you not meet him yourself, Miss Burnett? I would have been none the wiser."

"Well, to start, the jig would have been up the moment I arrived. It would have required an awkward explanation, to be followed by an even more awkward afternoon in the park together. No, I shan't set myself up for such humiliations. Especially when I have more important matters to attend to."

"He must think that I am you," Adeline whispered, as the implications began to crystalize. Adeline's brain whirred and clicked and put it all together: the duke must have thought that she was Miss Burnett. He must have thought that she was an heiress, and a woman of great social standing. He must have discovered the misunderstanding and that was why she had not heard from him.

It was to be expected.

Truly.

Even if they had this instant, magic connection. Adeline shook the thoughts out of her head and made a few more adjustments to the sleeve of the gown.

"I wore one of your dresses to the ball last night, Miss Black, and more than one woman gave me a long second glance and inquired after the designer. Where shall I tell them to find you when they wish to get your designs for themselves?"

"Madame Chalfont's, of course."

"Do you ever think of having your own shop?"

"I dream of it all the time."

"What's stopping you?"

"It takes money to open a shop, and I

haven't saved enough yet. I'm not sure that I ever will."

Given her wages, she would need to be saving for the next twenty or thirty years, but later was better than never, was it not? It wasn't just money, though, that kept her diligently cutting and fitting in service of Madame Chalfont. Adeline was unsure of how to make the leap from here to there. She was just a girl with a daydream and calloused fingers. How was she supposed to convince a landlord to rent to her, or clientele to come to her?

She had ambition to burn, but the confidence to pursue it and the money to do it eluded her.

"Perhaps your duke will swoop in and save you," Miss Lumley remarked from the settee. "They're always doing that in the novels."

"He's not *my* duke."

"No? Not even after a walk in the park together?"

"Everybody knows that lords and dukes only come to America in search of wealthy brides." There was a beat of silence in which each woman acknowledged that truth. And another truth: that Miss Burnett had money while Adeline did not. "Of course I have no plans to see him again. He will inevitably discover that I am not the heiress he needs *and* that he's been misled about it — if he hasn't already. I imagine he won't be too happy about it."

A sharp, insistent knock on the door interrupted her.

The women exchanged loaded glances.

The knock on the door had escalated to a harder, heavier pounding.

The knock of someone not used to being ignored.

Adeline's heart started to pound.

"It seems like the inevitable is happening," Miss Lumley said. "I told you, Harriet, that your matchmaking scheme wouldn't work."

Harriet shrugged. "But this should be entertaining!"

Adeline just took a deep breath and braced herself.

In an instant, the duke's presence filled up the space and sucked all the air out of the room. Every one of her senses sharpened their focus on him. She could see little else beyond him: the wide, cashmere wool-clad shoulders, the waistcoat highlighting his broad chest tapering to his trim waist. His dark hair pushed back from the beautifully defined planes of his face. There was something captivating about the way he stood, tall and proud and shoulders thrown back. He was so absolutely self-assured. Self-righteous even. Like he had centuries of proof that he mattered.

When he saw her, his eyes flashed. His lips pressed into a firm line.

There was no denying it: he was handsome when he was angry. And oh, he was angry. She badly wanted to press her mouth to his and kiss away his fury. Stroke her hands along the tense muscles of his shoulders and back until he relaxed under her palms.

But this was not to be.

It was a pity that this — whatever this was — would come to a definitive end. Here and now. In the middle of a dress fitting. Mindful of her professional reputation, she started to pray that this wouldn't involve a scene. How embarrassing.

"Good morning, ladies." He spoke in a clipped, ruthlessly elegant tone. He was polite, even when furious. How ducal.

The ladies murmured their reply, though each one was rendered somewhat mute in the face of such an overwhelming and awe-inspiring male. "I did wish to clear something up and it seems that I have done so. You two are not the same person."

His gaze shifted accusatorily from Adeline

to Miss Burnett and back again.

"No use protesting that one, I suppose," Miss Lumley said cheerfully.

"I'm Harriet Burnett. The one and only." She flashed a grin and stepped aside. "And this is Miss Adeline Black, my dressmaker."

"Seamstress."

Beside her, Miss Burnett elbowed her in the ribs. "Don't sell yourself short."

The point was moot in the eyes of the duke. Whether atelier or seamstress, Adeline was not an heiress and thus was a waste of his time.

Oh, but she could see that he had *feelings* about it. The man was positively wracked with all sorts of intense emotions as he was forced to conclude that she wasn't the girl he had imagined her to be.

It was an honest mistake.

Now he would think the worst of her character because of the fantasy he had spun about her — that she was a wealthy woman, an answer to his prayers — even though she'd never intentionally gave him reason to.

His jaw set.

He had been hurt.

Even worse, he had been embarrassed.

Like a wounded creature, he lashed out.

"That would explain your presence *here,*

but it does not explain why you allowed me to persist in believing you were a guest of this hotel and, as such, a woman I could consider making my bride."

How politely he lashed out.

How elegantly he insulted her.

The cut was sharp and effective all the same.

This. *This* is why she knew better than to dally with a duke, a man so high above her station. They could flirt around the truth, but there was no denying that when it came down to it, that vast difference in his status and hers mattered more than anything else.

Well. She did not have to stand for it or allow him to put her down because of it. This, *this* is why she insisted upon her independence; it gave her a measure of pride. Adeline couldn't imagine what she had to gain by the good favor of an irate duke and so she wasn't going to lose her own self-respect over his insults.

"It's perfectly fine," Adeline said in her best Fancy Lady Voice, which she had learned from hundreds of dress fittings with the ladies of the Four Hundred. "And you needn't concern yourself with my feelings; I'm not upset that you never once mentioned the fact that you were a duke, thus concealing an important facet of your identity."

He scoffed. As if that wasn't the same thing at all, wasn't just as important. But Adeline refused to be held to a separate standard because a man was upset.

Miss Burnett interjected. "This is all just a silly misunderstanding. Nothing to get your unmentionables in a twist about. Perhaps you might resolve this matter elsewhere. Perhaps over tea in the lobby? Miss Lumley and I have a very important meeting to attend this afternoon."

"I really question your priorities, my dear," Miss Lumley remarked. "One can always be late due to unfolding romantic drama."

"It's not romantic drama," Adeline insisted. "It is, as you said, a silly misunderstanding."

"More like a comedy of errors, I should think," Miss Burnett quipped, and Adeline winced. It was the wrong thing to say, to make light of the Duke's feelings. Like most men, he was not accustomed to them, especially so many, all at once. To find humor in this momentous situation was possibly devastating.

Adeline decided her presence was no longer required. The fitting had concluded and she had nothing further to say to the duke.

"My apologies for any misunderstanding. If you'll excuse me, I should go."

She gathered her things and made her way toward the door. Just as escape was imminent, his hand shot out and grabbed her wrist as she passed. "Not yet."

CHAPTER SEVEN

No, I will not settle for the imitation. Stop.
I must have the original. Stop.
— Telegram from Her Grace,
the Duchess of Kingston

Kingston had done the unthinkable: he had fallen for a seamstress. A seamstress! He had traveled to New York with the explicit purpose of finding and wedding an heiress and instead he found himself enchanted with a woman who surely possessed no fortune *and* was of the trade that robbed him of his. His mother and her desperate need for the latest fashions had drained the estate's dwindling coffers. Those girls, profiting off it.

And yet.

He had reached out and grasped her wrist. *Don't go. Not yet.*

The logical portion of his brain was still functioning and it informed him that this was all a simple misunderstanding that could be cleared up with a laugh. He was not *that* invested — after all, it had been just a walk in the park. He should have no further business with her, especially of the sort that necessitated touching her, even if it was only his big hand and her small wrist.

None. At. All.

Her gaze traveled slowly and pointedly from the sight of his hold on her, up the length of his arm and came to rest on his face. She fixed her cool, unflinching eyes on him. Kingston let her go.

"If you'll excuse me, I must return to the shop," she said. "Miss Burnett, we will have the rest of your wardrobe ready within the week."

She left.

And then *he followed.*

Kingston could scarcely believe it, but he couldn't stop himself. He was a peer of the realm, one of the highest-ranking men in one of the greatest countries in the world: he was *Kingston.* She was just a girl, just a seamstress. But there he was, taking one determined step after another, his footfalls silent on the plush carpet in the corridor. He was mesmerized by the sway of her hips and captivated by the rustle of her skirts as *she* walked away from *him.*

He had questions, that was all.

He would never see her again, certainly.

"Why did you not say anything about your real identity?"

She gave a little laugh as she walked the corridor, toward the elevator, that plush and intimate box where he'd forgotten the world existed and half fell in love with her.

"Such talk of *real identities* sounds so mysterious and dramatic. Honestly, it was all a simple misunderstanding. But for that matter, why didn't *you* say anything?"

"I didn't think I had to."

"I suppose you're right."

She acknowledged it. She knew. She had known who he was the whole time. After all, England's finest had been disembarking by the dozens from fancy ships, ensconcing themselves at this very hotel, throwing themselves into the social whirl until they snared their heiress and hightailed it back to England.

Look at his cousin Freddie, for example.

They were silent in the elevator. An agonizing silence.

The doors opened to the loud roar and crush of the lobby. She stepped out of the elevator and into the crowd. Not once did she glance over her shoulder at him to see if he followed, because what business could a man like him have following a girl like her?

None. At. All.

Still, he followed.

Questions. He still had burning, urgent questions. The kind that would surely keep him up at night demanding answers and robbing him of sleep. Surely, he would never see her again and so logic and reason dictated that now was the time to ask.

At the entrance of the hotel she paused. He caught up to her.

This was goodbye, then. Forever, most definitely.

Kingston did not care for the sensation in his chest that this fact produced. Like his heart was in the throes of a full-scale, violent rebellion. He couldn't breathe.

"Maybe I don't want to be wanted only for my position," he said plainly, giving voice to that feeling for the first time in his entire existence.

"Maybe I don't want to be perceived as any less than you."

She turned to the right and started down Fifth Avenue. He fell in step beside her, stealing and savoring these last moments with her. Because this was the end, of course. It had to be. He could not imagine a world in which a man like him married a girl like her.

"You knew who I was," he said.

"I suspected. Anyone of sense or who reads a newspaper would. Handsome, well-dressed Englishman shows up in the Fifth Avenue Hotel? Really, it can only be one thing. An English peer, wife hunting among the New York dollar princesses. I may be of the working class, but I'm not ignorant."

"Now you wound me."

She shrugged. "You're here to wed a rich girl and I'm not interested in marrying. I have dreams and plans other than keeping busy with seating arrangements and hosting parties and whatever it is that duchesses do all day. Am I the only one who thinks a walk in the park with a duke is just a walk in the park?"

Just a walk in the park.

She slayed him.

She was, quite possibly, the only woman in the world who considered a walk in the park with a duke *just* a walk in the park. Something clenched around his heart. Again. He had found her: the rare and elusive woman who cared not for prestigious titles. Who could, perhaps, love him for him.

Not that he could afford to love her. Or even be enchanted with her.

She probably wasn't even flattered that he was trailing her down the Manhattan streets like a lovesick swain. Which he was not. He was a gentleman, irate at being grievously deceived by some slip of a girl, and determined to get to the bottom of the situation once and for all and forever. That was all.

"I'm also a marquis," he told her, because he felt some powerful need to impress upon her how prestigious he was, and as such, how significant his attentions were. It would hint at the magnitude of this misunderstanding. This would explain how flummoxed and angry he was. Or so he hoped. "The Marquis of Westlake, Earl of Eastland, and Viscount Blackwood. Shall I continue? I have a few lesser titles that I never use."

"I cannot imagine your point."

"Nothing is ever *just* this or *just* that between a woman and a duke. Or a marquis, an earl, and a viscount."

There was a beat of silence.

"Is this the part where I am supposed to swoon?"

His mouth dropped open. He shut it quickly.

"Shall I ask around to see if anyone is carrying smelling salts?"

She craned her neck, making a show of seeing who around them on the street might be in possession of smelling salts. Perhaps a street vendor? Was there an apothecary nearby? Not a single other person on the city street was remotely interested in them.

She was making light of their situation.

She did not understand: she had made a duke fall for a seamstress after *just* a walk in the park. She had made an Englishman have intense feelings of the romantic variety. After little more than a chance encounter in an elevator and afternoon together, she had so swiftly and expertly bewitched him just by being herself. He was at a loss.

"You're supposed to be impressed," Kingston told her, matching his steps to hers as they walked at a brisk pace down Fifth Avenue before turning onto a side street. "You are supposed to understand the duties of my position are such that I am required to wed a bride with certain qualifications."

"Which I do understand and which I do not possess."

"Which makes it . . . inconvenient or perhaps distracting . . . for me to . . ."

"As much as I am enjoying watching you grasp about for the polite words to convey what can only be insulting, I shall cut to the chase for you. I understand the situation perfectly. You need a wealthy bride. I am not a wealthy woman. I do not move in the 'certain circles' that care to be impressed by your titles. I'm just an American girl who enjoys long walks in the park with charming company and who is trying to make something of herself without entangling a duke, a marquis, an earl, and a viscount in the process."

Kingston stood still.

She was doing him a favor.

She was refusing him.

He did not know a world in which this happened.

"So I really do not see what all the fuss is about," she continued. "You cannot be with me and I am not interested in being with you. Besides, you never asked."

They had stopped walking and had come to stand in front of a shop now. He peered up, noting a sign that said *Madame Chalfont: Dressmaker.* Adeline looked at him in the expectant way that he looked at his solicitors and estate managers: *Are you quite finished? I have other business to attend to.*

But he wasn't finished with her. Not yet.

Not that he could articulate what and why and how.

"You are not like any other women I have met."

"I'll take that as a compliment."

"I do find myself enchanted by you."

"So you said. When we first met."

Kingston noticed that her gaze shifted

anxiously from him to the shop. It was almost as if she didn't want to be seen with him. *That* never happened. Until now. Until *her.*

"But you do understand why I cannot pursue our acquaintance further." He cleared his throat. "Even if I may wish to."

There, that is what he'd been trying to say, however inelegantly. *I like you. But . . .*

She gave him a soft, sweet smile. Something twisted in his gut. "I did enjoy our time together," she said. "Even if it was just a ride in an elevator and just a walk in the park. Goodbye to you, duke, marquis, earl, viscount, and all your other titles. Good luck with the heiresses."

She turned to enter the shop but a short, stout, impeccably attired woman emerged to block her entrance. Her graying hair was coiffed into a towering arrangement and a length of pink measuring tape was draped across her shoulders.

"What is this?" She waved her hands dramatically to indicate that *this* included Adeline, the duke and whatever had just happened between them.

"This is nothing, Madame Chalfont," Adeline said. "I am just returning after Miss Burnett's fitting at the Fifth Avenue Hotel. You know she has committed to a very large order and has expressly asked for me."

Kingston thought that was a lot of information for a simple question.

Madame Chalfont narrowed her eyes. "Is that all?"

"Yes, that is all."

"Then why do you have this *gentleman* nipping at your heels and sniffing around your skirts?"

Such accusations were not to be tolerated. Especially not by this stout old woman who slipped in and out of a fake French accent.

Kingston drew himself up to his full height and squared his shoulders. In his most ducal voice he drawled, "Kindly take care not to make such unfounded accusations about the lady and myself."

He was a duke. He did not do something so pedestrian as sniff around skirts.

But Madame Chalfont was another one of those unimpressed females and would have none of it. "Oh, isn't this a gallant one. Why is he so gallant, Miss Black? Hmm? You have been gone for quite a while. What took you so long?" Madame Chalfont questioned, even though it was quite clear she had already formulated a conclusion and nothing on God's green earth would dissuade her from it.

"I told you, Madame Chalfont," Adeline

said with an admirable amount of patience. "I was making some final adjustments to Miss Burnett's wardrobe. I returned immediately by the most direct route."

"With a man. In broad daylight. Shameless hussy."

Adeline took a break from holding the gaze of Madame Chalfont to give Kingston a glance that took a year off his life, at least.

It was time for him to step in for a display of heroics and ducal powers. He was born and raised for such displays of authority.

"Madame — though I hesitate to use the word since you are not displaying any qualities befitting the appellation — I'll thank you not to make such aspersions on the fine character of this young woman. I was merely escorting her directly from the Fifth Avenue Hotel to this present establishment."

In England, this would be sufficient. In England, Madame Chalfont would already be begging his pardon and issuing heartfelt apologies for the misunderstanding. In England, the word of the duke was second only to the word of God and no one dared to cross it. If he said that fire was cold, then fire was cold.

But he was not in England.

He was in New York City. His lofty lordship routine did not have the desired — or usual — effect. Madame Chalfont ignored Kingston.

Then she turned to Miss Black and said, "You're fired. Effective immediately."

"Madame Chalfont, please!"

"You heard me! You're fired. I'm tired of hearing about your ridiculous, newfangled dress ideas. I'm appalled you haven't demonstrated more sense after all the effort I have made to impress upon you the importance of a woman's virtue. Take all your ridiculous designs and go plague another modiste with them. Or . . ." Here she paused to sneer, "Maybe your *friend* will set you up with a little shop of your own. Either way, I don't care. You, Miss Black, are fired. Good day."

"But Madame —"

She stepped forward only to have the shop door slam inches from her nose. She wasted not a second before pounding at that door. Her tiny gloved fists hardly made a sound audible over the din of the city.

"Allow me." Kingston stepped in and pounded on the door with his strong fists. *Heroics. Must display heroics.* Her life had just been ruined because of him and he felt the noble obligation to save her.

But the door remained firmly shut to them both.

Adeline whirled around to face him, righteous fury blazing in her eyes. "Look what you've done!"

Everything was ruined. Everything!

The door slammed in her face and remained stubbornly shut. Presumably Madame Chalfont had given orders that none of her fellow seamstresses were allowed to open it to her. She was done. Finished. Out of work and out of luck.

The duke — oh, that blasted, clueless man — still stood there, shocked, simply shocked by what damage he had wrought.

Adeline had known that Madame had it in for her; she always disregarded her "pesky" suggestions of how to improve a design. *I hired you to sew,* she'd repeat. Adeline should have known that she'd seize any excuse to get rid of her.

And here was the perfect excuse.

A six-foot-tall, impeccably turned out British aristocrat sniffing at her skirts and nipping at her heels. There was only one reason men like him engaged with women like her, and it had nothing to do with maintaining the moral standards any employer expected from her young female staff.

Of course Madame Chalfont made assumptions.

"Go. Just go." Adeline's voice was low and lethal, as she voiced the word she should have said a few blocks earlier. But no, it had been a perverse pleasure to have the city's most eligible bachelor following her down Fifth Avenue. A small part of her had been charmed by the spectacle and enjoyed, for a moment, being a woman that men lost their heads over.

That moment was over.

"Miss Black —"

"You've said enough. Take your fancy titles — all of them — and go."

"I'll make this right. If you'll just —"

She spared him a glance, a quick darting glance that she hoped he wouldn't see. His eyes were pleading. His countenance pale. It was obvious that guilt and regret were feasting on his conscience. *Good.*

She turned on her French heels — a week's wages, well spent? — and started toward the tiny room she let at a boarding-house on Fourteenth Street. She would have to economize in order to make her rent payment. Perhaps she could get by on just one meal a day.

On her way, Adeline would stop in every shop she passed to inquire about positions.

103

She could not afford to lose a day, an hour, a minute. Literally — there were not enough hours in the day for her work to make up for wages lost. Every penny was precious and essential.

She tried to focus on practical considerations and not the fact that she had come *so far* from being just another tenement girl basting sleeves. Differences aside, she'd had a good job with Madame Chalfont, one that at least allowed her to afford her own (small) room and independence. And she'd had that opportunity with Miss Burnett; pity, Adeline would never get to see her wear those dresses now.

And she still had a duke sniffing at her skirts and nipping at her heels.

"Miss Black — wait. I must apologize."

"Yes, you do. But I haven't got time for that now."

"Please forgive me."

"Forgive you? Do you think you and your notions of chivalry and soothing your conscience are really what is on the forefront of my mind right now?"

He pressed his lips together and said nothing. Yes. Yes, he did think that.

She could see the headlines now: *Woman strangles man with his own self-importance. Man chokes to death on his own sense of entitlement.*

"Wait —"

"I cannot wait. I must find another position."

"Immediately? Can you not take the day? An hour?"

She smiled, an indulgent smile reserved for children and fools.

"How little you know of the plight of a working woman. No, I cannot take a day off. Not if I wish to pay for my lodgings, or eat, or maintain my dignity. You feel destitute because your club membership comes due or a tradesman inquires about debts or *one of* your houses needs some repairs. Whereas I might not have enough money for bread or lodgings. And then I shall have no choice but to become the woman Madame Chalfont has just accused me of being."

"I will fix this," he said, in that ducal way of his, in which he just needed to say it to make it so. It was a pity that the world didn't work like that. "I have caused this catastrophe and I shall make it right. I'll have a word with —" Here he paused, as they realized that he did not know with whom to have a word about the plight of an unemployed seamstress he had no business knowing. Instead, he said, "I shall find you a position. And in the meantime, I can provide some funds to tide you over —"

An enraged Adeline imagined yet more headlines: *Man shredded to ribbons by scissors-wielding seamstress. Duke skewered alive by woman's hat pin.*

As it was, she felt the heat and color rise in her cheeks.

"And what will I owe you then?" Adeline asked hotly.

"Nothing, of course. My honor compels me to make the offer."

"And how shall I explain it to my friends? What will they say of me then? What will I say when prospective employers have reason to question my virtue because I have been kept by a duke?"

"What can I do? Surely there must be something I can do."

"Change the world, *Duke.*"

Adeline was too angry to pin down the thoughts swirling in her head. Something about how he could not just throw his money around and solve all her problems. Maybe *today* he could, but not for all the days and not for all the girls. The matter was bigger than just her, in just this moment. Perhaps if her employability didn't rest on *virtue.* Perhaps if she earned a decent wage — enough to save for a rainy day like this one. Perhaps if she had more choices, more opportunities.

Perhaps, perhaps, perhaps.

He shrugged and raised his palms in a gesture of defeat. "I cannot change the world. I'm just one man."

Adeline gave a bitter laugh. "Apologies, but I do not have the time or inclination to listen to a wealthy man lament his lack of power. Go find your heiress, Duke."

CHAPTER EIGHT

Do you need an introduction to Emma Goldman? You have seen supposed pictures of her. You have read of her as a property-destroying, capitalist-killing, riot-promoting agitator. You see her in your mind a great raw-boned creature, with short hair and bloomers, a red flag in one hand, a burning torch in the other . . .
— Nelly Bly, *The New York World**

Union Square
A few days later

Within a week, a duke had ruined her life. Last week, Adeline had been so close to success that she could feel it — like the finest silk and delicate lace against her fingertips. Now she was back at the bottom of the scrap heap, skipping meals and pleading for positions that were beneath her talents, all because Madame Chalfont had dismissed her without even a reference.

The stain on her satin was that she wouldn't even get to finish her order for Miss Burnett. Until she'd been fired, she had labored late into the night, pouring her heart and soul into the construction of those gowns. Now she wouldn't even get a glimpse of them.

It was cruelly unfair that even having a man walking with her in broad daylight was enough to ruin her reputation *and* professional prospects.

When Rachel and Rose invited her to join them for an evening out on the town, an invitation Adeline couldn't accept fast enough. She needed a distraction. Whatever it was.

"Where are we going?" she asked, once they were all out on Broadway.

"Union Square. Emma Goldman is giving a speech after she's just gotten out of jail," Rachel explained. "It's sure to be a crush."

"I don't know who that is, but as long as she provides a distraction from the wreckage of my life, I'm all ears."

"She's one of those reformers," Rose explained. Indeed, the city — America — was full of them these days, agitating for laborers and the working class, for women's right to vote or do anything other than get married, and some even fought for the rights of birds.

To say the square was a crush was an understatement. It was very nearly a mob scene. Union Square was full of people from all walks of life who had rallied to hear the anarchist reformer. In the crowd, ladies and gentlemen mingled with gamblers and prostitutes; there were rich bankers and crooked politicians next to common laborers and seamstresses like her; there were sportsmen and suffragists. Adeline had never seen such a mix, never even imagined it and here they all were, one seething mass of humanity, present to hear a *woman* speak.

She wondered what the duke would think of a spectacle like this.

"Come back to Madame Chalfont's. We miss you terribly," Rachel said loudly, trying to make her voice heard over the dull roar of the crowd while waiting for the speaker to take the stage.

"I was fired, remember?"

"That damned duke!" Rose said, her eyes flashing. "If I had known he'd get you fired I never would have encouraged you to walk in the park with him."

That damned duke, indeed. Not a day went by that she didn't think of him — and none too fondly, either. Sure, he was handsome in a forget-your-own-name, weak-in-the-knees kind of way. Sure, he had that accent and spoke in a voice of kings and wealth and power and security, which made mere flirting feel like something else entirely. And yes, he had been interested in her — asking and listening to her ideas, even if they contradicted his — and that was its own kind of seduction.

But none of that was enough to compensate for the fact that he might have just ruined her life.

He should have known what it looked like when a man of his station took up with a woman of hers and he should have stayed away. Yet they both let his prestige cloud their judgment.

Adeline didn't know if she were angrier with the world than with him.

"He owes you," Rachel said. "He should at least give you money to tide you over until you find a new position. It's the least he can do."

Rose scoffed. "She doesn't want his money."

"He offered and I refused. I didn't want to take his pity money to assuage his guilt."

Or did she? At night, as she tossed and turned and listened to every sound her neighbors made, she thought maybe she should have taken it. Especially when she thought of those massive beds in the massive bedrooms at the Fifth Avenue Hotel. Just a few dollars, just to tide her over would have been fine, right? Like a tax, or some other payment that she was owed. Perhaps she should demand it of him. She had only to march uptown and demand an audience.

He would see her. She knew he would.

What an interesting, tantalizing feeling to know that a man as powerful as he would drop everything to see her. His lips would turn up into a slight smile and his gaze would do not-unpleasant things to her insides. She might find herself tempted by him.

No, she would not go to him, asking for what was owed. She did not wish to grapple with any thoughts and feelings of desire.

She wanted her pride more than she wanted his money.

"I think he owes her," Rachel said.

"Well no one is disagreeing with that," Adeline replied.

"Shh . . ."

Then a woman took the stage. Alone. A petite woman in a blue serge Eton suit with a blue muslin shirtwaist and little heeled boots that peeked out from under her skirts. The people in the square went silent.

"It's *her*," someone next to Adeline whispered fiercely yet adoringly. All around her faces were turned upward in rapt attention. Adeline listened as this woman alone on the stage spoke of . . . love.

Of all things, she spoke of love and desire and *not* getting married.

Marriage and love have nothing in common; they are as far apart as the poles — are, in fact, antagonistic to each other.

Adeline snapped to attention. This she knew to be true. Her own mother was testament to that, three times in succession with not a drop of affection from any of her husbands. Just desperation — mother and child had to eat, after all. Adeline wondered: was the duke really any different? Her heart was almost moved to pity when she thought of the cold nights awaiting him if he married for a reason other than the deepest and truest affection.

Can there be anything more outrageous than the idea that a healthy, grown woman, full of life and passion, must deny nature's demand, must subdue her most intense craving, undermine her health and break her spirit, must stunt her vision, abstain from the depth and glory of sex experience until a "good" man comes along to take her unto himself as a wife?

And Adeline felt the heat unfurling within

her, from her cheeks to the tips of her toes in her little French heels, which pinched her toes. What a scandalous thing to even think, let alone to speak aloud, let alone to declare to this crowd of mixed company. That a woman might have those feelings and might freely indulge in them without marriage, and without censure, was a shocking idea to Adeline. One that, heaven help her, made her think of the duke. What if her desire wasn't wrong? What if they could exchange nothing more than hearts and bodies, without money and marriage getting into the mix? She had to admit to herself that the fire she felt for him wasn't entirely fury.

Love, the strongest and deepest element in all life, the harbinger of hope, of joy, of ecstasy; love, the defier of all laws, of all conventions; love, the freest, the most powerful moulder of human destiny. How can such an all-compelling force be synonymous with that poor little state- and church-begotten weed, marriage?

And Adeline thought, *Tell that to the duke.* Tell that to a man intent on marrying for money, not love. The more Adeline listened to Miss Goldman, the more she reaffirmed that love and passion she might welcome, but she would never, ever marry at all.

In the crush of women exiting the square Adeline got separated from Rose and Rachel, so she found a spot on the sidewalk to wait for them. She was standing in the glow of the streetlight when she heard someone call her name.

"Miss Black!"

Adeline turned and saw Miss Burnett strolling toward her, and she was wearing one of the dresses she had created. A lump rose in her throat because she was finally seeing one of her gowns on a real woman and not just in her imagination, and the experience was more emotional than she would have imagined.

It was the midnight-blue taffeta, with a deceptively plain skirt in front, while the bustle was a gorgeous bundle of fabric and ruffles cascading to the ground, like a waterfall at midnight. The fabric around the chest was shirred not only to add simple decoration but also to give an ease of movement. The decor on the gown was simple but stark: white mother-of-pearl buttons in a line from throat to tapered waist, as if to say *eyes up here*!

"Miss Burnett, what a surprise to see you here!" Adeline said. "Your gown is lovely, if I do say so myself."

"Thank you. All my friends have been jealous of my new wardrobe."

Adeline had scarcely noticed the three friends with Miss Burnett until one of them spoke. Miss Burnett introduced her to a Mrs. Dean and a Mrs. Bergen. Miss Lumley was in attendance as well, standing close to Miss Burnett.

"We have been plaguing her for the name of her dressmaker ever since she wore that forest-green afternoon dress to our last meeting," Mrs. Dean said.

"But we went to Madame Chalfont's to ask for you and was told you were no longer employed there," said Mrs. Bergen.

"I should think she would want you in her employ, because you have talent," Miss Lumley added.

"Well, I think so," Adeline replied, feeling the heat of shame and embarrassment rise up within her. She did not want to admit her situation to these fine women. "I cannot say the same for Madame Chalfont, though."

"Where can we find you?" Mrs. Dean asked. "I should like to commission some dresses for myself and my daughters."

Adeline did not wish to provide the address of her dismal, depressing lodgings, full of dismal, depressing people.

"I don't have an establishment at present," Adeline admitted.

The group of ladies did that thing women do, where they communicate volumes with only their eyes, never even uttering a word. When this silent conversation apparently concluded, Miss Burnett slid her gloved hand into one of the pockets that Adeline had lovingly sewn into her gown, removed a card, and pressed it into Adeline's hands.

"We take callers on Tuesdays."

"Be sure to come alone."

"Tell no one."

Adeline looked down at the card in her hand. The paper was plain white, but of an exceptionally fine quality. The words were printed in formal script with black ink.

The Ladies of Liberty Club
25 West Tenth Street
New York City

When Adeline looked up again, the women were gone, disappearing into the crowd that Rose and Rachel pushed their way through, casting backward glances at the women Adeline had just been speaking to.

"Who were those women?" Rachel asked.

"They look fancy," Rose remarked.

"Just some women who liked my dress,"

Adeline replied because she wasn't sure what else to say. Were they future clients? Fairy godmothers? Were they just figments of her imagination?

"Have you ever heard of the Ladies of Liberty Club?"

Both Rose and Rachel shrugged to say *nope, never heard of 'em.* Nevertheless, Adeline slipped the card into her own pocket and wondered if maybe she didn't need Madame Chalfont or the duke and his money after all.

Chapter Nine

Nora threatening elopement. Stop. Clara refusing wealthy suitor because of nonsense about love match. Stop. Solicitor says more repairs needed at Lyon House. Stop. Please tell him it is imperative that the Duchess of Kingston needs to be height of fashion. Stop. Ermine cape essential. Stop.

— Telegram from Her Grace,
the Duchess of Kingston

Meanwhile, uptown . . .
The Metropolitan Club
One East Sixtieth Street

Though it was newly established, the Metropolitan Club was, in Kingston's eyes, the Manhattan equivalent of White's in that it was the exclusive haven of wealthy, powerful, and privileged men. It was a place where they might not be plagued by the problems of the world, or females, or especially the female problems of the world.

It was a place where telegrams from his mother could not reach him, relating the very latest in family and fashion dramas, such as the one burning a hole in his jacket pocket now that the concierge had handed to him on his way out of the hotel. Putting her message out of mind was another problem, though, one he expected a drink at the club would help him forget.

The club was where he might take a break from the business of securing an heiress, what with the lack of scheming mamas and darling daughters present to potentially ensnare and entrap him. While they had all the wealth in the world, they did not have his aristocratic title — and they weren't used to not getting what they wanted.

But here, he could sit back, relax, sip a fine whiskey, and consider whether Miss Olivia Watson, the blond railroad heiress was The One. Or perhaps Miss Elsie Penny-packer, the brunette daughter of a shipping magnate, was his future duchess. After a whirlwind of soirees, musicals, and social calls, Kingston had narrowed his prospects down to these two women. There were certainly more eligible ladies for him to meet, but one of these two would have to do, for time was of the essence.

His mother *needed* an ermine cape.

Thoughts of marriage, money, and ermine capes made his thoughts turn to Adeline. Who was he fooling? He couldn't *stop* thinking about Adeline. She was a young woman alone, at the mercy of an unfriendly world. He was simply concerned for her welfare, he told himself.

But it was those fiery arrows of truth that she'd aimed and fired directly at him that really claimed his cognitive functions and held on tight.

You think being broke is when your club membership comes due or when you need to make some repairs to one of your houses.

Miss Black did not understand the position he was in, he protested, in a silent conversation with himself. Being a young woman alone in the world, she simply did not understand the number of people who relied upon him to protect them and provide for them.

His sisters.

His mother. And *her* dressmakers. To say nothing of the milliners.

His servants, who lived and worked in his houses and would like to do so without the roof crashing down on their heads. Some had even devoted their entire lives to serving the Kingston estate, and it felt like the worst sort of betrayal to let them go now.

His tenants were finding it harder and harder to make a living off the land, especially since his father had refused to allow a train station to be built on the estate. They were hardworking families who'd farmed the land for generations: the Smythes, the Blackwoods, the Harrisons. Families faced separation and poverty if he could not find a solution to the estate's pressing problems.

The world was changing. He admittedly fought it by holding on tight to tradition. After all, it had worked for countless generations of Kingston dukes before him.

Wed an heiress. So simple, that.

It was much, much easier than changing the world, as Adeline had admonished him to do.

With this fortune he could restore his world to rights. He could be the duke and gentleman that he'd been born and raised to be. He could ensure that everyone under his protection was provided for.

This loveless marriage of convenience was the right, honorable thing to do. So he would do it.

What will I say when prospective employers have reason to question my virtue?

Kingston sipped his whiskey and gave a hard look at the men around him. No one questioned their virtue as they schemed to obtain fortunes by methods both honest and dishonest. There was no question about their virtue as they told lewd and ribald stories about things they did with mistresses downtown, all while sipping expensive champagne and lighting imported cigars with hundred-dollar bills set aflame, in the vicinity of priceless works of art.

And she might not be able to *eat* because of him.

His stomach churned. The whiskey. It had to be the exceedingly fine whiskey, aged eighteen years, and selling for an astronomical sum. He did not even know how its price compared to a working woman's wages.

It was not the whiskey. Or the champagne or caviar or cake.

It was guilt. Hot, festering, churning guilt. It was the slow dawning awareness that while he might be a savior to some, he was undoubtedly the villain in her story. He had gotten a poor seamstress fired by his mere presence. By sniffing around her skirts and nipping at her heels.

Making matters even worse was the unavoidable and deeply uncomfortable fact that he had developed some sort of *feelings* for the woman, that spitfire female with the sparkling doe eyes and kissable lips. She teased and challenged him, forcing him to question the very foundations of his existence.

It wasn't every day a man had the pleasure of meeting a woman like that.

It wasn't every day a man lost her.

All because he'd been so blinded by anger. He never really believed that she had intentionally deceived him. If he was *emotional* at all it was because he'd had a glimpse of a future where he could please everyone: do his duty by the dukedom and find a bride he actually wanted. That possibility had been wrenched away.

He did not think he could fall in love with Miss Pennypacker or Miss Watson.

"What has you so glum?" Freddie strolled in and dropped into the seat opposite. "Let me guess — women troubles."

"You could say that."

"You've come to the right place. The club is an excellent spot to avoid women troubles. Hence my presence here. If you see my wife, tell her I'm very sorry for skipping her mother's birthday tea but I could not miss the races that day. Say, are you still debating between your two charming heiresses?"

"Yes. That. I cannot decide if I prefer blondes or brunettes. If I prefer railroad money or shipping money. The problems of a man of my position."

"You know, Duke, that some people work in coal mines."

"Yes, like my tenants when I cannot afford to keep the estates up and running. What is your point?"

"Some people have real problems and you're here sulking over which heiress you would like to wed. Some people even have to marry the only heiress who will have them." Freddie heaved a mighty sigh. Poor Marian. "You at least have the title. I had to rely on my boyish good looks, English accent and prospect as second in line. Fortunately, that was enough to charm Marian. And her giggling. But anyway, I can't imagine why *you* are having trouble landing an heiress."

He was not having trouble landing an heiress. Both the blonde and the brunette would say yes in a heartbeat. The problem was that he was enchanted with a woman who was the opposite of an heiress.

"As you pointed out, some people have real problems. Problems that make ours pale in comparison. For example, Miss Black."

Freddie lifted one brow. "I'm not familiar with her."

"I have taken a liking to a woman I believed to be the heiress Miss Harriet Burnett. But she was, in fact, Miss Adeline Black." Kingston took a swallow of whiskey and decided it was time to say the facts out loud. "A seamstress."

"A seamstress?" Freddie choked on his drink.

"Correction: former seamstress."

"You must have been blinded by her charms."

"You could say that."

She was enchanting. That smile. The sparkle in her eyes and the sway of her hips. The way she teased and challenged him and opened his eyes to give him a different glimpse of the city — another world, another life — one he found intriguing.

He wanted to be angry with her, but now that he'd had time to cool off, he acknowledged that the facts would not support it. Kingston had turned their encounters over and over again in his mind, looking for all the blatant falsehoods she had told him. But he came up wanting.

He had so badly wanted to believe that she was an heiress that he overlooked any clues that might indicate otherwise.

Because if she was an heiress he could have something like a love match.

A wife he wanted to cozy up with in his drafty old ancestral homes. Plural.

These were thoughts that verged precariously into the territory of *feeling* and he was horrified to think them and feel them, and they stubbornly refused to go away. But it was imperative that said feelings vanish, as quickly as they had come. He had a duty. A sacred duty to uphold tradition. He couldn't be a mess of emotions over a woman he couldn't marry.

He should think about Miss Olivia Watson (the blonde) or Miss Elsie Pennypacker (the brunette).

Or drink more whiskey.

He should not think of Miss Adeline Black, despairing seamstress whose life he ruined and had no way of fixing.

Whiskey. Definitely more whiskey.

"I might have been responsible for her being relieved of her position."

"What. Did. You. Do?"

Kingston recounted the discovery, the heated walk, the ridiculous altercation with the shop owner. The way Adeline had summarily dismissed him and vanished into the crowds. The least he could do was disappear and get out of her way; clearly his stalking her steps did her no favors and he had no desire to force himself upon her. But now he wanted to see her again and had no way of finding her. He had to admit this was probably for the best.

"Well, you're an ass," Freddie said.

"I know. I have to make this right. I'm just not sure how one would go about it."

"Do you though? No one expects it from a man of your position."

"It is the honorable, responsible thing to do. I cannot bear the thought of her starving on my account. Or worse."

"Chuck her some coin." Freddie shrugged. "I know you think that you're broke, but you can afford to spare enough to tide over a seamstress between jobs. Just one of those drinks ought to keep her for a night at least. Who knows, maybe she'll enjoy a new career as your mistress."

"I cannot."

"Why ever not?"

But Kingston didn't know how to repeat what she had tried to explain to him. That it was not merely a simple fact of having coin or not. That it could not even be a simple matter of love or lust, so long as the disparity in their wealth existed. He did not understand, and he was shocked, slightly horrified, and somewhat aghast to discover that he wanted to.

Change the world, Duke.

What did that even mean? Where did a man even begin?

Not with Freddie, that was certain. His cousin thought nothing of leaving his wife uptown and spending her dowry on other women downtown. As long as he suffered Marian's giggling, this was somehow owed to him. For the first time, Kingston started to wonder about the lives of those other women. He knew, instinctively, that Freddie did not. A curious fissure in the connections between the two friends and cousins opened up — Kingston saw it, noted it, kept the fact of its existence to himself.

And then there was this unfortunately true fact: "I don't know how to find her."

He had stood on the sidewalk and watched as the city swallowed her up. One minute she'd been beside him, then a swarm of pedestrians surged around her, engulfing her, hiding her, sweeping her along. It would be a fool's errand to walk the streets of New York in search of a petite brown-haired and brown-eyed seamstress with a fiery gaze and a mouth he hungered to kiss.

He did not have the time. The debts were crushing and coming due with a ferocious speed that left him little breathing room.

He didn't have a good enough reason to, either.

Not when roofs were leaking, tradesmen's bills were due, tenants were struggling, and his sisters were threatening elopement. Not when finding her was only half the battle; she would make him change the world. No, he needed an heiress, the sooner the better. No matter how he may — or may not — feel about the matter.

"Well then," Freddie said. "I repeat my original question. Which heiress will it be? The blond one or the brunette? If you're really struggling, might I suggest that you flip a coin for it?"

CHAPTER TEN

It is a curious phenomenon that the respectable ladies of the city are now occupying their days with the formation of clubs for the purpose of improving their minds and communities. One is prepared to tolerate it — as long as wifely duties at home aren't neglected.

— *The New York World*

Tuesday
25 West Tenth Street

Adeline paused in front of 25 West Tenth Street, a fine and impressive redbrick townhouse nearly indistinguishable from any other house on the pretty, tree-lined street. Her heart was thudding hard in her chest and echoing in her ears.

We take callers on Tuesdays, they had said.
Tell no one, they had said.
Come alone, they had said.

For what? They did not say. It was nerves

and fear making her heart beat so, but she told herself such feelings were ridiculous. This street was perfectly nice and clearly well-to-do and not the sort of place where Dangers Might Befall You.

She allowed herself a small sigh of relief.

Besides, how dangerous could a group of *ladies* be?

What would they do, prick her to death with their hat pins? Tighten her corset until she couldn't breathe? Hang her from the ceiling by her bustle? Absurd!

Adeline climbed the stoop to the front door. And she paused. What was she afraid of, anyway? The unknown, of course. Miss Burnett had not been very forthcoming about the purpose of this call or whom she would meet. Why, it could be anyone, with any nefarious intention.

They could poison her tea. Elegant, polite, clean, and lethal. That was how ladies would do it, if they were determined to do it.

She wore her best ensemble for the occasion — the one she'd been wearing when she met the duke. If the circumstances were good, she wished to make a favorable impression, and if she was going to meet her maker, she would like to be finely attired.

She had come all this way. She would have

to take the risk.

She also did not have any other options. Every shop she'd called upon to inquire about positions was not interested in hiring a woman without a reference — which Madame Chalfont steadfastly refused to give, despite entreaties from Rachel and Rose on her behalf. Soon, Adeline would have to swallow her pride and return to the tenements and find a position basting sleeves or something equally tedious and low-paying.

Finally, Adeline raised the brass knocker — in the shape of a woman's head, with a riot of curls that upon closer inspection, were *snakes* — and rapped on the door, which was opened swiftly by a person who she could not immediately identify as being either a man or a woman, despite wearing the traditional butler's attire. But regardless, this kind and friendly face smiled at her and said, "Come in, love."

Just like that, no questions asked.

Adeline followed her through a recently refurbished foyer — one could still smell the fresh coat of paint. It was decorated in a simple style, but with fine materials and furnishings that suggested old New York money. There was none of the glitzy, gilt new-money style, designed to dazzle, impress, and conceal a sense of inadequacy that their fortunes didn't stretch back for generations.

Like the duke. She wondered what his house — houses — were like. Probably monstrous old castles into which could fit the entire neighborhood in which she'd grown up.

The butler opened the doors to the drawing room and stepped aside for Adeline to enter. The sight that greeted her was hardly one that would inspire fear, or cause for concern, or even be the remotely remarkable.

A group of women sat around, sipping tea. As women do. As women had done. For centuries.

It was such a benign scene, Adeline almost wished for weaponized hat pins and bejeweled vials of poisons. Had she really come all this way merely to take tea, even if it promised to be quality tea?

"Miss Black!" It was Miss Burnett, smiling at her. "How lovely to see you again."

She performed introductions. "Miss Black is the dressmaker I was telling you all about, the one who makes the beautiful and flattering dresses *with pockets.*"

This was greeted by *oohs* and *aahs,* and suddenly, the women's faces became friendlier. Somehow, this feature made her and her work more amenable to this society's purpose, which still remained a mystery to Adeline.

"What a darling ensemble," complimented a woman wearing a pinstriped day dress.

"Is it your own design?" asked another.

"Yes, thank you. I get bored sewing simple cuts and styles, so I like to be more inventive with my own attire." Since the ladies seemed interested, Adeline continued. "I like garments that feel good to wear, but I don't wish to sacrifice style, of course. I just think life would be a lot easier for women if they needn't bear the weight of seven pounds of corsets and petticoats, or if they had someplace to keep their things without having to mind where they put their reticule."

"We couldn't agree more with your assessment on women's attire," a woman who introduced herself as Miss Parks remarked. "Many of us are active in the rational dress movement. We believe that liberating women from her skirts will make it easier for them to move about the world freely."

"Who knows what shall happen when we are free from corsets and can take a deep breath?"

"There will be no stopping us then!"

Adeline was startled when the ladies then emitted whoops and hoorahs. They did so in a very ladylike way, but still, they were whooping and cheering about women taking over the world while enjoying afternoon tea.

How curious.

Adeline had to admit she was intrigued.

"Miss Black, welcome to our meeting of the Ladies of Liberty society," Miss Burnett said. Her gray green eyes crinkled with amusement. Like she had a secret. Like she possessed magic. "I am the founder. Our shared purpose is the advancement of women in the professional arts."

"I'm sorry, I'm not familiar with your group."

Adeline remembered Miss Burnett's vague mentions of important afternoon teas, but she had not revealed more than that and Adeline thought nothing of it. Fancy ladies like these were always forming societies and foundations to lecture on hygiene or the evils of drink and to aid poor, unfortunate girls in unfashionable neighborhoods. They handed out Bibles and mittens and it was all right, she supposed. Adeline was going to be tremendously vexed if she had donned her best dress and come all this way only to receive a Bible and a lecture.

"You mustn't apologize. You are not familiar with our work because it largely takes place behind the scenes. In fact, the women of our club take a vow of secrecy. We cannot have many people aware of us."

"Yes . . . of course," Adeline murmured, confused.

Miss Burnett continued. "While our sisters clamor for the vote — as they jolly well should and we support them — we take more direct, but discreet, action. We have no wish to wait for laws or society's expectations to change. We will not seek permission. We simply place ladies in positions where they might do good, honest work for a fair wage. We believe that the more women thusly employed, the more powerful a force they'll be together, and the more men will have to acquiesce to our demands for equality."

Adeline wasn't sure if this was absurd or audacious. Or both. But at least it didn't sound as if they were going to distribute Bibles or mittens. They looked like such respectable, traditional women, and yet Adeline felt as if she might have fallen into the clutches of a revolutionary ladies collective.

"Sometimes girls in trouble come to us," Miss Lumley explained. "And we help them get on their feet and give them employment opportunities that preserve their safety and dignity."

"For example, some are given positions as sales girls in my salons."

"Your salons?"

"I'm Madam C. J. Walker, how do you do?" A dark-skinned woman smiled at her. Adeline gasped in recognition and shook the woman's outstretched hand. Madam C. J. Walker was a remarkable entrepreneur; she had created her own line of hair products specifically for dark-skinned women like herself and was rumored to be a millionaire. Rose was such a devotee of the products that she occasionally spent her spare funds on them rather than her beloved dime novels.

"Those with literary or journalist aspirations are given employment with the suffragette newspapers — like the *Women's Journal* or *The Revolution*. You've heard of it?"

Adeline shook her head no. The only periodical she read regularly was *Demorest's Illustrated Monthly,* which included dress patterns and design ideas.

"We have connections at all the papers, numerous activists, and even a female physician among our members," a woman in a blue day dress added. "We help women with whatever they might need, but we mainly help women find good jobs."

"The other members here are either professional women themselves or married to open-minded professional men who are willing to hire females for their offices," Miss Lumley said. "We are in a position to make a difference and we don't take the responsibility lightly."

"I suppose the short answer is this: we are a placement agency," Miss Burnett said. "One with noble and revolutionary aims. Now, how can we help you?"

Adeline understood *placement agency*. There would be no Bibles and mittens making her feel like a charity case — there could be a job, an opportunity to stand on her own two feet again and prove her worth. She would never, ever make the mistake of getting starry-eyed by a man and letting him walk her to her place of employment or *anywhere* again.

"I would like employment in the dressmaking trade."

"I would be happy to make an introduction and put in a good word with my dressmaker. She is always looking for good help and the quality of your work, Miss Black, speaks for itself," one woman offered.

It was a generous offer. It was the reference Adeline desperately needed in order to find a good position worthy of her talents. This was the miracle that people prayed for. This was an unprecedented stroke of good fortune.

But Adeline noticed that one woman, Miss Parks, was wearing a Worth dress. She was so wealthy that she wore Paris couture to afternoon tea. The woman wearing the pinstriped dress complimented her attire with a hat bearing the expensive feathers of a snowy egret. All of the women, in fact, were exceedingly well turned out. Even the women who did not obviously display great wealth on their sleeves wore well-made hats and gowns that were not cheap.

Adeline had an eye for these things.

These women had influence, yes. But they also had money. Even better, they had ambition; after all, they were all here together conspiring how to help her.

Adeline's spirit of brazenly seizing every and any opportunity had long served her well; it had gotten her out of the tenements, into Madame Chalfont's shop, and it had gotten her here. Now she would test how much further it could take her.

"I am a seamstress and I am in need of a position, preferably at a fine establishment.

I'm very qualified," she began. Then she paused, dramatically. "Or you could help me establish my own shop."

She had harbored this dream and spoke of it to anyone who would listen — her mother, family, neighbors. But people had only laughed. Even Rose and Rachel smiled politely but distantly whenever Adeline mentioned *if I had my own shop . . .*

Adeline braced herself for laughter. Or polite smiles, or renewed offers for a good word at their local dress shop — something simpler, less risky.

These ladies expressed themselves in murmurs of shock and resistance. But they were considering it. Adeline held her breath.

"But the expense!"

"But it hasn't been done!"

"But how!?"

"Is it necessary?"

"Too much, too much . . ."

"You could place me at another dressmaker's shop, but I am just one woman," she said, finding her courage with each word she spoke. "However, if I had my own shop — making stylish yet sensible gowns that make women feel as if they could conquer the world — then I could employ scores more girls."

Miss Burnett was gazing at her intently

and Adeline couldn't read the look in her gray-green eyes. Had she gone too far? She might have gone too far. The ladies chattered among themselves, debating the merits and drawbacks of supporting some seamstress to this degree.

Finally, Miss Lumley spoke and the room quieted down. "Miss Black does have a point. We could help more girls if we established new businesses rather than cajoling existing business owners to make room for one more girl, here and there."

"Yes, but what do any of us know of running a business?"

"Plenty, I daresay! We manage households and servants. Such skills must be transferrable."

"They are. I would be happy to advise," offered one woman. "I discovered that I have a knack for accounting when balancing our household books and have since taken over the accounting for my husband's firm."

"The expense though. It must cost a tidy sum to establish a shop," one nervous woman pointed out.

"What are our membership dues for? What are we all contributing our pin money for, if not this?"

"We do use these funds to support

women," Miss Lumley explained to Adeline. "We use our own allowances and occasionally pilfer from household funds, which is why no man can know what we do."

"The minute they discover we are appropriating their money to empower women is the minute we are likely to be cut off," Miss Parks added.

"I hope we can count on your discretion," Miss Burnett said pointedly.

Come alone. Tell no one. It made sense now. She had nothing to fear at all.

"My hopes and interests are aligned with yours," Adeline said solemnly. "I promise I will never breathe a word of this club or your efforts to anyone."

Whether they helped her or not, succeeded in their efforts or not, Adeline recognized these ladies were saviors for what they were attempting. Oh, how different her mother's life might have been if she'd had a collective like this to turn to instead of a series of wretched husbands. She'd do anything to spare other women her mother's struggles. Thus, when Adeline promised secrecy, she meant it with her whole heart and every fiber of her being.

"Establishing a dress shop does fit the spirit and mission of this club," Miss Burnett said thoughtfully. "Miss Black makes excellent points about how many women we could serve — from the seamstresses and shop girls she'd hire, to say nothing of changing the prevailing fashions to those that encourage women's freedom. I motion to approve and support this venture."

Adeline's heart went still.

So often people had laughed at her when she had shared her dream of owning her own shop. And now? Silence reigned and it was excruciating. Was it approval or disapproval lurking in that quiet?

Finally, one woman spoke up. She'd been silent thus far and even now seemed very nervous about speaking in front of the others. Her fingers clenched and twisted around a lace-edged handkerchief. "As you know, my husband owns many buildings with space to let," she said quietly. "The other night at supper he was grumbling tremendously because one of his tenants had fallen through at the last minute, after he'd gone to the expense of preparing it. There are new floors, electric light fixtures . . . I wonder if we might . . . perhaps . . . be able to rent it for Miss Black's shop?"

"That is a wonderful suggestion, Mrs. Harris."

And that seemed to settle it. A shy, quiet

woman mustering the courage to speak up had just made all the difference in Adeline's life.

"What do you think, Miss Black?" Miss Burnett asked.

"I have dared to dream of such a world where this happens, but I never imagined that I might live in it."

Change the world, she had told the duke. But instead, perhaps she and these ladies would change the world themselves.

CHAPTER ELEVEN

Tradesmen at the door demanding
payment and attention. Stop.
Please fix. Stop.
— Telegram from Her Grace,
the Duchess of Kingston

Two weeks later
In the afternoon

The brunette. Definitely the brunette. Her name was Miss Elsie Pennypacker, sole heiress to her father's shipping fortune and a descendent of an old Knickerbocker family on her mother's side — the Manhattan equivalent of a prestigious and distinguished lineage, even if it only went back an adorable 100 years (compared to his family's title, which dated to 1066).

She would be the future duchess of Kingston.

Probably.

Kingston had been feeling immense pressure to marry someone — anyone — quickly. Between the telegrams from his mother and missives from his secretary, the situation with the estates was becoming dire. Crops were failing. Mortgages coming due. And more tradesmen's bills, too.

Of all the women he had met at that point, Miss Pennypacker seemed to have the most promise. She had an amiable disposition, a voice that did not grate the nerves, and ambitions for motherhood.

He had been courting her exclusively for the past fortnight. Besides possessing the requisite fortune, she was also in possession of dark hair and velvety brown eyes and a bow mouth that reminded him of . . . Adeline.

But an Adeline without the propensity to tease him about marriage proposals or lecture him on the significance of the shirtwaist. He missed being made to feel like just a man, and not only a lofty title. He certainly did not receive any sharply worded rebukes from Miss Pennypacker challenging him to change the world or at least question his position in it. Instead, she told him about her passion for floral arrangements, her strategy for seating at dinner parties.

She did not make him think or feel like

his heart was bursting at the seams, like Adeline did.

But Miss Pennypacker's way with a guest list was *legendary.*

Which was everything he wanted in a duchess.

Probably.

"So you are going to propose to Miss Pennypacker," Freddie said as they walked through the city streets on an errand.

"Yes," he said with a certainty that he did not feel.

"Excellent. Marian will be pleased; they are friends. They can sip tea and complain about us cavorting at all hours."

"Unless we do not cavort at all hours," Kingston replied. They'd had their fun during their university days but as he'd grown older, he'd also grown more sedate in his pleasures. A sense of duty and responsibility tended to slow down a man's cavorting. "Might I even suggest that we don't give them anything to complain about? You know I have some notion of gentlemanly behavior."

Freddie just laughed.

"Spoken like a man who has never been married. Allow me to paint a picture of your future: you return to cold, dreary England with your bride. You will be consumed with all the necessary work on the estate while she will become bored, lonely, and needy. This will make you bored with her. Affairs will ensue. Feelings will be hurt. Before you know it, you'll be trudging along the Ladies' Mile in search of some apology trinket."

They were, at present, trudging along the Ladies' Mile in search of an apology present for Marian. Apparently she had taken issue with the hours her husband had been keeping, though Kingston suspected it might have been the company he kept during those hours that upset her.

"I can't imagine *all* this to become true. For one thing, I intend to be faithful."

"Oh well, all *intend* that. And it's one thing if you marry for love. But if you marry for money?" Freddie shrugged. "She's interested in your title. You're interested in her money. It's hardly the stuff of great passions and grand romances."

"That is unexpectedly astute, coming from you."

Kingston also hoped it was wrong.

"I have learned the hard way. Just as I have learned to take my pleasures where I may."

Any further thoughts and conversation on the matter came to an abrupt halt, as he did, when Kingston saw a freshly painted sign hanging over a certain storefront on Nineteenth Street.

THE HOUSE OF ADELINE

Could it be her? How many Adelines were in New York, anyway?

Kingston resumed his steps, involuntarily drawn toward her name and the possibility that he might see her again. He got close enough to see a large display window, revealing a vibrantly colored pink gown on display. There were sparkly bits on it and ruffly bits, and being a man who took no interest in the attire of women (save for knowledge of removing it), he lacked the vocabulary to describe it. But Kingston was instinctively aware that this dress was different from the gowns ladies tended to wear.

It *had* to be her. How many women named Adeline who created such fantastic gowns were there in New York, anyway? Actually, probably a few, because that was New York for you.

As such, that meant it would behoove him to confirm whether or not this was in fact, the one and only Adeline who haunted his thoughts and desires. If she was proprietress of her own establishment, it would assuage his guilt for the circumstances in which he last saw her. This would even be a great improvement in her situation. He could stop losing sleep over her, for wondering what had become of her, how he might find her, and how he might make things up to her.

How many women named Adeline who had captured his heart were there in New York, anyway? Just one.

"Might I ask why we are entering a ladies' dress shop?" Freddie inquired as Kingston opened the door and resolutely stepped inside.

It was a very fine shop, one that clearly catered to a wealthy clientele, or hoped to. The dark hardwood floors were covered in a plush crimson carpet, the walls were a bright white plaster, all the better to set off the stunning array of gowns on display. Massive gilt-and-crystal chandeliers provided a warm, flattering glow to the space.

But the shop was empty. Other than a girl, but not *the* girl he sought.

"Good afternoon. May I help you, gentlemen?" The woman behind the impressive mahogany counter had dark hair and eyes, similar to Adeline, but with a no-nonsense air about her that suggested she was excellent at managing anything and everything.

"This is the House of Adeline?" Kingston asked.

"That's what the sign says."

"As in, Miss Adeline Black, formerly of Madame Chalfont's dressmaking shop?"

The shop girl's eyes flashed, then narrowed, the manner that suggested that she suspected who he was. Because he had been discussed. At length. Not entirely favorably.

"Yes, the one and only."

Kingston began to assemble the pieces together: this woman was likely a friend of Adeline's, who was aware that he was the reason Adeline had been relieved of her position. She likely had thoughts and feelings upon the subject of his person that were not entirely charitable. And now she was the gatekeeper between him. And her.

"How do *you* know her?" she asked, just to confirm, it seemed.

"Yes, Duke, how do you know her?" Freddie quipped.

The shop girl smiled and it was not reassuring. Kingston groaned inwardly because dukes did not groan outwardly.

"We had a chance encounter once upon a time."

"How romantic," she deadpanned.

"It was very romantic."

"Stop. I might swoon."

"I'll catch you. I'm known for my impressive displays of heroics."

She scowled. "Save your attempts to be charming for Miss Black. I suppose you would like to see her?"

"Well, he's not here for a gown," Freddie answered, with a dashing grin as he leaned against the counter, quite oblivious to the woman's decided lack of interest in his flirtations.

"I'll see if she's free."

The shop girl disappeared behind a thick velvet curtain that was insufficient to conceal the sound of a furiously whispered conversation between two women.

She was here. The woman who had slipped into all his waking thoughts and nightly dreams was here. His heartbeat quickened. Kingston did not try to slow it down.

How could he, when he might soon have the opportunity to gaze at those dark, sparkling eyes, to breathe her in, to discover how she'd gone from down-on-her-luck to mistress of her own shop in less than a month's time?

Besides, he owed her a groveling apology.

But the girl returned with terrible news. "Miss Black is busy."

As a rule, people were never too busy to see a man of his position. As such, he was not accustomed to being refused or accepting failure. For a moment, he was stunned.

And then he was determined.

Kingston glanced around at the finely appointed but utterly empty shop. "Busy? Is that so?"

"She says you must make an appointment," she said authoritatively. She began to dramatically flip through the pages of the appointment book — Kingston noticed they were all devoid of ink. "Shall we say for the first day, in the month of Never, in the year of our lord 1899?"

Well, then.

It was really time to turn on the charm.

Kingston smiled at her. He disbanded with his I-Am-A-Duke posture and leaned casually against the counter.

"What is your name, may I ask?"

"Rachel. But it's Miss Abrams to you."

"Hello, Miss Abrams. I would like to make an appointment."

He heard a muffled guffaw from the other side of the shop, where Freddie was giving a close and thorough inspection to the bodice of a gown on display while eavesdropping on the entire matter.

"Certainly. And when would you like your appointment? Perhaps December?" she offered with a smile.

It was June.

Yes, she was definitely in the category of

enraged on her friend's behalf and determined to enact some sort of revenge for slights real and perceived. Oddly enough, this made him *like* her. One should feel thusly on behalf of their friends. The smile he gave her was genuine.

"I was hoping for June. June seventh, perhaps."

"That's today."

"I know. How about three o'clock?"

"How about right now, you mean?"

Kingston leaned forward and dropped his voice. "I am desperate to see her."

Miss Abrams leaned forward and spoke quietly, "So you can get her fired from this shop, too?"

"Ah, that."

"Yes. That."

"Would it make a difference if I told you that my express purpose was to grovel at her feet and to beg for her forgiveness?"

"I'd rather you bought a dress."

"I can buy a dress."

Miss Abrams smiled devilishly. "We only do custom work. You'll require a fitting."

Kingston paused and considered all the things that men had done for love and he didn't think twice when he said, "Then I should like to make an appointment for a dress fitting. Immediately."

CHAPTER TWELVE

Rational dress reformers want to know:
why can't a woman's attire offer
the same comfort and ease of movement
as a man's?
— *The New York World*

A chance encounter with a duke was —
alas! — the most interesting thing to happen to Adeline that afternoon. She'd been hoping that a queen of New York City society would enter her shop — or any woman interested in buying a dress, really — but it seemed she would have to be content with a duke.

The duke with the marriage proposals and public displays of heroics. With those strong arms and, oh, and that devastatingly attractive accent.

It was almost enough to make her forget the grudge she'd harbored against him for nearly ruining her career. Almost. But tell that to her heart, with its rapid-fire beating. Her hands — always so steady — were trembling.

How had he found her?

What had brought *him* into *her* shop?

After an initial flurry of orders from the members of the Ladies of Liberty club, all of which were being made by Adeline's small group of seamstresses, customers had been scarce. It was to be expected — newspaper advertisements were not yet within her budget and no one had seen her gowns modeled by real women in the real world, so no one quite knew to schedule a fitting for her inventive gowns. Yet.

Yet. Oh, how she clung to that word.

She told herself that as soon as the first batch of gowns were made, delivered, and worn out on the town, she would certainly entertain more customers. She *had* to. Those ladies had taken a chance on her when no one else would; she could not fail them.

In the meantime . . .

The duke. Was here. He had found her.

According to Rachel, he wanted to speak with her. He had even agreed to this whole nonsense about a fitting, a charade she expected the Lofty and Proper duke to refuse. Now that he hadn't, she either had to go through with it or let him call her bluff. Which was of course unsupportable.

Resolved, Adeline pushed through the heavy velvet curtains into the small, intimate and enclosed space where dress fittings were conducted. Privacy would protect her from anyone seeing them together. But privacy could be dangerous, too.

Because there he was: the duke of Kingston, her downfall.

The damned man was as handsome as ever. Yet Adeline was more determined than ever to resist the temptation that he posed to her. Whether walking in the park with him (and nearly losing her heart) or walking to Madame Chalfont's with him (and losing her job), this duke was dangerous.

She had plans for her life that did not include a duke, marquis, earl, or viscount. Her plans did *not* include losing her head or heart or anything over a man.

He smiled when he saw her. A slight upturn of his lips, a genuine warmth in his deep blue eyes. Her heart did a stupid fluttering thing when he murmured her name.

"Adeline . . ."

Oh no. Absolutely not.

There could be none of that seductive smiling, which led to flirtation, then kissing, which everyone knew led to all manner of dire fates. It would not do. Not now, when women had taken a chance on her and helped and were counting on her to repay their investment and revolutionize ladies' attire.

Adeline's heart was really pounding now. Her temperature was spiking, too. It took every ounce of her self-control to keep her demeanor cool.

"I understand that you're here for a dress fitting?"

She gave him a small smile and snapped a length of measuring tape in her hands like a whip. She desperately wanted to appear absolutely in control of her feelings. Even though she was feeling quite dizzy, like there wasn't enough air in this fitting room.

His gaze dropped to her hands. Her slightly trembling hands. His eyes widened ever so slightly when he noticed that she wasn't joking about measuring him for a dress.

"Adeline, I had to see you."

The plaintive notes of longing in his voice almost undid her. From his voice, she knew that he had been thinking about her, probably with a tortured mix of feelings: guilt, desire, unanswered questions. If they spoke honestly and openly, they would discover they liked each other, that she never meant to deceive him and he never meant to get her fired.

And then what?

Adeline *needed* the anger she harbored toward him. Otherwise she might have to admit that her hot-hearted feelings were those of lust and liking, a potentially fatal combination indeed. She had too much at stake to risk a kiss or a full-blown affair with him.

Now, though, she had women she respected and admired counting on her to succeed.

Busy. She would keep busy.

He was here for a dress fitting, so she would fit him for a dress.

She ought to focus on the task at hand.

"You'll need to remove your jacket."

"Adeline, you cannot be serious about taking my measurements. My tailor in London has them all recorded. Never mind that I do not actually wish to have a dress made."

"Then this appointment is over."

"Fine."

He shrugged out of his jacket.

He wore his shirtsleeves, a vest and a smile that said *two can play at this game.*

Adeline had to admit that this was probably a mistake. Not aloud, of course. But privately, to herself.

The same spirit that had propelled her from the tenements to here urged her to brazen this out.

She began her measurements with his chest, stretching the length of the tape across the wide expanse of linen- and silk-clad muscle and bone and skin and man. Memories of their collision were still vivid: she still knew how it felt to rest her cheek against the firm warmth of his breastbone, just above his beating heart. She still hadn't quite recovered her equilibrium. Worse, she still yearned for that intimate touch. This was a convenient excuse for an indulgence.

"Forty-two inches." She paused to write it down in a small notebook for such purposes, then she slid it back into her pocket.

"I haven't been able to stop thinking about you, Adeline. I have been worried."

"As you can see, I'm quite fine." She stretched the tape from the length of his shoulder to his elbow, then from his elbow to his wrist. Twenty-three inches in total. *Concentrate on the numbers.* Twenty-three inches of finely wrought muscle and bone. Twenty-three inches of strong arms that could hold a girl all night.

Perhaps she would not concentrate on the numbers.

"I hope you'll forgive the intrusion, but

when I saw the sign, I had to see if it was truly you. When we last spoke, your fate seemed . . ." Kingston seemed to be at a loss for words.

"Dire? Hopeless? Desperate?"

"I must apologize for my part in the events that transpired that day. My pride had suffered a blow, thinking I had been deceived. I so badly wanted to believe you were —"

"An heiress who would solve all your problems? I suppose I should be flattered."

She was close enough to him to feel his low rumble of laughter.

"Call it wishful thinking," he murmured in her ear as she turned to measure his other arm.

"You needn't lose sleep on my account. As you can see, I have my own shop now."

"A remarkable state of affairs."

She felt his eyes on her, wondering *how.* How an impoverished seamstress on the verge of ruination suddenly appeared in possession of a fine establishment of her own. He would never suspect the truth: that the Ladies of Liberty had invested in her dream with their pin money and personal fortunes because no bank would lend to a woman. Especially one like Adeline, without a husband or family connections.

The Duke would never think of that. And she had taken a solemn vow to never, ever breathe a word of it.

"I admit I am curious as to how you have achieved this."

"How or who?" she said, answering the unspoken question in his eyes, the subtle accusation in his tone. He probably thought she had taken a lover, a wealthy one who set up his ladybird with a little shop to occupy her days while he occupied her nights. "Duke, I daresay you sound jealous."

"I might be."

"You have no right to be."

"I am well aware."

She could disabuse him of the notion that she had a lover but, she thought — as she took the measure of him from shoulder to waist — why? Why not let him think that she was spoken for? It would help keep some distance between them. Distance she badly needed.

Besides, she could never tell him the real reason — the Ladies of Liberty had sworn her to secrecy.

"It is none of your concern," she told him.

"I had offered to help you," he said, and she understood him to mean, *who is he? And why not me?*

She turned around to take a deep breath

to cool her pulse, her temper. She had achieved something with this shop and he wanted to know whom she had dallied with to do so. He was jealous he hadn't been the one. He was making her great achievement about his hurt feelings, his wounded masculine pride. She didn't know whether to direct her anger at *him* or the state of the world that made his assumptions have some validity.

She looped the tape around his waist. Abdomen: firm. Waist: thirty-three inches. Sense of his own self-importance: inflated.

This whole insistence on measuring him for a dress was a spectacular failure.

Because she had to get close to him to do it. Close enough to breathe in his scent of fresh linen and soap and man. She kept touching him, too, and savoring the feel of fine linen and wool, warm from his body, and it made her want to feel his bare skin under her palms. And his mouth! Always so close that if she just turned her head or tilted her face up, his mouth would be right there, wanting and waiting to claim hers for a kiss.

They would not stop at a kiss.

Not when she felt desire coursing through her veins like electricity coursing through the city. Hot, potent, *new.* Combining her arousal with her still simmering anger was a dangerous combination.

"Step up on the box, please."

He did.

It was a mistake.

She had wanted to avoid kneeling in front of him. But his navel was practically at her eye level which meant that a certain portion of his anatomy was now close to her mouth. The air in the dressing room became heavy and thick. Comforted by the knowledge that he was as tortured by this as she was, she quickly took the measure of his inseam.

He was either excited at the prospect of a dress of his own or he still wanted her. When her hand accidentally brushed against his arousal, she heard a quick hiss of breath. It was her. He wanted her. Their desire was mutual and that was all the more arousing. Damn.

"Step down, please."

"As you wish."

She turned away to write down his measurements for no purpose other than to maintain the pretense of a fitting and, frankly, to take a moment to compose herself.

It was just the way he took up so much of this small intimate space and made it impossible for any thoughts to remain in her head. Correction: any decent thoughts. She had plenty of wanton ideas that would involve discarded clothes and fevered kisses and skin against skin. Given the way he was looking at her, his thoughts were straying into the same wicked territory.

"Did you land your heiress yet?" she asked, desperate to introduce a subject that would cool this fevered state between them. "Are you still deciding between Miss Watson and Miss Pennypacker?"

"Those damned newspapers. What does one have to do for some privacy in this town?"

"Be a nobody."

"Either one would make a fine duchess," he said. "But . . ."

The remainder of his sentence was left unsaid. It hung in the air between them for a moment. His eyes locked with hers and she feared she knew which words were on the tip of his tongue. Pretty ones like, *but they are not you. But I want you.* Or bitter-sweet ones like *but I am not in love.*

Adeline thought that if he wasn't going to marry for love, then he damn well better marry for heaps and heaps of money. And so she finished his sentence for him:

"But only one of them is actually an heiress."

■ ■ ■ ■

Not actually an heiress?

This was news to Kingston. If it were true, this was information worth enduring an oddly erotic and utterly torturous dress fitting for. This was information that cooled his blood enough for him to resume thinking with his brain instead of something else.

"That was not how I was going to finish that sentence, but I'll admit, I'm now intrigued. Not an heiress? Explain yourself, Miss Black, before my entire future is wrecked."

She smiled devilishly. "Like you wrecked mine?"

"Clearly, given that you are now proprietress of this very fine shop in a fashionable neighborhood. A dictionary definition of dire straits and a hopeless case. Tell me what I need to know. Please."

"I happen to know that Miss Pennypacker — or rather, her father — is often late paying bills, if they are paid at all. However, she receives so much attention in the papers for what she wears that it still behooves the dressmakers to attire her. And those are just the dressmaker's debts. One can only imagine what other bills are left unpaid."

"If that is true, then I shall be in a worse position than I am currently, should I marry her and assume her debts. Why in that case, I might as well marry you, Miss Black."

"There you go again with the marriage proposals."

Their eyes met. Lips parted. His heart slammed against his breastbone.

"I suppose Miss Watson is the future duchess of Kingston then." There was no joy in making the announcement.

"I wouldn't count on it. She just did a large order of traveling dresses and plain day dresses from Madame Chalfont. A friend who still works there told Rachel, who told me."

"So? What is the point of such information?"

"That suggests a simple lifestyle, one quite at odds with her current one as a Park Avenue Princess. Or future duchess."

"A woman with simple tastes who won't deluge me with bills from dressmakers and milliners. Splendid. I feel an increasing fondness for her already."

"My hunch is that she is planning to elope. Probably with someone her parents will never approve of, especially when she has a duke nipping at her heels and sniffing at her skirts. You'll want to act quickly with your proposal if you intend to make one. Though you will certainly risk a runaway heiress if you do. Her parents would never allow her to refuse you."

"Bloody hell." Kingston pushed his fingers through his hair in a gesture of frustration. Weeks of late nights in ballrooms, long evenings enduring the opera, endless afternoon social calls and polite walks in the park were all for nothing.

All that wasted time and effort.

The clock was ticking.

Kingston was inclined to believe Adeline, because she kept refusing him and she clearly didn't need him. This shop was testament to that. And it burned, oh it burned, to think that he hadn't been able to provide for her. He did not want to think of what arrangements she had entered into to get this shop. Honestly, he did not know what was worse: the feeling of jealousy that she was with another man or the feeling of failure that he had been unable to provide for her.

Or was it the fact that she didn't need him at all?

He should be thinking about his own dire circumstances. Although, if Adeline spoke the truth, then she had just saved him.

"I do wonder which newspapers you are

reading. They are certainly not the same as the ones I have read. Nor has this information been shared with me at the club. I have all the stock tips in the world and can tell you about all the best haunts for women of negotiable affection, but I haven't overheard anything like this. I had no idea."

Adeline laughed. "Oh, this information you won't find in any one of the city papers. No, this information is exchanged exclusively between ladies, their dearest friends and their maids during dress fittings. Because seamstresses are little more than servants, we're considered invisible, yet we are privy to so much of a woman's secret life."

"I had never considered it."

"Of course you haven't. Think of what you unwittingly share with your valet, for example. Consider what your chambermaids might have observed."

Though they never once had a conversation about it, his valet always ensured that Kingston was sufficiently stocked with rubber shields, for example. In order to do so, he must take note of when they were in need of replacement. He had never paused to consider what attention was paid to his personal habits.

And so Kingston believed her. He believed

her because she alone was not impressed by him and his title. Because her ambitions were incompatible with being a duchess, and so he trusted that she was not sabotaging the competition. He trusted her because he suspected that she did like him, as inconvenient as such feelings were for them both.

"How quickly and expertly you have ruined my prospects."

"Now we're even."

"Bloody hell. Now I must go back to the start — the introductions, the flirtations, the courtship." He rubbed his jaw, wearily, like this was all a great trial, which he did find it to be. Oh, he was happy enough to charm and enjoy the company of all the young women. But he was painfully aware of each day that passed in which he was no closer to solving the problems of his estate or honoring his legacy. The pleasures of courtship tended to wither when under such unrelenting pressure. "I am eager to return to London. My sisters need guidance. My mother needs . . . management. To say nothing of my estates."

"You'll find someone," she said consolingly. "How hard can it be for a duke to find a duchess in New York City?" Adeline now held up a swatch of fabric near his face

— he caught a flash of lavender. "Honestly, you'd think she'd just trip and fall into your arms," she teased, and he couldn't help but laugh a little.

"It is harder than I had anticipated. To think, I thought I had met the girl on the first day."

Adeline held his gaze for a moment, then looked away.

"Lavender doesn't suit you."

"Try a blue. It goes with my eyes," he said. And as she rummaged through her swatches — were they still maintaining this charade? — he said, "Now my two candidates are revealed to be all wrong."

"You have problems, Duke. Real problems."

He gazed into her eyes and said, "I do."

He could only hope that when he returned to the cool, gray shores of England with his bride, he would forget about Adeline. Perhaps in time he would think of her the way he thought of the barmaid who had divested him of his virginity — with a genuine warmth and fondness for what they shared, but with no bearing upon his present.

But until then . . .

It seemed impossible to forget her now that he knew where to find her. How could he put her out of mind when there was a chance that he might turn the corner and run into her? Manhattan was a small island, after all. Inevitably Fifth Avenue ballrooms would be filled with women wearing her gowns. She was talented; he had no doubt she would succeed. Just as he had no doubt that whatever he felt with her wasn't finished. Yet.

But they would have no reason to see each other again after this farce of a dress fitting concluded. Unless . . .

"I have an idea how you might solve all my problems," he said the split second that the idea occurred to him.

"Oh? Do tell. I've been in want of a hobby. Solving the problems of dukes might be just the thing to do in all my free time."

He sighed with mock impatience. She grinned.

"Obviously, I must continue on my quest for the perfect bride — an heiress with impeccable manners and a sterling reputation. A woman who will restore Kingston to its rightful glory. It seems that I need you and your intelligence network to help me choose the right woman to be my future duchess."

"I can hardly spill all my customers' secrets. What kind of business practice would that be to betray their confidence and potentially wreck my chances of dressing the best women in society? I think not. It violates the sacred trust between women and serves no one."

Her chin tipped up, resolutely. Adorably.

"You're right. You cannot betray any of your customers' secrets." He paused, about to say something that might hurt. But his intentions were noble. "However, I do not see any customers. I have not heard the trill of the bell on the shop door. I did not see a full calendar of appointments in Miss Abrams's book. In fact, I daresay I didn't see any at all."

"I believe you are here for a dress fitting," she replied icily.

"Which brings us to another problem we could solve together. You require customers. High-quality, fashionable customers. This, I can help you with. Come with me to the opera and wear one of your stunning creations. You'll be a sensation. The ladies will come in droves and your appointment book will be full for weeks."

She was tempted. He could see it in her eyes.

"And then tell you all their secrets? No."

"Don't tell me any of their secrets. Simply give a shake of your head if I indicate an interest in a woman who would not make a fitting duchess. Or better yet, indicate which ones I ought to pursue. Please. I owe this to my family. While I will sacrifice my own opportunity to marry for love, I cannot ask the same for my sisters."

She was really tempted now. He could see it. She had stopped holding up fabric swatches and was now thinking. Kingston kept going.

"My sister, Nora, has fallen for an impoverished scholar and I should like to see her kept in a manner at least somewhat befitting her station. My other sister, Clara, has my mother in an uproar because she refused a wealthy husband because she doesn't love him. And who can blame her? He is old enough to be her father. If I seek an heiress, it is not so that I might redecorate my houses, it is so my sisters may have a chance to marry for love, not money."

To say nothing of the roofs and tenants and acres of verdant green hills that he'd rather not spoil with a mining operation and a train station.

"A very interesting proposal, Duke."

"One that serves to benefit us both. And my sisters."

She pressed her lips together.

"Just a night at the opera."

175

"It's just a little free advertising, isn't it?" she mused, and he could tell she was on the verge of acquiescence.

"The last time we were seen together, it was written about in three different papers, and if memory serves, your dress was described in great detail by Jennie Jones."

Kingston badly wanted her to accept. It would give him the pleasure of her company, which he truly wanted even more than the information she might share.

Furthermore, this seemed like an opportunity to use the power and influence of his station to encourage her success. It was more valuable than the pity money he had offered her previously or a loan he'd never call in. He would simply redirect the attention that *he* normally attracted to her, where it might do some good.

Kingston didn't know how to change the world, but he could see now how he might use his position to change hers.

"This old title has to be good for something."

"You know it's not just your title," she replied. "You will be the perfect accessory to show off my creations." Her gaze traveled slowly from his head to his toes and he felt his flesh warm under her obviously approving gaze. How intrusive. How possessive.

How arousing.

After the exquisite agonies of being measured by her, and now this smoldering appraisal that had him hard again, Kingston thought he would probably die if he ever actually made love to her.

And she was probably only thinking of how he would show off her gowns.

Who knew dress fittings were so sensual and emotionally devastating?

"And all you wish for is to know who pays their bills, or who might cause a scandal?"

"That's all."

That, and the pleasure of her company. That, and the nearness of her body, the chance to touch her, however chastely, properly, and politely. Even if his heart was pounding, his blood pulsing, and his nerves thrumming in anticipation just from this unusual interview.

"Just one night at the opera?"

"Just one night." He wanted a thousand nights but he would settle for one.

Finally her eyes had that glimmer and her lips tipped up into a smile. "You have a deal, Duke."

CHAPTER THIRTEEN

No pocketless people has ever been
great since pockets were invented, and
the female sex cannot rival us while it is
pocketless.
— The New York Times*

The Metropolitan Opera House
Thirty-ninth Street and Broadway
A night at the opera in the company of a
duke might have been the most glamorous
thing to ever happen to Adeline. Very well:
it absolutely was.

She had never experienced such refined
entertainment in such a glamorous establishment, with such impressive company. It
went without saying that she was nervous
about what to expect, how to act, how *not*
to make a fool of herself before the best of
Manhattan society *and* that damnably dashing duke.

She disguised her anxieties with fashion.

178

She obsessed over her dress.

The dress.

The one that would declare her as *the* dressmaker of the moment.

It was made with a pale pink blush satin, in a shade one would describe as *a woman's cheeks after a delicious first kiss.* Over the skirts she had layered tufts and swathes of white chiffon upon which she'd spent many, many midnight hours sewing tiny faceted beads. She wanted to sparkle.

The bodice was fitted and cut to reveal a generous hint of her breasts; enough to tease and tempt but not so much as to be indecent. The delicate cap sleeves were composed of more chiffon and satin and designed to rest at the far edges of her bare shoulders, only appearing as if they might slide down, taking the rest of her gown with it. She wanted to entice.

Her hair was upswept. Her lips ever so slightly reddened.

Gloves, she had decided after an embarrassing amount of consideration. Black satin elbow-length gloves.

"Don't look now, but everyone is staring," Kingston murmured privately to her as hundreds upon hundreds of faces turned to stare as they arrived in their box. They stood and paused for effect, both aware of their purpose this evening.

"Oh really? I hadn't noticed."

"It's simply a fact of my position. People tend to stare."

"Don't be silly. They're looking at my dress."

The truth was that the two of them together had captivated everyone's attention. The duke, even without the title, would turn female heads. The dress, on its own, would have men and women lusting, though for different reasons — women to wear it, men to remove it.

That Adeline was unknown to society only inflamed their curiosity. Who was this dark-haired, doe-eyed beauty on the arm of the season's most eligible bachelor? Was she the mystery woman with whom the duke had previously been sighted? If so, this would be their third known outing, which suggested something serious.

To the marriage-minded mamas and their daughters, it suggested competition.

Adeline was keenly aware of more than a few opera glasses trained upon her. Would it be wrong if she, say, turned slightly so that she might show off the back of the dress? She was rather proud of how the fabric was gathered at the bustle, from which tumbled a cascade of tufts and ruffles and silk and tulle.

As if he were trying to make tongues wag even more, Kingston leaned over and murmured into her ear: "It is a very fetching dress."

She smiled. Because he hadn't seen anything yet.

"It has pockets."

Adeline slipped her hand — clad in a black satin glove — into the small pocket she had sewn into the pale blush pink skirt. All around the room, women leaned forward, some even gasped. And some of the stodgier frowned in outright disproval at the sight of a lady's hand disappearing into the volumes of her skirt. How mysterious. How suggestive. Exactly how a proper woman should *not* be.

The style of gowns included layers and layers of fabric; it was easy enough to create a small enclosure where a woman might keep things, yet most dressmakers overlooked this opportunity.

Having sufficiently made a scandalous and notable entrance, Adeline took a seat, arranging her skirts around her, and pretended not to notice everyone staring at her. The duke sat beside her. Close. Very close.

"What does a woman need pockets for?"

"The same things a man uses his pockets for, of course. For instance, to carry money."

"A woman needn't carry money. She has accounts at the various shops. Or, if she is traveling with a gentleman, he would carry it."

Adeline had a vision of women followed around by men whose purpose was merely to hold things for them — human pockets, essentially. Like horses, they would require feeding, watering, and long pauses to rest their legs. A woman already had enough people in her life to care for. Sewing pockets into a gown seemed like a much easier solution.

"And what if she hasn't accounts at the shops? What if there is no man to count the change for her?"

"She should stay home."

"That is absurd. What if she is home alone and needs bread?"

"Send a —" She could tell that he was about to say *send a servant* and caught himself. The duke, it seemed, could be taught about how the rest of the world lived. Unfortunately, this only made him more appealing to her. She wanted to think of him as merely an accessory. But as he continued to prove himself to be a man who listened, who considered, who enjoyed the challenges she presented to him, she found it harder and harder to harbor a grudge.

"Love letters," she said. "Don't tell me a woman needn't carry love letters."

"Love letters," he scoffed. "I suppose in the context of a proper courtship one might pen some romantic lines. I can't imagine otherwise."

So the duke was not the love-letter-writing type. Noted.

"What of a husband and wife?"

"Love letters assumes a love match, does it not? Which we both know not all marriages are, even in this day and age."

"In case you are too obtuse — and I worry that you are — this expression on my face is one of shock, horror, and pity. Your lack of romance is a crushing disappointment and I hope for your sake that none of your heiresses can hear you."

"A man of my position does not often have the liberty of marrying for love. They know it as well as I. It is simply the way things are."

She gave him a patronizing smile and drawled, "Tell me more about all the things a man of your powerful position cannot do."

"It is the truth. There are things my station compels me to consider: the management of the estates and the tenants whom they support, my family, particularly sisters and mother. I must ensure they are provided for. I must consider my family's legacy. It is my duty. My honor. It is impossible to consider matters of the heart as well."

Adeline studied him; he was absolutely serious. She could not fault him for taking his responsibilities seriously. If anything, it was very admirable and attractive that he should place everyone else's concerns above his own. Yet it seemed grievously wrong that one should be required to sacrifice love and happiness. The only logical solution was to fall in love with an heiress.

Or — Adeline thought of the Ladies of Liberty, of the suffragists' rally cry that had struck a nerve — to change the world.

"But it is still a choice to do your duty and to uphold tradition."

"It is a choice I have made." The duke spoke in a calm, firm tone that conveyed that his decision had been made and it would not be revisited.

"Lip paint," she said. "A woman might also carry lip paint."

"Only certain kinds of women would do so, and I can't imagine they're the sort you want seen wearing your gowns."

"At the moment, perhaps. But fashions change."

"Love letters. Lip paint. Cash and coin. It seems to me that pockets in a dress lead to all sorts of scandalous female behaviors."

"That is precisely the plan." She gave him a winning smile. "Women shall subvert the order of things with pockets in our dresses. Perhaps one day we shall even wear trousers, drink brandy, and rule the world."

Kingston laughed, a low rumble. "I wouldn't know heads or tails in such a world."

"Actually, if a woman were wearing pants, I think it'd be much clearer what was heads or tails."

"Stop. You're making me blush," he deadpanned.

"Am I offending your modesty or sense of masculine superiority?"

"I do have some notion of trying to be a gentleman," he said. "Between your scandalous ideas and that tempting dress, you're making it rather difficult."

Their eyes met again. A smile played on her lips. She was playing with fire now but having so much fun. "I would apologize, Duke, except I'm not very sorry at all."

The lights dimmed, the opera began, and Kingston's torture intensified. Freddie and Marian still hadn't arrived — it was their usual box at the opera — and so Kingston and Adeline were sitting alone together in the box, chaperoned by the watchful eyes of hundreds of rabidly curious audience members.

Adeline was beautiful, softly scented of lavender, and *right there.* She was saying things about pockets, love matches, and women in trousers. He was shocked at how resistant he was to the image she painted of the world: women roaming freely with their pockets full of money, love letters, and lip paint, marrying only for love, if at all.

It was radically different from the world in which he'd been raised, indeed anything he had personally witnessed. It was so very different from the expectations he had internalized for himself. It was damned unnerving to discover that at the ripe old age of thirty-one, he was old-fashioned and unromantic.

"Now about this business of finding you a wife," Adeline began, and he was glad to get down to business. The matter was becoming increasingly urgent and he felt as if he'd already met every eligible woman in Manhattan. "Tell me: other than a fortune, what makes a woman duchess material?"

"I shall need my duchess to bear my children."

Adeline nodded. "The all-important heir and spare."

"She should also be an accomplished hostess," he said, thinking of what he had seen his mother and other peeresses do. "A man of my position must often entertain — everything from intimate dinner parties to balls. She shall also need to manage my various households."

Whatever that entailed.

"This sounds more like a job than a marriage," Adeline replied. "Here I thought duchesses just dressed and undressed and drank champagne."

"Many do."

"Can you just imagine?" Adeline sighed. "I would last about a week. Then I'd be bored out of my mind."

"When duchesses get bored, they go shopping. They ride all around town in the carriage, leaving their calling cards and sipping tea. They plan parties. They gossip. They redecorate. They run up enormous bills with the milliners and dressmakers and whatever other fripperies are foisted upon women as essential."

He had seen this repeatedly.

"I'm certain you'll find many women here tonight, any of whom will make an excellent duchess. You have come to the right place."

He watched as her gaze skimmed over the inhabitants of the various boxes indicating the families were subscribers to the opera. Many faces were familiar to him, but still more were not. Finally her gaze settled on a particular woman.

"Miss Edith LaRoche, two boxes to the right in the green taffeta dress. I recognize her from Madame Chalfont's. Her father made a fortune in steel production and she is known to organize many charitable luncheons to benefit municipal hygiene efforts. The family has newly arrived in the city as well."

Kingston looked and saw a perfectly fine-looking woman who was actually paying attention to the opera, suggesting a level of refinement and maturity that many in attendance (namely, those gawking at him) were lacking. At this distance, without making her acquaintance, he could see nothing wrong with her, and yet he could muster no interest, mainly because she was not the scandalous, shocking, tempting woman beside him.

"Perhaps someone a little more . . . young," he said, grasping for a reason. Any reason.

"Of course," Adeline said dryly. "A brood-mare ought to be young."

After a moment, she pointed out another potential candidate. "Miss Cooper — three boxes to the left in the lilac gown — is young. Just twenty, I believe."

"I have already made her acquaintance. She speaks every sentence as if it were a question, which I imagine might become trying after a time."

"What about Miss Elena Howe, in the pale blue watered-silk dress?" Adeline subtly inclined her head to the left. Kingston nodded and pretended he understood what watered silk meant and instead looked for a woman in a blue dress. His attentions settled on a young, pleasant-looking woman whispering to her friend.

Adeline continued: "I have dressed her at Madame Chalfont's as well. Her family is not the wealthiest, but they are one of the oldest and most respected families in Manhattan. In fact, they trace their arrival to the seventeen hundreds and are one of the original families to settle here. Her mother is always harping on it."

"The seventeen hundreds are considered old? How quaint. I have barns on my properties that are older."

"Don't you find it remarkable that Miss

LaRoche's advanced age is considered a detriment but the older a family is, the most prestigious it is? It's almost as if when a woman does something, it loses its prestige."

"It is just the way of things."

Adeline pursed her lips. He knew what she was thinking: *Old-fashioned. Unromantic.* He had only one thought immediately: *no.* He did not like this vision of himself that he saw in her eyes. He did not want to be old-fashioned and unromantic. Not yet. He had been raised to see the world in starkly drawn lines in black and white, with clearly proscribed roles and duties. He had simply accepted this lack of any alternative vision. *This is how things are.*

And then there was Adeline, sashaying into his life, painting in color, and blurring the lines he'd always existed within. She actually made him think about writing love letters that she might carry around in her pockets.

And so, when Adeline suggested one heiress after another, he easily found fault with each one. Some he had already met at parties and discounted due to quirks of personality — a cackling laugh, a tendency to fidget, a heavy hand with perfume. Others didn't have the right connections, the right fortune, the right "look" of a duchess.

Which was to say, perhaps he didn't *want* to find a woman who was duchess material. Perhaps he wanted to be with a woman who sparked some excitement within his heart and head and elsewhere. Kingston did not have the words to admit to these radical thoughts raising a rebellion in his heart. And so he just said, "I don't think she'll do," again and again.

Finally Adeline gave a huff of exasperation with him.

"This is ridiculous. *You* are ridiculous." He was momentarily taken aback. No one ever told him he was ridiculous. "I have suggested more than a few good potential duchesses and you have dismissed them all."

Because they're not you, Adeline.

If he could marry without concern for money, he'd propose to Adeline as soon as he could find the right ring. He suspected he would never be bored by this woman who fearlessly called him ridiculous and challenged him at every turn. To say nothing of the temptation of kissing her, the tantalizing promise of her breasts swelling from her bodice, the burning desire to remove this marvelous gown and make love to the woman beneath.

But he lived in the world, with rules and expectations and debts; how selfish would he have to be to marry purely for his pleasure?

And it would be purely *his* pleasure.

Society would not welcome a dressmaker to the ranks of duchess. Being cut from the haute ton would damage his sister's prospects. The roofs would still leak. His tenants would still hunger. And Adeline would probably *hate* being a duchess, especially if it meant giving up her craft.

"It's almost as if you don't actually wish to wed," she pointed out.

"What I wish is to do my duty to those who depend on me, to honor my family's legacy," he said, surprised at how deeply the words resonated. For better or for worse, this is what the world asked of a man of his position and he wanted to provide. It was simply in his nature, who he was, to do the decent, gentlemanly thing. He would do it by wedding an heiress; there was no other way.

"If you're truly intent on this, then the real one to catch is Miss Alice Van Allen."

Adeline inclined her head to the right and discreetly pointed out a fair-haired young woman in a golden yellow gown that put him in mind of canaries. "Her family has been here since it was still just the colonies and had the foresight to buy up vast tracts of Manhattan real estate. I've heard their cottage in Newport is a sight to behold. It's a mansion with all the modern conveniences. To say nothing of their palace on Fifth Avenue."

"She is beautiful," he said without emotion, as if it were a mere fact, which it was. Honey-hued hair piled atop her head, a creamy complexion showing off cheeks flushed pink with excitement at whatever was happening on the stage. She seemed like a ray of sunshine in the darkness of the opera house.

"As you can imagine, she has countless suitors. You might even have competition."

There was no good reason for him not to at least make her acquaintance tonight; indeed, it seemed absurd that they had not already danced twice and been linked in the newspapers. No good reason, other than she wasn't Adeline. And that was not a reason he could share.

The curtain dropped at the conclusion of the first act and by mutual agreement, Adeline and the duke retreated to the back of the box. He had said something about champagne and she had thoughts of a respite from everyone's attentions. Heavy velvet curtains created a small, dimly lit and private alcove between their seats and back of the box.

Adeline was not accustomed to being so noticed. She may have turned heads on the sidewalks, but that hardly compared to the height of Manhattan society focusing their attentions upon her.

Or her dress.

She hoped they were focused on her dress.

The duke followed her to the back of the box. Between the darkness and close quarters, it was almost inevitable that he should misstep and accidentally place his shoe on the small train of her gown. When he did, she was inadvertently tugged back, back, back into his arms.

She gave a sharp exhale as she slammed against his chest. Again. His arms closed around her. Instinct, probably. Nothing more, she told herself.

But heaven help her, Adeline surrendered to the urge to take a deep inhalation and breathe him in. She couldn't quite describe his scent — all sorts of good, clean smells — but it had an effect on her. Made her crave more of him, all of him.

"My apologies," he murmured. "Are you all right?"

He was still holding her, clutching her to his chest. She did not mind. It was decidedly erotic feeling his breath steal across her neck as he murmured low words only she could hear. His hands were splayed across her belly, her waist.

"More importantly, how is my dress?"

"It doesn't matter. You've already made your first impression."

"So I could go home right now," she teased. But she undercut her own words by sinking against him. Reveling, for just one second, the feeling of someone else supporting her weight. He stood still and strong and held her. With each passing second, the expectation, the *desire* that something more would happen increased.

Adeline waited for him to make a light-hearted quip, something to diffuse this explosion waiting to happen. Instead he simply whispered, "Stay."

Undone. She was utterly undone. The simple sweetness of his request had something to do with it. That heat unfurling within her was not irrelevant either. Her body was aching for more of his touch.

The duke, ever the gentleman, obliged.

His hands skimmed higher, higher but not high enough.

Lower, lower but not low enough.

It was a caress, to please her. It was an exploration, as if he wanted to memorize her for later.

He might even be mussing up her dress and she did not care.

Because desire was a mighty feeling that had a way of drowning out all other concerns. Adeline reveled in it. She did not want to subdue her most intense craving, as that lady speaker had claimed. She was a woman of life and passion with a devilishly attractive man intent on pleasing her, only because they both wanted it. Needed it. Now.

She tilted her head back and turned her face up to his in a pose that said *kiss me.* He slowly lowered his lips to hers.

She'd be mad to deny this indulgence.

Just a kiss. Just this once.

Then the door to the box burst open. The duke jumped back at the intrusion and swore mightily under his breath, and Adeline was *quite* in agreement.

"Freddie. Marian." The duke greeted the two interrupters. "How good of you to turn up to your own box at the opera . . . now. You have only missed the first half of the performance."

Lord Hewitt looked from Kingston to Adeline and back again.

"Did I miss anything else?"

"No. You did not," Kingston said tightly.

But I did! Adeline thought. *I missed a kiss I've been hungering to have!*

"I should think the best entertainment is right here," Freddie said, and the woman on his arm giggled. She didn't see her husband give Adeline a roguish smile. Like he knew. Like he thought she let just anyone muss up one of her dresses and almost claim her lips for a kiss. "Everyone is buzzing about the mystery woman you are attending with tonight."

"Miss Black, this is my cousin, Lord Hewitt. He has a knack for showing up when he is unwanted. Freddie, this is Miss Black."

"The seamstress!"

"The dressmaker," she corrected.

"The one with the shop. I remember," Freddie smiled. "It's not every day the duke drags me into a ladies' dress shop for a fitting. Or for any reason. I have heard all about you."

"Have you really?" She glanced at the duke, intrigued by the idea that he might be discussing her. He smiled, but it did not reach his eyes.

"Somewhat," Freddie said with a laugh. "Although, he's a British male, which means he's not very forthcoming with sharing his innermost thoughts and feelings, especially if they pertain to women. But I'm now putting the pieces together. You must be the seamstress who has captivated him completely —"

"Freddie."

"— who has remade herself into a dressmaker and is now in the process of enchanting him again with that dress, which everyone is talking about."

"I do love your dress," Marian cooed. She glanced up at her husband with a pout. "Freddie, I want a dress just like hers."

"I know just the place to get you a dozen, darling wife." He patted her arm. "I'll take you tomorrow."

Adeline smiled. This whole evening was now so, so worth it. The duke, however, was scowling.

"Oh, look, there is Miss Pennypacker!" Marian said. "I must go say hello. Care to join me, Kingston? I know she's been asking why you haven't called upon her recently when you were so attentive before."

"I should stay with Miss Black."

"All right." She giggled. "Ta-ta."

"So what's your story?" Freddie asked, once his wife had gone. He leaned against the closed door and gave Adeline a wolfish smile, like he was the lord's gift to womankind. A good number of women had probably not disabused him of the notion: like the duke, Lord Hewitt was handsome in a dark and dashing way. He spoke with a cultured and attractive English accent. Plus, he had a title.

"You must provide everyone with some explanation. You obviously cannot tell the truth," Lord Hewitt said.

"Much as I hate to admit it, Freddie is right," Kingston said. "We do need a story."

He stepped toward their seats in the front of the box and Adeline and Lord Hewitt followed. In moving from here to there, Lord Hewitt's hand brushed against hers. An accident, certainly. Lord Hewitt was married. Rachel had mentioned that the duke's friend was "handsy" when he'd been in the shop with the duke, but Adeline hadn't given it much consideration — she had too many other matters on her mind. She thought of it now, though.

"So, Miss Black, what shall we tell everyone? What will explain what a duke is doing at the opera with a woman like you when he is in the throes of heiress hunting?"

"A woman like me?"

She glanced at Kingston and his expression was dark. She glanced back at Lord Hewitt. Surely he did not mean it the way she feared he did. But his gaze tracked from her lips to her breasts to lower still. Something about the way his attention lingered on her felt different from when Kingston took a long, deep look at her.

Perhaps it was because Lord Freddie had a wife.

Perhaps it was because she did not want his attentions.

"Not exactly duchess material," Lord Hewitt answered. Adeline glanced at the duke and saw that he, too, possessed the same tight, polite smile as her.

"The story should be something that confirms my respectability," she said pointedly. "The sort of women I wish to attract as clients won't frequent dressmakers who are not respectable. I am already taking a risk in being seen with the duke."

"We'll tell everyone that she's the widow of a school friend," Kingston declared. "Someone we went to Eton or Oxford with."

"And you, ever the noble gentleman, wish to ensure that she is faring well, not too lonely in this big city, that sort of thing," Lord Hewitt added. He turned to Adeline. "As a widow, you'll have more freedom."

She smiled blandly.

"As a widow, I will take pains to remain respectable."

It was a sound explanation. Many dress-makers established their businesses after the loss of a husband forced them to find their own employment. Others merely pretended to be widows as protection.

"I shall bring Marian to the shop tomorrow. The missus does love to shop." He sighed in the manner of long-suffering husbands everywhere, but Adeline paid him no mind. Dressing Lady Hewitt would be a stunning achievement, but unfortunately Adeline had a feeling there would be a catch.

CHAPTER FOURTEEN

The Duke of Kingston was seen attending the Metropolitan Opera House with a woman unknown to polite society and all anyone can talk about is that her gorgeous evening gown had pockets!

— *The New York World*

The House of Adeline

The last person Adeline expected to see barging into her shop the next morning was Madame Chalfont, but there she was, in a huff and shaking a newspaper clipping. She paused — briefly — to survey the shop, taking in the chandeliers and extravagant gowns on display and she smiled. A wry, bitter, *I knew it* kind of smile.

"Good morning, Madame Chalfont. How good of you to stop by."

Adeline stepped from behind the counter. Her former employer marched forward until she stood directly in front of her, nose to nose. Last night she had felt glamorous and adored; now she felt like a young, recalcitrant girl about to get in trouble.

Big trouble.

"I knew it was you the minute I read about the pockets," Madame said, thrusting the newspaper clipping at Adeline. She didn't even bother with her feigned French accent, and her Midwestern voice rang true. "Just as I knew he wasn't just a friend or whatever nonsense you tried to tell me the day I fired you. I knew you were up to something . . . something nefariously wanton."

"I'm sure I don't know what you are speaking about." Adeline took a step back.

"A night at the opera with a duke?" Madame laughed. "For a girl of your position, it can only mean one thing. It doesn't flatter you."

Adeline's cheeks reddened. Yes, they had concocted that story to protect her reputation, but it wouldn't wash with anyone who actually knew her. Like Madame.

"I assure you, it's not what you think."

"Don't play the fool with me. I know you, Adeline. I took a chance on you — a poor girl from the tenements — when no one else would and when you had no one else in the world. I trained you myself, spending hours teaching you to sew, cut, and fit. And what have you done? Set up your own little shop. You stole my two other best girls, Rose and Rachel. Ungrateful girl." She threw up her hands in outrage. "Unforgivable!"

"Might I remind you that *you* fired *me*, Madame."

"Because you were walking the streets with a bachelor in broad daylight when anyone could have seen you!" It was the truth and yet not the truth all at once; Madame made it sound like she committed the worst sin imaginable.

"I'll thank you not to make such aspersions on my character," Adeline said icily, in an effort to adopt the duke's imperious tone. But it had no effect on Madame.

"Then don't act in such a way as to invite them. I see I failed to impress upon you the importance of a dressmaker's impeccable reputation. Not for lack of trying, though."

Adeline didn't argue. She'd heard Madame's lectures before and knew she was right, but Adeline couldn't get past how unfair it was that people thought women doing honest work outside the home were up to no good. The only defense was to be perfectly virtuous and give no one cause to think otherwise.

But how was she to succeed if she stayed

cooped up in her shop and never showed off her dresses? And the truth was, Adeline was perfectly virtuous. And that hadn't protected her at all.

Madame turned and stalked around the room, making sharp note of every detail, from the plush crimson carpet to the way the light reflected off the cut-crystal chandeliers. To the way everything was new, fresh and full of promise, whereas Madame's shop was . . . well established. When she finished her perusal, she turned to Adeline, a jealous, seething fury in her eyes.

"You took my customers, too. You took Miss Burnett. Others followed when they heard she'd found a new dressmaker."

They must be Ladies of Liberty, Adeline thought, for the women of that secret club were her first customers.

"I'm sorry for that." It was easier and kinder to apologize than to point out that if Madame had just listened to her and trusted her about both the pockets and the duke, Adeline would be in her employ right now and making all those customers happy indeed.

"The facts of the matter are this, dear girl. Your business success is a threat to mine," Madame Chalfont said in a voice laced with menace. "And as long as you associate with that duke, giving rise to questions about your morals, then your business is a threat to all dressmakers."

Adeline knew a warning when she heard one and a grand exit when she saw one. She also knew that Madame was right: further entanglement with the duke would be dangerous to her business, to say nothing of her heart.

Later

Adeline was in something of a state after Madame Chalfont's visit when Lord Hewitt came to call with his wife a short while later. Her feelings were mixed upon seeing them. On one hand, Lady Hewitt was considered a tastemaker among the Four Hundred. To dress her would be a coup and would help assure her success as other women strove to emulate her style.

But Lord Hewitt had given her an uneasy feeling at the opera with his lingering gazes and insinuations. Adeline told herself that she was probably just reading too much into the situation. It seemed like the height of self-flattery to assume that he had designs upon her person, a lowly orphan dressmaker.

To have this fashionable and attractive young couple in her shop was another lucky opportunity that she should seize without a second thought. One did not come this far — with so many dear people relying on her success — to suddenly develop qualms or worries. No, she needed every customer she could get. Especially if Madame Chalfont was determined to run her out of business.

Adeline greeted them both with a warm smile.

"Good afternoon, Lord Hewitt. Lady Hewitt. How lovely to see you both again. Welcome to the House of Adeline."

"Hello again, Mrs. Black," Lady Marian said, easily adopting the *Mrs.* that Freddie had added to her name for her protection. "I so loved the dress you wore last night that I've decided I must have a few made for myself. Especially with pockets. I'm forever losing my things," she said with a giggle. Her husband winced.

"Then we shall make you some beautiful gowns with pockets. You will look stunning — and you won't lose anything."

"How perfect." She giggled.

"Rose will help you get ready for the fitting." Rose emerged and guided Lady Hewitt to the fitting room in preparation for a conversation about the gowns she liked and the fabrics she preferred, and to have her measurements taken.

Rose and Adeline exchanged excited looks at having such a fashionable and chatty society darling frequenting their shop. She and Rachel had left very secure and decent positions to join her in this mad and risky venture, a fact that was never far from Adeline's mind, especially on days when business was slow.

Which was, until today, most days.

But now Adeline felt hope rise in her chest. Perhaps this scheme with the duke would work. Perhaps she would be a successful dressmaker after all. Perhaps all her hard work and mad risks would pay off. Perhaps she could live the dream. Perhaps she wouldn't change *the* world but perhaps she could transform her own.

Smiling she turned back to the shop and to Lord Hewitt, who had not yet taken his leave. She didn't think her establishment was the sort where a gentleman would want to linger, but . . .

. . . Oh, very well then. Apparently it was. Lord Hewitt was leaning against the counter now, effectively entrapping her where she stood.

"I told my wife she could have whatever she wants."

"What a *good husband* you are. Not all of them are."

"Well, it is her money after all," he answered with a laugh. Adeline managed a smile. They both knew that he was the one who controlled how it was spent and which bills would be paid. Or not. He joked, "You know what they say: happy wife, happy life. If I keep her well dressed and adorned, she doesn't question how much time I spend at my club. Or elsewhere."

Adeline issued a perfunctory smile. This was far more information about the marriage of Lord and Lady Hewitt than she wished to be privy to.

"If you'll excuse me, I should go see to your wife's fitting."

He moved back *just* enough for her to pass. But nevertheless her body brushed against his. Or it might be more correct to say that his body caressed hers as she passed. A subtle but important distinction. She thought she might have felt his hand linger for a second on her waist, but that would be forward and untoward. He was a gentleman, wasn't he?

In her head she heard Madame Chalfont lecturing her about being seen in such a close, intimate position with a married man. In her head, she argued back: *Well, I would rather not be!*

But Adeline did not feel she could say

anything to Lord Hewitt, keeper of the purse, and payer of the bills. Instead she would go to the back to warn the girls and would see to the fitting and put this whole awkward encounter out of her mind. He likely wouldn't return to the shop. She likely wouldn't encounter him again.

"You must be wondering about Kingston."

She stopped. She did not want to turn around. She did not want to admit to him or herself that he hadn't quite left her thoughts since the previous evening — and she'd already had quite a day. After their charade last night, she couldn't be angry at him anymore. He had put himself on the line to help her succeed and asked for nothing indecent in return.

Attraction to him was one thing.

She didn't want to actually *like* him.

She turned around.

"I really must go see to your lovely wife."

"Yes, my wife . . . Impoverished nobleman meets American heiress. A love story for the ages," Lord Hewitt said in such a dry tone that she was given to understand that his was not a love match. Not that she'd been laboring under that impression. "But enough about me. Kingston is calling on Miss Van Allen now."

Her heart stopped, just for a beat or two,

but it was enough to reveal her own feelings to her. Something like dismay. Jealousy. They were stronger than she had wanted them to be.

"That's what men like us do," Lord Hewitt continued on, coming closer. "We marry for duty and find our pleasure elsewhere."

This time there was no mistaking his meaning and no dismissing his touch as an accident. Lord Hewitt slid his hand around her waist and gazed into her eyes. Every fiber of her being rebelled — well, except for the one that was acutely and uncomfortably aware of what it would cost her to refuse his advances. He could refuse to pay her bills, *after* she and her seamstresses spent hours to create gowns for his wife.

But she also could not afford to have her name linked with his in the same breath. A dressmaker's good reputation was the foundation of her business. Madame Chalfont was right about that.

Every second that she struggled to find a polite response that would neither encourage nor enrage was another second that could be misconstrued as encouragement.

"I should go see to *your wife*. I hate to keep such an important client waiting."

She stepped away. He dropped his hand. He flashed a grin anyone would have described as friendly — anyone other than her, that is — and said, "A dressmaker must keep her clients happy, hmm?"

He winked at her.

Dresses. She wanted to make dresses. The only encounters she wished to have with clients' husbands were receiving their money for payment for her dressmaking work. That was all. Was it really too much to ask?

CHAPTER FIFTEEN

Nora is on the verge of compressing
herself with Dashwood. Stop. Clara
says she won't wed at all now. Stop.
When will you return with heiress? Stop.
Starting to think about my dress for the
wedding. Stop.
— Telegram from Her Grace,
the Duchess of Kingston

The next day
The House of Adeline
The workroom was full of chattering female
voices discussing sleeves and hems, hairstyl-
ing techniques, society gossips, and landlord
dramas, among other things. Rose and Rachel were there, along with some new addi-
tions to the shop, all of whom had been
referred by the Ladies of Liberty: Margaret,
Annie, and Lila. They all went silent upon
the arrival of a young man in the uniform
of the Fifth Avenue Hotel.

He presented a letter to Adeline.

"Go on, open it now," Rose urged when Adeline started to slip the letter in her pocket to read later, in the privacy of her room.

She knew it had to be from Kingston. She recognized the strong slant of his handwriting.

There had been no word from him since their night at the opera, which she had presumed meant that the terms of their agreement had been satisfied, and that *something* between them was purposely left to die.

This was for the best, she told herself.

Because she was shocked and dismayed to discover that she felt *bereft* with his absence. She missed the way he looked when she teased him: startled, before his features eased into a relaxed and delighted smile. She missed the way one deliberate glance from him could make heat unfurl in her belly, course through her body, wake up her nerves, make her feel hot and alive all over.

She didn't just miss him, she craved him.

And now she had a letter in hand from His Grace.

What could he possibly want now? Nothing good. Nothing *decent.*

"Open it now," Rachel said with an air of authority. "You know that we will plague you until you tell us everything, so you might as well read it aloud now."

Rachel. She was always so practical and efficient.

"Fine," Adeline said. "I'll open it."

She did. And she read:

Dear Mrs. Black,

I have called upon Miss Van Allen and she possesses everything a man could want in his future duchess. However, I do believe that I should continue to make the acquaintance of other potential brides, just to be prudent. For this, I shall require your expertise.

Which is to say, I find myself missing your enchanting company and should like to see you again. Will you join me tomorrow night at Mrs. Mellon's ball?

— Kingston

"Well, if that isn't right out of one of my novels I don't know what is," Rose replied. She had since forgiven him for his role in getting Adeline fired and once again embraced her firmly held devotion to all things romance. "The dashing duke whisking you off to fancy ballrooms for champagne and waltzing . . ."

"You are overlooking the part where he asks me to help him find a wife. I'd hardly say that's romantic."

"Those lords *cannot* be trusted," Margaret said. "A girl finds herself charmed by their accent and the next thing you know . . ." She paused in her sewing to rest her hand over the bump in her belly.

"I should not risk being seen with him, let alone —"

"— being alone with him," Margaret finished.

"People have already begun to talk," Adeline said. "I overheard two women gossiping about us during their fitting the other day. I cannot risk my reputation being besmirched."

"It won't matter if he marries you," Rose pointed out.

This was probably true. However, it was also highly unlikely such an event would come to pass.

Before her love-struck seamstresses could further campaign to soften her heart, put stars in her eyes, and blind her to reality, Adeline penned a response and handed it to the messenger, who had been waiting.

I'm afraid I must decline your invitation. Would you believe me if I said I had nothing to wear?

— Mrs. Black, dressmaker with a
reputation to mind

And with that she put the matter out of her mind. The chatter about sleeves and society gossip, about courtship dramas and landlord dilemmas resumed. Adeline breathed a sigh of relief.

It was done. This *something* between them was over. There would be no more teasing marriage proposals for her to refuse and no more moments where she thought he *might* kiss her. There would be no more heartache of wanting the world — or him — to be different so that they could be together. No more heated thoughts about them just being together, forgetting about the whole world, if only for one night.

For approximately one hour, Adeline mourned the end of her *something* with the duke. This was also the amount of time it took to deliver her missive, have it read by the intended party, and a reply composed, and for said reply to be delivered.

Adeline scowled when the messenger was back, with another letter in hand.

No. Wear one of your fancy frocks and show it off.

> — Kingston, who promises to be a
> model of propriety

"Nothing more vexing than a handsome man who is a model of propriety."

"Maybe in the novels you love," Margaret retorted. "But a bit of propriety might have spared me a lot of bother."

She didn't entirely mean that. Anyone could see from the affectionate way that she rubbed her growing bump that she was coming to love her baby already. But it was hard on her to be cast out of her family and society, losing her friends and means of support. All because she had dared to love where she shouldn't.

Margaret reminded Adeline of other risks that she faced, should she continue to see Kingston, who seemed intent upon seeing her.

"I know of a female doctor downtown . . ." Adeline said. Mrs. Phoebe Jane Babcock. She was a member of the Ladies of Liberty club.

"Information too late to help me now, but perhaps you would benefit?" Margaret ventured the suggestion.

The thought had crossed Adeline's mind.

But also considered Madame Chalfont's warnings and remembered the hard experiences of her mother, who'd been reliant on bad men her whole life. What choice did she have, given that she had a young daughter to support? Adeline knew her mother had endured so much to protect her daughter; she just wished she hadn't had to. It all renewed her determination that nothing — especially a dalliance with a man — could distract her from her dream of making this shop a success, which would provide her the independence and security she craved.

"I am married to this shop," Adeline said. "I shall be faithful to it. And to you lot as well."

"Then you really must go to the ball with the duke."

It was Rachel — Rachel! — who said this. She who was practical above all else, who was not swayed by pretty words and flights of fancy from handsome men. She who was proving herself to have a hard head and heart for business.

Adeline's jaw dropped open.

"You, too, Rachel? I expect as much from Rose, but you?"

"He's good for business," Rachel said bluntly. "We can't deny that. Our customers increased after you attended the opera with him in that dress. It logically follows that we will gain more customers if you attend a ball with him as well. I'm not being romantic but practical. We need more customers for this shop to succeed."

This was all true.

"And we're all counting on this shop to succeed, Adeline," Rachel said in softer tones.

They all relied on the wage to support themselves and others. They all benefited from the sense of purpose, too, and the camaraderie of the workshop. Their lives *all* were intertwined with and dependent on this shop. And they all relied on Adeline to make it a success.

"You can and should go to show off your gowns and drum up more business," Rachel said. "No other dressmaker would have such an opportunity."

Later

That was how Adeline came to be making her grand entrance in Mrs. Mellon's ballroom arm in arm with the duke. This was for business, she reminded herself, not pleasure. But as she stepped into the most beautiful room she'd ever seen, with the man she was falling for standing beside her, she thought business was indeed a pleasure.

For the occasion, she wore her most stunning creation yet: a deep cerulean-blue satin gown upon which Rose had painstakingly embroidered stars, moons, and constellations in gold and silver thread. The satin was tufted and layered around the hips and bodice, which was the height of fashion and which conveniently concealed pockets.

She wore her hair upswept. Her eyes were bright and her cheeks were flushed with genuine delight and a dash of nervousness.

And she had the perfect accessory in Kingston.

He commanded attention because of who he was, and he held people's attention with the confident, utterly assured manner in which he carried himself. In his black-and-white evening clothes, he provided the perfect complement to whatever Adeline wore.

"You cannot say I haven't lived up to my end of the bargain," he murmured as they began to move through the room, with murmurs and stares surrounding them. "You and your dresses have certainly caught the attention of all society's tastemakers."

"Well, then our work here is done. I could turn and go right now."

His hold on her tightened as if to say *no, not yet.*

"After you've gone to all the trouble to get so dressed up, you might as well stay. Have some champagne at least."

He plucked a glass from a tray held by a passing waiter and handed it to her. She gave the delicate flute of golden, sparkly champagne a moment of consideration before taking her first sip, imagining how she might design a dress inspired by it. Delicate pale gold silk, swirls of the palest yellow chiffon and tulle, shimmering crystals.

She raised the glass to her lips. "If you insist."

"I do." He just had to gaze into her eyes as he said those words. As if he wasn't speaking merely of staying late at the ball and drinking champagne, but something more *forever* instead. Adeline couldn't help it: her gaze connected with his and she dared to imagine more. Voluminous white dresses and celebratory champagne and Kingston vowing to be hers forever.

Intoxicating stuff, that.

And she hadn't even tasted her champagne.

That, of course, was the moment Lord Hewitt emerged from the crowd to interrupt.

"Mrs. Black. We meet again. What a lovely

surprise." He gave her that charming, rogue-about-town grin that she knew better than to fall for. She nodded hello. "And my dear cousin the duke, too."

"Freddie, good to see you."

"Where is Lady Hewitt?" Adeline asked.

"She ventured off to the ladies' retiring room with a group of friends, as women are wont to do. She's wearing one of your gowns."

Just wait until you see the bill for it, she thought. She considered adding a *handsy husband* surcharge.

"Don't look now," Freddie said, dropping his voice and leaning in. "But it seems our hostess is advancing in this direction."

Indeed Mrs. Mellon, whose husband had obtained his fortune from oil and finance, was moving purposely toward them, dripping in green silks and blue sapphires and some heavy floral scent. She could not decide which was a more fascinating object of her attention: a handsome duke or the mystery woman on his arm.

"Your Grace, what an honor to have you join us. You must introduce me to your guest. And I don't mean this rogue that follows you around town."

"*Lovely* to see you, Mrs. Mellon," Freddie said with a wink.

"Don't flirt with me, boy. I know your kind. Your pretty words are wasted on me."

Kingston cleared his throat. "May I present Mrs. Black. She is the widow of an old school friend of mine from Eton."

This was the story they had agreed upon to circulate in society to explain their connection. It made her seem respectable. It made their unchaperoned occasions together in public acceptable — for now. And it made the duke seem kind enough to squire around an old friend's tragic widow.

"May he rest in peace," Freddie said somberly. "Dear old Reggie is missed."

"Dearly, dearly missed," Adeline said, adopting a forlorn expression. "It was a love match."

Kingston scowled at the two of them. "When I learned my good friend's widow was also in Manhattan, I called upon her to see how she was faring. I thought she might enjoy some of the city's finest events after her period of mourning for her late husband."

"His Grace is nothing if not friendly, especially with lonely widows," Lord Hewitt quipped.

Kingston gave a tight smile. "Freddie, you make me sound untoward. Rest assured, Mrs. Mellon, I am the model of propriety."

"Pity that," she replied. "Your Grace, I thought you would like to know that Miss Van Allen is here this evening. I'm sure she would love to see you. I heard from her mother that she greatly enjoyed your sojourn in Central Park together. It was very sporting of you to join her for a birdwatch."

Adeline stilled. She had not known that birdwatching was something one even did, let alone as part of a courtship.

"We had quite an adventure in search of the black-throated blue warbler."

"And in the rain, too! Miss Van Allen said it was a lovely introduction to England," Mrs. Mellon said to a round of polite laughter.

At least Kingston seemed as uncomfortable with the conversation as Adeline, who busied herself with pretending not to care in the slightest that this man went mucking about in the shrubberies looking for birds with one of Manhattan's most sought-after heiresses.

Adeline had even suggested that he pursue Miss Van Allen. She ought to delight in such an obliging male. She ought to delight in being right.

And yet, just because her brain knew better did not mean she took the knowledge to heart. She leaned a little against his arm and accidentally on purpose brushed gently against his chest, just because she could do so now and probably would not be able to ever again. Was it wrong that she craved the feeling of his arms around her once more?

She wouldn't mind another display of heroics.

Perhaps in a more secluded, private location.

With fewer interruptions this time.

Her desire for him was strong and stupid but there was no denying its existence.

"Kingston, you ought to say hello to Miss Van Allen," Lord Hewitt said. "Don't worry, I shall keep Mrs. Black company."

"Actually, I —"

"We shall take a turn around the ballroom to give everyone a chance to view her magnificent dress. Isn't it magnificent, Mrs. Mellon?"

Their hostess agreed.

"Thank you, if you'll excuse —" Adeline tried to make her escape. Perhaps she might find a pack of ladies to safely escort her to the refuge of the ladies' retiring room. Really, that was the ideal location for her purposes this evening: a captive space with prospective clients. But it was not to be. Mrs. Mellon was leading Kingston away to his likely bride and Adeline was alone with

Lord Hewitt. And his hands.

Kingston hated to leave Adeline alone, but when duty called, a man of his position answered. Nevertheless, he watched from across the room and saw that Freddie was saying something and she was laughing, and he bit back a howl of anguish.

Never mind that. He had a duty. Honorable intentions. A noble purpose.

Her name was Miss Van Allen and she was lovely.

Truly.

She possessed all the most admirable qualities: she was amiable, kind, well-mannered. She had a passion for birds and birdwatching. She had been quite sporting about traipsing around the park in the rain with him and proved to be a veritable fount of information on the local flora, fauna, and birds.

Miss Van Allen had interests and as such, was rather interesting.

Any man would be happy to have her as a wife, and not just because of her enormous dowry. Her father had made a fortune investing in Manhattan real estate and made his only daughter his sole heiress, too. She was a catch.

Kingston smiled warmly at her. "Miss Van

Allen, it is a pleasure to see you again. Especially in more favorable weather conditions."

"Hello, Your Grace. How are you enjoying the ball this evening?"

"I am enjoying it now," he replied smoothly. But this was a hideous lie. Freddie was promenading around the ballroom with Adeline on his arm, and so Kingston was in agony. He felt jealous. And helpless. Hardly feelings befitting a man of his position.

He *wanted* to storm across the room and dispatch his cousin and ask Adeline to dance. But gentlemen of his position did not cause such scenes. Neither did they neglect the female company in their immediate vicinity.

He focused again on Miss Van Allen. "And how are you enjoying this evening?"

"Our hostess has outdone herself," she replied, which was a polite way of saying the party was everything a party should be and yet she was not enjoying herself at all, probably because of his caddish behavior.

He had arrived with another woman, to start.

And now his gaze kept straying toward her and his cousin. Miss Van Allen was a shrewd observer of behavior — the bird-watching, you see — and this did not escape her notice.

"You haven't introduced me to your friend," Miss Van Allen remarked, following his gaze. "I should like to ask who makes her dresses. They're very . . . enchanting."

That word. She had to use *that* word.

"They have pockets," he said because it was all that came to mind as he tried to both maintain a conversation with Miss Van Allen and keep track of Adeline's whereabouts in the ballroom. Freddie had always been a bit of a rogue and, in his book, a girl like Adeline would be fair play.

"Do they?" Her eyes lit up. "How novel."

"How is your luncheon coming along?"

Miss Van Allen was organizing a charitable luncheon for the Audubon Society. They were on a crusade to save whole species of birds from being hunted to death for the purposes of millinery and other women's fashions. She had told him all about it over tea after their birdwatching expedition.

As she gave him the latest update on the lineup of speakers and guests, he nodded at appropriate intervals and wondered what the devil was wrong with him. Here he was, in the midst of a courtship with this wonderful, charitable, thoughtful, beautiful woman and he couldn't keep his attentions focused on her.

Not when Freddie was whispering to Adeline.

Not when Freddie escorted Adeline out of the ballroom.

Not when Freddie clearly had a death wish.

They seemed rather . . . friendly. Though he hated himself for even considering it, Kingston wondered if there was something *more* between them. A wealthy lover was a likely way for a woman to secure the necessary funds to launch her own shop, especially such a fine one in such a fine location. Freddie did have a weakness for women. And, thanks to his giggling dollar princess, plenty of money.

Was it possible?

Of course it was *possible.*

But it was Not. His. Concern.

If it were true, it was none of his business. Kingston knew that he had no claim on her heart, her body, her mind. He was not her husband, or her lover, he had made no declarations or promises of affection. There was no reason for him to feel wounded because Adeline took a turn about the ballroom and laughed at another man's humor.

If it were true, he could not judge her for it. Not when he was currently trading in on his position, his charm, his title in order to seek the funds he required. Was his heiress hunt really any different?

If it were true, he still wondered, why Freddie? More to the point, why not him?

This question brought him to the crux of the matter: his feelings for her were beyond logic and reason and well into the realm of lust and possibly love. He was jealous because he wanted her. He was vexed because he was jealous and not even righteously so. He was all restrained fury because he *wanted* to storm across the ballroom and destroy his cousin and claim the girl, but a man of his position did not do such a thing.

He could not even make some excuse of "concern for her well-being." His cousin was a rogue, but not some vile seducer. She was a grown woman, free to make her own choices. Even if he found them personally enraging and downright devastating.

Because he wanted her. And could not — would not — act on his desires.

He had a duty. Honorable intentions. A noble purpose.

There was only one other question to consider: How could he expect Miss Van Allen to hold his attention for the rest of their lives when he couldn't even focus on one conversation?

Adeline couldn't help but wonder: how many turns about the ballroom must a girl take with Lord Hewitt to keep him happy but not cause rumors? One she could pretend to enjoy, but two was veering into troubling territory; three would be too many indeed.

Adeline dispatched him in search of a glass of champagne.

She sought refuge in a corner of the ballroom and savored a moment to take it all in. The unapologetic display of such massive wealth was breathtaking, mind-boggling, perhaps even infuriating. Massive chandeliers hung from soaring ceilings. Every inch of wall space was covered with enormous gold-framed paintings depicting wild country landscapes, and dignified portraits in the old style. The orchestra played soaring, elegant music. People danced, chatted, and laughed as if they hadn't a care in the world. They probably didn't.

She paid particular attention to the gowns and the way the women wore them, how they moved in them, how the light of a ballroom enhanced or diminished certain colors and fabrics. She would apply all the observations to her future designs and would create better, more flattering dresses as a result.

This evening would not have been in vain.

Adeline turned at the sound of her name.

"Miss Black!" It was Miss Burnett, her patron saint, her fairy godmother, her generous benefactor. Miss Lumley followed closely behind. Adeline was happy to see them both and greeted them with a genuine smile, not the polite ones she'd been forcing thus far this evening. Like the opera, this ball made her so very anxious.

"Hello, Miss Burnett! How wonderful to see a friendly face."

"How remarkable to see you here, Miss Black! I heard you have been busy with the shop and I see you are wearing another one of your splendid creations."

Wonderfully, Miss Burnett was wearing an Adeline original as well. That meant *three* of her gowns were out in the wilds of Fifth Avenue and Adeline had never known such a feeling of joy and satisfaction.

"It's *Mrs.* Black actually. It so happens that I am now presenting myself as the widow of an old school friend of the duke."

"Is that the story?" Miss Burnett and Miss Lumley shared A Look.

"It is the excuse that allows me to join

him at events to display my dresses and catch the eye of potential customers. I have already dressed Lady Hewitt, thanks to my arrangement with the duke. I think of it as free advertising," Adeline said proudly.

"Very clever," Miss Burnett replied.

"But nothing is ever really free, is it?" Miss Lumley asked.

"I know. In return, I am to help him in his search for his future duchess."

Miss Burnett's eyes did not alight with the genius of this exchange. In fact, she gave a concerned glance to Miss Lumley. Adeline suddenly felt nervous and possibly even foolish. Had her desire for the duke led her to be duped by his proposed scheme? Was she making a terrible mistake?

"That is a very clever exchange" — Miss Burnett started.

"But one fraught with risks," Miss Lumley finished.

"You know that I have always championed you, Adeline, and only wish you the best. So I must ask the question: are you certain that's all it is?"

"Of course," Adeline replied with a confidence that wasn't entirely genuine. "What else would it be?"

"I'm so glad to hear it," Miss Burnett replied, breaking into a smile. "So many of my friends have been focused and ambitious — until they meet a man who sweeps them off their feet. Before you know it, they are distracted by wedding plans and babies and they have hardly any time for their old unmarried girl friends, to say nothing of the ambitious dreams they once harbored."

Adeline nodded sagely. Men were a distraction. She knew that well.

"Miss Susie Howell, for example," Miss Lumley said.

"Such a dreadful situation."

"It breaks the heart."

Adeline did not dare inquire.

"But it cannot *always* be the case that men ruin women's prospects," Miss Lumley added thoughtfully. "Look at Mrs. Clinton or Mrs. Lafayette, from the club. Or even the great Elizabeth Cady Stanton. They all have children and husbands and households, and it has hardly slowed their work."

"It helps that they have husbands who are supportive of them, which not all husbands are." Miss Burnett turned to Adeline. "I wonder if your duke is one of those men."

"He's not *my* duke," Adeline corrected. He was supportive of her shop now, but would he be if she was his duchess? Given his determination to uphold tradition, she doubted it. Not once in his definition of an ideal duchess did he say *dressmaker* or even *gainfully employed.* "I daresay he would not encourage his duchess to work. But the point is moot, as he has his sights set on a woman of wealth and prestige. And I have no intention of marriage."

"None?"

"None," Adeline confirmed. "I have also seen it wreck too many women's ambitions or break their spirits."

"I don't worry about you too much, Adeline," Miss Burnett said affectionately. "You have a gift and talent, determination, and the support of all the Liberty Ladies. I know you won't squander all that on a fling with some man, handsome as he may be."

Adeline glanced at him now, as he was wending his way toward her through the crowd. His gaze was fixed upon her with such focus and determination that she wondered if he even saw anything else besides her.

"I promise," Adeline said solemnly. So solemnly she thought of white dresses and forever. But she knew what Harriet and Madame Chalfont said was true: men were a distraction, a danger, and they could wreck a girl's reputation. Thus far, their arrangement had served her well — the gossip wasn't unfavorable and she hadn't fallen in love with him. But every encounter with him increased the risk that she'd lose everything — her heart, her shop. Adeline knew she couldn't compromise her life's ambition for a man who wouldn't — couldn't — provide her with the life she longed to live.

Tonight would have to be goodbye.

CHAPTER SIXTEEN

Overheard in the Fifth Avenue Hotel
Lobby: one is occasionally reminded why
young ladies ought to have chaperones.
— *The New York World*

Later that evening, Adeline was ensconced
in the carriage with her silk and satin, her
ruffles and embroidered trains, and the
duke. Kingston sat opposite her in this
small, enclosed, intimate space. Light from
the street lamps shone into the carriage il-
luminating just enough to reveal the slant of
his cheekbones, his sensuous mouth, his
evening clothes covering his firm chest and
strong arms.

It was enough to tempt her.

Even in spite of the warnings from women
she respected, Miss Burnett and Madame
Chalfont. Even in spite of her determination not to let a man distract her from her
dreams. She would NOT be the silly female

who threw everything away for a handsome man who would never do right by her. To his credit, the duke never tried to mislead her about what he would offer her.

Any flights of fancy were of her own creation.

It was one thing to risk going to a ball with him for business reasons. It was quite another to be alone in the carriage with him. Here, in the dark and unmarked carriage, no one could see them. While the privacy offered a measure of security for her reputation, it still felt dangerous because of that palpable desire between them.

"The evening has gone well," she said. Because conversation meant *not kissing* and being alone in a dimly lit carriage certainly suggested kissing. That *something* between them definitely suggested kissing.

"Yes," he agreed. "You seemed to enjoy yourself. With Lord Hewitt, particularly."

Adeline hesitated. She wanted to say something about how the man plagued her, but a hint of venom in his tone that she hadn't heard before made her reconsider. "I daresay he has taken a liking to me," she said with a shrug, as if it were nothing of any consequence at all. "I received many compliments on my dress," she said, changing the subject.

His lips turned up into a wry smile.

"Including one from Miss Van Allen. She called it *enchanting.*"

"Interesting choice of words."

"I thought so as well."

Their eyes met and their gazes held and they were both thinking it: *she* was his enchanting girl. It was his word for her.

"I hope you feigned ignorance about my dressmaking."

"Of course. There is no good reason that a man of my position would know anything about women's dresses." He paused. "Except for how to remove them."

She laughed softly, nervously.

"I couldn't very well speak to that with my likely future duchess."

His likely future duchess.

That sounded so much fancier than *enchanting elevator girl.*

"Besides," he continued, "for me to say anything remotely knowledgeable on the subject would cast you in an improper light, which would hardly serve our purposes. We'll leak the name of your shop to the newspapers. I'm sure they'll all be clamoring to identify the Mystery Woman who was spotted with me multiple times now — and what, or who, she was wearing."

Her lips curved into a smile in spite of her

tumultuous feelings.

"That is brilliant. You are brilliant. We should send word to Jennie Jones of *The New York World.*"

"Consider it done."

Once their names were linked in the newspaper, her shop wouldn't want for customers. It would still be up to her to impress them and keep them as clients, so if she succeeded it wouldn't be entirely attributable to him. But she wouldn't have been able to do it so quickly without him.

Consider it done.

She could consider this something between them done, too. After tonight, they could have no further business with each other. He had found his heiress and she had achieved just enough attention from their liaison without irrevocably endangering her reputation.

She ought to savor these last few moments with him.

"You never did tell me how you managed to build your own establishment," he remarked. "One day you are penniless on the streets and the next you are mistress of your own very fine shop. It is a marvel. I'm impressed."

"Thank you."

"I confess that I am curious how you did it."

There it was again: that subtle something sharp in his tone that she didn't care for.

"I'm afraid I can't say." Adeline didn't think twice about refusing him an answer, for she had made a solemn promise to the Ladies of Liberty and she certainly wasn't going to break it for a man, even if she liked him and trusted him, as she did with the duke.

His eyes narrowed and she was taken aback by it. Inquiring dukes wanted to know: "Can't or won't?"

"Both."

She met his gaze from across the carriage, but he looked away, out the window, at the sights of Broadway as the carriage rolled past on its way downtown.

"Did Lord Hewitt have anything to do with it? I only ask because I saw you with him tonight and, as you said, he seems to have taken a liking to you."

Adeline stilled. How dare he ask her that. How dare he do so without looking her in the eye, as if he knew what an indecent question he had posed to her.

Only then did it strike her just what the Ladies of Liberty club had inadvertently asked of her: allow the world to wonder what she did to suddenly earn a significant sum of money.

It occurred to her that Lord Hewitt's "innocent" flirtations were anything but; they were downright dangerous.

It didn't escape her notice what the duke was really asking. She watched him, the shadows flickering over his face — those slanting cheekbones, that sensuous mouth, those blues now seeming black in the darkness — as he avoided looking at her. He wanted to know: was she *that* kind of woman?

He could have his reasons. Jealousy — not that he had a right. Or perhaps he wanted to know if there was another way to come into funds, rather than wedding a woman he didn't love. Either way, she would not answer with the truth because she had made a promise that she had every intention of upholding, even if it made Kingston think less of her.

"Do you really wish to ask me that?"

"No." He turned to her, his expression imploring. "Please forgive me. And I hope you have forgiven me for getting you fired from that shop."

"I suppose you've made it up to me."

"You suppose?"

"I'm just teasing you, English."

"I don't think Miss Van Allen will tease me."

"She won't. Because what you want in a wife is not compatible with a wife who would tease you."

"And what is that?"

"Independence."

"What do you mean?"

"If she is reliant upon you for fortune or status, she won't risk your ire. If the security of your affection is in doubt, she won't risk upsetting you." The speech she had seen had opened Adeline's eyes and was beginning to see how love, money, and marriage were all tangled up in ways that didn't always lead to happy ever after.

The duke lifted one brow. "So if I want to be teased and tormented I should marry you?"

Marry you. Yes, please. What?! Her breath caught at her own thoughts. In order to conceal her feelings, she turned that hitch of breath into a dramatic sigh. "There you go with the proposals again."

"You think I'm teasing?"

"Be careful, Duke. You never know, I might just accept. And you're the sort to be honor bound to follow through."

She was teasing him again. What fun it was to watch his restraint crack so she might catch a glimpse of the real man beneath the title. She had a feeling those moments were as shocking and intriguing to him, too. While he might need an heiress, he really needed a woman like Adeline who would remind him not to take himself so seriously.

To have a little fun. A little pleasure.

Adeline watched as his eyes locked with hers and dropped to the swells of her breasts rising above her bodice, to linger for a second before lifting higher to settle on her lips. They had not yet kissed.

And this moment was probably their last chance.

Kingston had tried to be a gentleman. But the sound of satin and tulle rustling in the dark was its own kind of siren song. The way she bit her lip was its own kind of torture. To look at the mischievous glimmer in her eyes, to gaze at the swell of her breasts in that dress was to truly know yearning for the first time in his life.

He knew, too, that this was the last possible moment that he would have to kiss her in this lifetime. Now that his penance had been paid, he would see Adeline no more and his pursuit of Miss Van Allen would begin in earnest. She would experience the full force of Kingston's courtship. He would do whatever it took to woo her: more bird-watching in Central Park, waltzing in ballrooms and escorting her to Audubon Society functions, taking her for supper at Delmonico's.

But a part of his heart would always and forever belong to Adeline.

"Adeline . . ." He said her name softly. It might have been a question.

The carriage rolled on through the city streets. They were alone and enclosed in the shadows, save for the occasional flash of light from the streetlights they passed.

"Hello, Duke," she whispered in reply as she leaned forward. "I still don't even know your name."

"My name is Brandon Alexander Fiennes, Duke of Kingston, Marquis of Westlake, Earl of Eastland, and Viscount of Blackwood . . . I have a few more lesser titles, too. Shall I go on?"

"You should definitely stop talking."

He leaned forward to close the distance between them. "And?"

"Kiss me."

He traced a line along the bodice of her gown where the sleek blue satin contrasted with her soft skin. Her sharp intake of breath was the sweetest, most seductive sound.

"Kiss me before we lose the moment," she whispered and her gaze locked with his.

He touched his fingertips to just under her chin, tipping her face up to his.

"Kiss me before it's too late," she whispered.

And so, he kissed her.

Because the lady told him to. Because he needed to. Because he couldn't live the whole rest of his life without knowing how she tasted or knowing how her unimaginably soft lips felt against his own, or how a simple kiss could turn a man's world upside down and inside out.

This kiss, though. God. This kiss was hot, molten desire — he was hard and wanting and their lips had only just touched. When her lips parted, when their kiss deepened, when he really tasted her, Kingston knew he was in trouble. Her every touch and his every taste of her only made him want her more.

More, his heart pounded.

More, his cock begged.

More, his brain demanded.

And *why not*? asked the devil on his shoulder. There was no expectation that they should marry; she did not rely on him for anything; she had no chaperone and the night was still young, relatively speaking.

The need to hold her as he kissed her was impossible to deny.

So Kingston tugged her into his lap and she did not resist. She landed with a soft laugh and a swish of fabric. He was enveloped in satin and silk and woman and it was something like heaven.

"This is a magnificent dress but it is not conducive to kissing in carriages."

"Tomorrow I shall design a gown for such an occasion."

Then she kissed him deeply and passionately and he was too drunk with the pleasure of her touch to think about how she could make a million of those dresses and he would never experience her in one of them. Ever. Forever.

Instead, he kissed her.

Instead, he held her.

He explored the curve of her bare shoulder and moved his hand lower to the swells of her breasts. She moaned and arched her back as if to say yes, please, touch me like that. So he did, tugging the bodice down to free her gorgeous breasts so he could be the one to tease her, for once. This he did with his hands on her breasts, his mouth on her nipples, until she was moaning with pleasure and writhing against his hard cock.

"Adeline . . ." he whispered as his hands

moved to her legs, grasping the soft flesh of her thighs. "I want to touch you."

"Yes."

He found that sweet space between her legs, where she was already wet with wanting, and he began to touch her with slow, steady, deliberately torturous strokes.

"Oh God," she sighed as he intensified the pressure.

"Just a duke, actually," he murmured, teasing.

Her soft laugh turned into another moan of pleasure as he dipped one finger inside her, moving in and out slowly, steadily increasing the pressure to match her quick, shallow breaths. He found the spot that made her throw her head back and moan and so he lavished his attentions there. She clutched the lapels of his coat like she was drowning. She moved with him. She kissed him. His cock was straining to be inside her. He kept on teasing and stroking and caressing and kissing her until she was writhing and crying out in pleasure.

And he felt truly powerful for the first time.

He had given her that pleasure. Not his title, not his legacy, not anything he'd been taught in school. This was a triumph that belonged to him alone.

It was for the best that the carriage stopped.

She collapsed against him, her breasts against his chest, arms around his neck and lips on his for a deep kiss. And he thought *maybe.*

Maybe he didn't care about his honor or acting noble.

Maybe he didn't care about his duty to everyone.

Maybe he wanted to selfishly indulge in the pleasure she offered now, or even forever.

Maybe he didn't want to be the man he was trying to be.

And because of these thoughts of *what if* or *perhaps,* Kingston knew it was time to say goodbye to Adeline for good.

CHAPTER SEVENTEEN

The mystery of the Duke of Kingston's unidentified female companion — and even more important to many female readers, the name of her dressmaker — has been solved. This sensational dressmaker can be found at the House of Adeline on Nineteenth Street near the Ladies' Mile.
                                 — *The New York World*

Two weeks later
The House of Adeline

Their mad scheme had worked. Actually, unbelievably worked. After the name and address of her shop appeared in Jennie Jones's newspaper column, the fashion-forward ladies of New York descended upon the shop in a mob of muffs and millinery. They clamored for evening gowns, asked for tea dresses and ordered walking dresses by the dozens. They all wanted dresses with pockets.

Adeline was kept busy from morning to night, sketching different designs and adapting them to best fit each customer's unique shape and needs. With Rose's help, she oversaw an ever-growing staff of seamstresses whom she'd hired and trained to cut, fit, sew, and embroider. The business of the shop didn't manage itself — Adeline was learning on the go and getting by with Rachel's knack of numbers. Help from the more business-minded women of the Ladies of Liberty club proved to be invaluable.

Adeline was living the dream and it was more demanding and fulfilling than she had ever dared to imagine. She was an independent mistress of her own burgeoning empire.

There was no time to moon over the duke.

Absolutely none.

She scarcely had time to breathe.

Yet she managed to think of Brandon — Kingston — constantly. As she rushed around the city, she wondered if she might walk right into him again. As she took a customer's measurements, she smiled at the memory of the time she had taken his measure. She thought about him rather a lot for a woman who had repeatedly professed no interest in romantic entanglements, especially none in marriage.

She still was not interested in marriage, per se. Intimacies with the duke, however, were another matter. As she fell asleep at night, she thought of him. She closed her eyes and relived that delicious experience from the carriage. She touched herself the way he had. She brought herself to a climax by imagining what would have happened had they not stopped.

It was good. It was *great.*

It was not enough. Her desire for Kingston — his kiss, his touch — seemed to be insatiable.

Then it was morning and she was at her shop, full of women who wanted dresses that would get the duke's attentions. They thought she had the secret.

So there was no time to notice that weeks — weeks! — had passed without a word from him. No charming notes, no invitations, no strolling into the shop unexpectedly.

Yes, she noticed his absence.

Yes, she counted the days.

Yes, she scolded herself for caring.

It was a little thing, but she felt it keenly, like a straight pin accidentally left in a garment. Occasional and painful little pricks reminding her *this isn't finished.*

There was also no time to read the newspaper, which diligently detailed his whereabouts and with-whom-abouts with an earnest dedication that ought to have been reserved for actual wars.

Not that Adeline knew about it. While her seamstresses avidly devoured the gossip columns, they also ensured that she knew nothing about the latest blow-by-blow reports of his courtship of Miss Van Allen.

Until she did.

It was a Wednesday.

A Wednesday at half past three. The doldrums hour of the week, when nothing but work stretched before or behind. Adeline had a few minutes to prepare for the next appointment. It was Lady Hewitt, who had the unfortunate tendency to bring her husband, who had the lamentable habit of being a little too enthusiastic in his appreciation of seamstresses and dressmakers. As Lady Marian's dress order progressed with increasing extravagance, it became more and more imperative that Adeline remain in the good graces of Lord Hewitt, keeper of the purse. So she kept her seamstresses out of the way and dealt with him, and his hands, herself.

Adeline was not looking forward to the fitting.

"Do we have the muslin ready for Lady Hewitt? She has an appointment in ten minutes and —"

Adeline stopped short as she entered and saw her seamstresses not at their stations but huddled around a newspaper.

Rose and Rachel were among them. They were joined by Lila and June, who had each suffered a bit of bad luck — a stint in the tombs, a stint on the street — but they could sew well and they were lovely company in the workroom. And Margaret, who was expecting. Adeline was glad to have their help, but also deeply proud to be able to offer them a decent wage for honorable work, especially since it was unlikely they would find employment elsewhere. She did not even want to think about what their alternatives were.

But not one of them was helping now. They were all frozen, clutching an issue of *The New York World.*

"What is it?" Adeline asked. "What is the news?"

"Nothing."

"Nothing interesting."

"Nothing newsworthy."

This Adeline found hard to believe, given that the headlines she glimpsed included the words *Death, Bribery, Arrests* and *Poi-*

soned by Cheese.

"I feel stupider for having read it," Rose said. "I implore you not to do the same."

Rose loved the newspapers and delighted in sharing choice bits aloud. For her to say this suggested that she was deliberately hiding something from Adeline.

She reached out to grab the paper. "You're hiding something from me."

Rachel snatched it first and held it behind her back.

"Didn't you say Lady Hewitt had an appointment?"

"I hope she leaves her husband at home," Lila muttered and no one disagreed.

"Is it news about the shop?" Adeline asked. "Has someone written something bad? I got the feeling that Miss Delamere wasn't completely happy with her gown. Has she said something disparaging?"

"Always thinking of work. And dresses. And work," Lila said.

"I haven't time for leisure," Adeline replied. "You all know that. Now what is in that newspaper?"

"Oh, it's just something about the duke," Rose said. "He's really old news by now, isn't he?"

Ah. Yes. Of course.

It was always all about the duke.

And no, he was not old news.

"Oh. How is he? Is he still tall, dark, handsome, and the most eligible bachelor in town?" Adeline quipped. She was determined not to care about him and if that was unmanageable, then she could at least not appear to care about him. So what if it had been two very long weeks since she last saw him?

"As of this printing . . ." Rose said sheepishly.

"As of this printing? What does that mean?"

Adeline grabbed the paper. First she looked at the date — yesterday evening's post. Then she started scanning. Blah blah blah *potential war* blah blah blah *serial killer at large* blah blah blah.

Then she saw it:

To the surprise of no one who has been following my reports, the duke of Kingston was spotted at Mr. Tiffany's shop on Union Square. One doubts he was there to inquire about the purchase of a lamp. Those watching the courtship of the duke and Miss Van Allen expect his proposal of marriage to be imminent.

Adeline stilled as she read it, keenly aware that her band of misfit seamstresses were all anxiously watching her to see how she would react. Would she fling patterns and half-made dresses in the air and storm about the room in a fit of despair? Collapse in a heap on the floor and sob her heart out?

No. She would display not such theatrics.

Even if she did feel her knees wobble.

She had known from the minute she stumbled into his arms that they had no future together. And that was *fine* because she had no wish to surrender her independence to a husband or lover. She had known it when they walked in the park and kissed and took his measurements that witty banter and passionate kisses were all that they would share. She had known it when he was bringing her to heights of pleasure she'd never imagined.

She had known and the knowledge had done nothing to soften the blow of this moment. The truth of it hit her hard and fast knocking the wind right out of her. She had fallen for him; one had to admit that now. She still desired him with a hot, intense longing that kept her up at night. And he was going to marry another woman, which would make him off-limits forever.

Anything she might have been feeling right now — say, sadness, longing, regret, and all those heartache-y, might-have-been feelings — was her own fault because she had forgotten her rule.

Men were a distraction.

She was right. Miss Burnett was right. Madame Chalfont was right.

None of this could be admitted to anyone, of course, especially her team of seamstresses, who were all holding their breath and waiting for her reaction.

Adeline delicately set down the newspaper and said, "My felicitations to them both."

"Shall we send flowers or a card of congratulations?" Lila offered.

Adeline didn't think twice before replying, "Let's not get carried away."

CHAPTER EIGHTEEN

Mrs. Van Allen is already planning the
wedding of her daughter to the Duke of
Kingston. Can a proposal be far behind?
— *The New York World*

Later that afternoon
The Fifth Avenue Hotel

Though the duke's sprawling suite had
captivating views of the sun setting over
Fifth Avenue and Madison Square Park, his
attention — and Freddie's — was fixed on
the small, hard object between them.

Kingston reached out to touch it tentatively, finding the surface smooth but firm
under his fingertips. Then he moved to
ensure that Freddie had a good, unob-
structed view.

"Do you think she'll like it?" he asked.
Everything depended upon it being to her
taste.

"How could she not like the pride and joy

of the Kingston family jewels?" Freddie quipped, looking down at the hard object in the duke's hand.

The diamond they admired sparkled in the setting sun. The ring featured one large, princess-cut diamond in a gold setting, flanked by deep blue sapphires. It was nestled into a velvet box after having been reset and polished by Mr. Tiffany himself.

It sparkled and reflected wealth, prestige, former glory, and grand promises for the future.

"The roof of Lyon House may be leaking but we still have the family jewels," Kingston said dryly. "My mother fainted — actually fainted — when I suggested selling some to settle debts."

"Priorities."

"I do need a ring befitting my future duchess. It must be something that will stand out among Miss Van Allen's other jewels."

"That one is certainly large enough."

It would be the wedding of the season. The visiting English Duke would wed New York City's richest and prettiest heiress, Miss Alice Van Allen. After his near misses with Miss Olivia Watson and Miss Elsie Pennypacker — and his impossibly distracting attraction to Miss Adeline Black —

Kingston had finally found a suitable bride to supply him the fortune he needed, and presumably an heir, a spare, and a pleasing face across the breakfast table so long as they both shall live.

Everything was progressing as planned.

He should be ecstatic.

He had yet to formally propose, but he'd spoken with her father and learned that Mrs. Van Allen had already reserved Grace Church for a Sunday in July. There was already talk of the gown, the guest list, and a honeymoon at their cottage in Newport.

For his part, Kingston was already making specific plans for her dowry, which couldn't come soon enough. A fire at his stables had recently caused significant damage — the horses and groomsmen were unharmed, thank God, but it was another urgent and crucial expense. Despite his advice, his mother had acquired the desired ermine cape — along with a matching gown and complementary hat. He thought Adeline would at least want the dressmakers and milliners to be paid.

Adeline . . .

These were good reasons, noble and honorable reasons to wed a woman he did not love. He would be kind, faithful, and would certainly try to be a good husband to her. He would put her dowry to good use, not just wager it all away. Before he'd met Adeline, Kingston thought that would be enough to bring to a marriage — never mind his title and status, too. But now he felt like he was cheating Miss Van Allen out of something.

Maybe even cheating himself, too.

Had he known when he stepped into the elevator with Adeline that she would force him to review and revise every expectation he had for marriage and the rest of his life, would he still have stepped in with her? Would he still have let himself be charmed and enchanted and *changed*?

Could he still go on with his plans, even if he had known something like love?

These questions were the reasons he had not slept and why he still had not popped the question, though everyone was expecting it at any moment now.

"When will you propose?" Freddie asked. "I imagine there is some urgency."

"Soon."

As soon as he could stop thinking of Adeline and plan a proper proposal. Or even sooner, so he could *stop* thinking about Adeline. He had abruptly cut off all contact with her after that kiss — for what purpose did they have to connect, other than to torture himself with wanting to kiss her again? He thought the distance would spare him the torture of wondering *what if* or *if only* or other emotional, romantic nonsense.

He was wrong.

Grievously, achingly wrong.

He thought of her constantly.

"Soon," he repeated firmly. "Within the week, after they return from Newport. I imagine her mother will want time to plan a ball announcing the betrothal."

"Nothing says true love like logistics."

"You know love has nothing to do with it."

"Wrong," Freddie said sharply, to Kingston's surprise. "Love has everything to do with it. Perhaps you don't love your bride yet, but you are doing this out of love for your dukedom, your family, your tenants, your legacy. Your honor. Your duty. Love."

Kingston felt his chest tighten. Love. Of course.

Leave it to Freddie to surprise him with such an astute observation.

"When you put it like that . . ." was all he could say. This was verging precariously into the territory of emotion.

"Enough of the sentimental talk," Freddie said. "Let us go out to celebrate your impending betrothal and the end of your freedom. I know just the place."

They were nearly ready to depart when there was an urgent knock on the door.

"Are you expecting anyone?"

"No."

The knocking was accompanied by the sound of a commotion in the hall.

Freddie tilted his head. "Does that sound like — ?"

"Oh bloody hell, it does." Kingston closed his eyes.

Or maybe he winced.

He definitely cringed.

A chorus of women's voices rose up in the hall. English-accented voices. Two of them bickering and one voice rising above with a "now now" of mothers everywhere.

The door burst open.

Sisters.

His two sisters and his mother. Here. In New York. Unexpectedly.

He *knew* that silence from telegrams was too good to be true.

"Mother. My dear sisters. You are not in London. Where you live."

"We simply had to see New York!" That was Nora, pushing into the room and heading straight for the window to admire the view.

"I thought about it, darling . . ." his

265

mother began, as she removed a hat decorated with an atrociously colorful assortment of plumage and he wondered how many exotic birds relinquished their lives so that his mother could feel *fashionable.*

Ah, Miss Van Allen was having an effect on him already.

". . . and I decided that I just couldn't let my only son make such a monumental decision as to who should replace me as the duchess on his own. A mother's guidance is needed . . . or something."

"We wanted to see New York," Clara explained, flopping down onto the settee and making herself right at home.

"And Clara was plotting to elope with some impoverished academic, who studies philosophy of all the useless things," Nora said. "She had to be stopped."

"We're in love!"

"There were also creditors plaguing us," his mother murmured.

"*Plaguing* you?"

"Yes, and your secretary refused to extend credit to my dressmaker and I simply couldn't be the only one who wasn't wearing a fox-fur stole. We are *Kingston;* we have standards to uphold."

"And what rare bird supplied the feathers in this hat?"

"Oh, who even knows? Do you like it? They're all the rage in London."

"The hat pins are studded with precious gems," Clara added.

"It all looks very expensive."

"All the best things are." The duchess patted his cheek affectionately. As if he were still a small boy and not a grown man tasked with controlling her spending and serving as head of the family and saving a dwindling empire.

"Mother, did Father ever make you feel like a caged animal? Is that why you want an ermine cape and a fox-fur stole?"

His three female relations paused to stare at him, mouths agape, in stunned silence.

"Wherever would you get an idea like that?"

"Just something that occurred to me one day."

Beside him Freddie murmured, "Sounds like something Miss Black would say."

Kingston turned sharply to his cousin; why did Freddie know what Adeline would say? He hadn't realized his cousin knew her so well. He also hadn't anticipated such a thought would result in a fiery burst of jealousy but there it was, burning him up.

What was it to him if she and Freddie had . . . something? His cousin might not be faithful to his wife, but Kingston would be. He meant to sacrifice his happiness to fulfill his duty to those who relied on him. It was his honor. His duty.

He'd made his choice. He had done the math, weighed the options, and made his decision. Kingston's hand fisted around the diamond ring in his pocket as if it were a lifeline, which it was.

Marry me, Miss Alice Van Allen.

For the feathers. For the birds. His mother had needed some diversion from her train wreck of a husband; he could not begrudge her some millinery.

So Clara and Nora could marry for love, respectably. For the tenants and the roofs.

It was all more important than his own happiness.

CHAPTER NINETEEN

Many New Yorkers enjoy taking refuge from the hustle and bustle of the city in one of the rooftop theaters popping up around town.
— *The New York World*

Later that evening

Kingston was a duke in need of a diversion. Between his impending, unwanted betrothal and the unexpected arrival of his mother and sisters, a drink was definitely in order. He gladly accepted Freddie's offer to join some friends — the Rogues of Millionaire Row, the press had dubbed them — for a rollicking night on the town.

It might just be his last hurrah.

A farewell to his bachelor days.

Tonight they eschewed the formal society entertainments and headed for more *democratic* haunts where one might hear music or see a show, have a drink, and take in the

269

vibrancy of the city. The crew of rich, rowdy men — plus the duke — dropped in at the Casino Theater on Broadway and Thirty-ninth Street. They took in a musical show — *The Belle of New York* — and then they headed *up.*

Kingston had never seen anything like it. A garden had been established on the roof of the theater for public enjoyment, where anyone might procure a beverage, enjoy entertainments and other company, and simply enjoy the (relatively) fresh air and quiet, both rare finds in the heat and din of the city. It was a welcome respite for the stay-at-homes, otherwise known as those who could not afford to leave the city for, say, a Newport cottage. This was not an exclusive enclave of the Four Hundred or a private pleasure ground for men; it was open to all.

From this vantage, the city rose up around him, some buildings meeting him at eye level and others demanding he look heavenward. On the street, one could easily feel overwhelmed and downtrodden by the force and size and stink of the city. But to stand at this height and look out at those increasingly towering buildings — built by nobodies, with nothing but ambition, desperation, and hard work — was to feel the desire to conquer the town and to get excited by the possibility of it.

When one experienced something new and exciting on one's travels, the instinct was to share it with someone. Kingston was no exception. The problem was that he wanted to share this with Adeline. *Isn't that view of the sun setting over the skyline stunning? No, there is nothing like this in London. Can you imagine having the vision to build something like this, that has never been done before? Yes, I imagine you can, Adeline . . .*

Freddie and his rogues had wandered off to pair up with whatever lovely ladies they could strike up a conversation with. From his position near the balustrade, Kingston watched them laugh, flirt, carouse, and generally act as if behavior had no consequences and fortunes lasted forever. He spotted a few of the gents he'd met at the club or at various parties, and they, too, were clearly on the prowl for women with whom to spend the night.

This place, this night, was about a moment's pleasure. Not one's duty, not forever.

"Kingston!" Freddie calling out to him. "Look who I found!"

He looked over to where Freddie was waving at him in a manner too enthusiastic to be dignified, but admittedly there was no other option for getting someone's attention in this crush.

It wasn't as if this was Mrs. Astor's ballroom, after all.

Freddie, being Freddie, was not alone. Nor was he devoid of female company. He stood in the middle of three dark-haired beauties whom Kingston happened to recognize.

Adeline. She stood stiffly, with Freddie's arm around her waist. She was with her friends Rose, the world's most wonderfully bad chaperone; and the no-nonsense Rachel (Miss Abrams, to him though).

Of course. Of all the rooftop gardens in Manhattan, they had both gone to the same one. On the same night. At the same bewitching hour of dusk, between daylight and darkness. Had he been a more superstitious man, he'd have thought it fate. Instead, in a sign that the city was getting under his skin, he thought it so very New York.

"Isn't it our lucky night?" Freddie grinned.

Lucky night indeed.

"Fancy seeing you here," Kingston remarked to Adeline. Just seeing her transformed him from forlorn, foreign-born bachelor to just a man standing in front of just the girl his heart desired.

"We need to stop meeting like this," she said with a little laugh.

"Do we?" He lifted one brow. At least Rose appeared charmed.

"We're out for a last hurrah," Freddie explained with a devilish grin. "Before my cousin pops the question and gets himself committed."

There was a beat of awkward silence.

"Congratulations are in order, I suppose," Adeline said.

"It's too soon for that," Kingston replied, meeting her gaze.

"Have you not yet proposed?" she inquired, and he couldn't tell if she was just repeating her lines from their first encounter or genuinely asking. He was struck by how much it mattered.

"He's got the ring. But he hasn't got the girl," Freddie interjected. "He's dragging his feet for some reason."

"What reason could that be, I wonder?" Rose said, pointedly.

"I honestly could not imagine," Rachel added.

"It defies logic and reason," Adeline said.

"Drinks?" Kingston offered. "Would anyone care for a drink? Some champagne, perhaps?"

He dispatched Freddie to procure a bottle

of champagne. With any luck, he'd get distracted from his task and leave Kingston alone with Adeline and her friends.

Rose and Rachel flanked her like guardian angels who would lose their wings if they so much as *glanced* away from their friend. There would be no stealing away alone with Adeline tonight, much as he may desire to. Her lovely, charming, and somewhat terrifying friends made that abundantly clear.

"Well, if it isn't the Duke of Kingston," Rose said stepping forward to enclose him in their circle.

"The most eligible bachelor in town," Rachel added.

"The stuff of dreams and fantasy," Rose continued.

"Stop," Adeline said, cheeks adorably pink. "Stop! You are all embarrassing me."

"I should be the one embarrassed. What high standards I am held to. I couldn't possibly live up to them. Unless I am succeeding at being the stuff of your dreams and fantasies?"

Adeline's cheeks reddened considerably now, confirming that yes, he was the stuff of her dreams and fantasies. His chest might have swelled with pride.

"Seems like it's my turn to tease you," he murmured.

"Adeline has told us all about you," Rose cut in, coming to the rescue of her friend.

"Has she now?" He leaned in. This he wanted to hear.

"If we don't change the subject, I think I might actually die of mortification," Adeline said. But everyone ignored her.

"Oh yes," Rachel said, eyes bright with mischief. "She raved and raved about the fine tailoring of your suit on the day you first met."

"My suit, not what's inside of it?"

"Adeline has her priorities in order," Rachel countered.

"Yes," Adeline echoed. "Priorities."

Her cheeks were now pink in a way that suggested she wasn't envisioning the fine tailoring of his suit, but what it concealed. Stuff of dreams and fantasies indeed.

It meant something to know that this *something* between them was not one-sided. An infatuation of his own was more easily dismissed than a real and deep attraction between the two of them.

But it was too early in the evening for such a discussion.

"What brings you all out this evening?"

"Can't working girls have a little fun after sewing all day?"

"On a fine night like tonight, how can one

stay in?"

"If anyone deserves a little fun, it is the ladies of the House of Adeline," he said. "I see your dresses everywhere I go now — ballrooms, social calls, Fifth Avenue after church on Sunday. I am always reminded of you."

"What torture that must be for you," Rachel said.

"You have no idea," he replied.

"Oh, isn't he a romantic one," Rose commented.

"Stop, you might make us swoon," Rachel said.

"Don't you all carry smelling salts in those famous pockets of yours?"

"I would think you might, Duke, with all the swooning ladies you leave in your wake," Adeline said.

"Alas, I don't have any with me tonight, so take care not to be overcome with desire or emotion," he replied. "But I see plenty of women here tonight wearing House of Adeline dresses, so perhaps someone else has some tucked away."

"We can hardly keep up with the demand," Rose said proudly. "You don't even want to know how long our waitlist is."

"Our appointment book really is full now," Miss Abrams added. "In case you were in the mood for another dress fitting."

He laughed.

"Congratulations on your success. May your appointment book always be full."

He meant it: he had every wish for their good fortune. There was no overlooking the fact that these women had worked hard — from the long hours diligently stitching and sewing each gown, to the great risk of creating something new and presenting it to the world — and they deserved to enjoy their success.

To think, these women had started with nothing, truly. Adeline was right — he had thought being broke was when his club membership came due, he did not know the fear of not having a place to live or a way to earn his bread. Only now did he even stop to consider what that must feel like for them.

He hoped, for their sakes, that this dressmaking enterprise brought them riches. In fact, he had to wonder just how much of a fortune a dressmaker could make. Lord knew he certainly forked over obscene amounts for his mother and sisters' wardrobes. And they were but one family. And by the looks of it, the House of Adeline was now *the* dressmaker for the Four Hundred.

She did not need him. Not anymore.

This ought to have made him feel wretched. Instead it made him feel wanted in a way he'd never felt before.

The evening progressed — Freddie eventually did return with champagne, and they all enjoyed a glass together before Freddie wandered off in search of more obliging company. Rose and Rachel drifted a few feet away to chatter about Rose's recent suitor. He and Adeline were left alone in a spot with a breathtaking view of the sun setting over the city.

"My friends like you," Adeline said.

"I like your friends."

"I'm rather fond of them myself. They took a big risk to join me at the new shop. I know what they had to lose and I wouldn't have blamed them if they'd stayed."

"That's probably why they thought you were worth the risk."

"I'm glad someone thinks so," Adeline said softly. He didn't know what to say to that, but he felt it. He really did.

He wondered if Adeline had hoped that something might change for him. And maybe things were changing, as she opened his eyes and challenged him to see opportunities he might have missed because of his narrow-minded focus on an heiress.

For example, these women — alone in this

big city, dependent upon no one but their own wits and talents — had risked all for Adeline. Kingston had thought of himself as brave and courageous, but next to those girls he could not lay claim to it.

"It seems their risks have been rewarded," he said. For her. And frankly, for himself. It was worth noting that these women had attained such success after starting out with so much less than he possessed. He thought of the excuses he had made for himself. He now reconsidered them.

"That's the thing about this town," Adeline said, leaning against the railing and staring out over the city. He watched a smile play upon her lips as she gave him a quick glance. "It's a place of big risks and greater rewards. Those grand fortunes haven't come from playing it safe but from taking big risks. And, frankly, by taking advantage of those less fortunate. But the lesson I choose to take away is that one must seize opportunities presented. Even if they make your heart stop in fear and make you wonder if you're crazy."

"That sounds like a dare."

She stepped closer to him.

"Take it as you'd like, Duke."

His hand found hers, hidden in the folds of her dress.

"No other woman has challenged me the way you do."

"Is that a good thing or a bad thing?"

He stroked her palm gently with his thumb. It was the littlest touch, but he needed this connection to her. He watched her features soften at the pleasure of his touch.

"I can say that you're the only one I can think about, Adeline."

She looked up at him, meeting his gaze. "I'd be lying if I said you never crossed my mind," she said quietly and he wanted to live in this moment forever.

Kingston wanted to kiss her urgently. Here. Now. Forever.

Take her in his arms and take her away to someplace more private, more secluded. His hotel room, perhaps, or even that hunting lodge of his in the wilds of Scotland.

He had to face how much he wanted her. This was not just desire — though it was that, with an intensity he'd never before felt — what he felt was verging on love. And love was notorious for making men think mad, irrational, insane thoughts.

Like discarding one's eminently sensible plans to marry an heiress and taking a chance that there was another way to obtain the fortune he sought. He would be putting everything of his at risk — centuries of privilege, the legacy of his dukedom, his forthcoming marriage, the future he had always expected.

The very way he had always imagined himself was at stake. Ever since he was a child, he'd been the dutiful son, and he'd grown into the responsible duke upon whom everyone could rely for continued protection.

He was a respectable gentleman who did not throw everything away because of a pretty New York City girl.

Except maybe he was the kind of man who threw everything away because of a pretty New York City girl after all.

Because Adeline, oh Adeline. Those lips smiling at him recalled the memories of their frantic, heated kiss. The way she looked at him with a sparkle in her eye made him think anything was possible. She had the Manhattan skyline as her backdrop. Buildings were starting to rise higher than ever before, and so many were works in progress but projecting so much promise. The city was just beginning to be electrified. This was a cityscape new to history, made by those who dared to dream of things that did not previously exist, and

those who dared to take the risk.
    The question was, could he?

CHAPTER TWENTY

Everyone is talking about Mrs. Carlyle's upcoming masquerade ball. The hostess is promising a spectacle of grandeur and wealth, the likes of which this city has never seen, and that is saying something.
— *The New York World*

The House of Adeline

The Duchess of Kingston herself arrived the next day. She came without the duke, but she did bring his sisters. The three ladies entered the shop in a burst of ruffles, swishes of petticoats, and girlish chatter in English accents, declaring they had just arrived and desperately needed gowns fit for New York City society.

The duke did not accompany them, likely because he had spent more than enough time in the House of Adeline than was seemly for a gentleman. Likely, too, because most men considered joining ladies for trips to the modiste to be akin to torture.

And because of last night.

Nothing had *happened.* Nothing happened that one would write home about, print in the newspaper, or that would make for interesting gossip among the girls. But Adeline had sensed a change in him. His sheer bloody-minded narrow focus on wedding a fortune was dissipating and he was considering other options. Either she or the city was having an effect on him, opening his eyes, challenging him, and inviting him to stay.

And now his mother and sisters were here, interested in acquiring gowns from the House of Adeline, while the dressmaker in question was entertaining a seriously scandalous thought.

And then the words were actually leaving her mouth.

And then the duchess and her daughters left in a swish and a huff. Along with their ruffles and petticoats and massive feathered hats. And the honor of dressing their esteemed, aristocratic selves.

Adeline returned to the workroom, leaned back against the wall, closed her eyes, and exhaled the breath she had been holding.

"What just happened?" Rose asked, looking up from some lace embroidery.

"I refused to dress the Duchess of Kingston."

"You refused to dress a duchess? *The* duchess?" Rachel asked, aghast.

"Oh my God. I need to sit down," Margaret said.

"Is it the baby?"

"No, I just realized my employer is insane."

"Insanely in love, perhaps," Rachel said. But her voice wasn't as snarky as it might have been. Kingston had been quite successful at charming her friends last night. He dispensed with any Lofty Lord act and treated them as . . . equals. Unbelievably charming, that.

Adeline did not disagree with her friend's assessment.

But all eyes were on her as each one of her girls expected an explanation as to why Adeline would refuse the honor of dressing a duchess.

"I have more than once heard him complain about dressmakers' bills being an expense he struggles to pay," she explained. "I refuse to add to his debts."

"You mean you refuse to make it more necessary for him to marry his heiress," Rose said softly.

"You know that she will just go elsewhere,"

Margaret said. "She will go to someone else who will show no such restraint."

"Like the dressmaker of her current ensemble?" Rachel replied, wincing at the recollection of it.

The duchess had arrived in a gown that couldn't say *no.* Ruffles, fringe, and beads all competed to draw the eye; no flourish was deemed too much. And the hat — oh dear God, the hat. Her Grace wore an entire aviary on her hat, along with sufficient flora to feed them. There was more nature on her hat than Adeline had seen while growing up in the tenements of Lower Manhattan. The duchess was a woman screaming for attention with the only way she knew how: through attire that dared you to look away.

Dressmakers, milliners, and mantua makers must have seen her coming from a mile away and taken unfair advantage.

"Perhaps I should have agreed," Adeline said. "And perhaps I might have — free of charge, or at a reduced rate — but she was determined to have an "eye-catching" costume for the upcoming masquerade that 'would have the whole town talking.' "

"Oh dear."

"Indeed.

"Besides, we also have a significant request from Miss Burnett." *My benefactor.* "Her letter arrived just this morning. For this upcoming masquerade ball, she and five of her friends wish to go in complementary costumes, which we are to make. And Rose, I shall need you to fit me because, by Miss Burnett's invitation, one of them is for me."

Later that day

For all that their lives were strangely intertwined at the moment, Adeline had never actually met Miss Alice Van Allen and her mother. She knew plenty about them from the gossip columns; their fortune derived from Manhattan real estate and they regularly appeared at Fifth Avenue soirees and generously patronized a variety of charitable endeavors, with Miss Van Allen being particularly devoted to fundraising and organizing for the Audubon Society. Their family held a subscription at the Metropolitan Opera House, but only since the opera house favored by old Knickerbocker families had been demolished.

Though Adeline had no way of confirming it, she would wager that Mrs. Van Allen was a devoted subscriber to *The Titled American,* a periodical that listed the American women who had married into the British aristocracy . . . and that also listed the eligible, titled bachelors, their holdings, and

287

annual incomes.

In other words, she was *that* kind of mother.

"Good afternoon. Mrs. Van Allen. Miss Van Allen. How are you today?"

"Well, it seems the gossip is true," Mrs. Van Allen stated, and Adeline's stomach lurched. *Did she know? What did she know?* "This is a lovely shop."

"Thank you." Adeline breathed a sigh of relief.

"Your dresses have become quite the sensation, so when we needed a dress for my daughter for a special occasion, it seemed natural to call upon you. It wouldn't do to wear something other than most au courant fashions on the most important day of my daughter's life so far."

Before she could ask, *what occasion?!* Mrs. Van Allen continued on. "But she doesn't need pockets in her gown."

"Pockets are one of my signatures," Adeline said, confused.

"Yes, so they say. But I don't agree with it. It's too masculine. I can't imagine what a woman needs a pocket for, anyway."

Money. Lip paint. Love letters. Adeline's gaze dropped to Miss Van Allen's gloved left hand and thought: *A place to keep her gloves after she has removed them so one might see if she is wearing a betrothal ring.*

"We know that you are a friend of the duke's," Miss Van Allen said in a sweet, girlish voice. "The widow of his friend from Eton. I'm so sorry about your husband's passing." Adeline could scarcely whisper thank you for the very unnecessary condolences. "We wish to support the duke's friends. His interests and concerns shall soon be ours."

Oh damn. She was sweet. She was kind, pretty, and sweet.

Adeline glanced again at Miss Van Allen's hands as she delicately tugged each fingertip of her gloves for the slow, delicate process of removal. *Is there a ring? Is there a ring!?*

"And what is the occasion for the gowns?" Adeline asked, doing her very best to adopt the demeanor of Disinterested Dressmaker Who Was Not Personally Invested in the Occasion At All Whatsoever.

"We need gowns for my daughter's betrothal ball."

Ah.

Well then.

That. Was. That.

Adeline had no business feeling that pang in her heart, so sharp that her breath literally caught in her throat. For a moment, she couldn't breathe. After last night she had thought . . . *maybe.* Maybe they would have a chance. But apparently not.

"My congratulations," she croaked.

Miss Van Allen had removed her gloves now, gently draping the soft blue kidskin leather across her lap. No ring adorned any of her long, elegant fingers.

"Oh, it's not official. Yet," Mrs. Van Allen replied with a wink. "But we expect him to ask soon. And then we won't have much time to plan the betrothal ball and the wedding. Best to get a head start on these things. We don't want him to slip through our fingers now, do we?"

"Of course." Adeline smiled tightly. But so did Miss Van Allen. And that piqued Adeline's interest. That royal *we* told Adeline just what she needed to do next.

"I shall need to take Miss Van Allen's measurements. While we do that, Mrs. Van Allen, perhaps you would like to have some refreshment and consider fabric options in the other room? You must have something in mind."

"Excellent, thank you. I'm thinking a lovely shade of ivory. Or perhaps pearl."

"Oh indeed. Both are excellent options," Adeline agreed, ushering the meddling mama out of the room. The velvet curtains swished shut behind her and they were alone.

"Ivory or pearl? Does that mean anything to you? Aren't they both just shades of white?" Miss Van Allen asked after her mother was out of earshot.

"It absolutely means something," Adeline began to explain. "It means that your mother has a very specific idea of what perfect happiness is for you. It means that she has been considering the finer points of this event for quite some time. It means that everything must be just so."

"That is the difference between ivory and pearl?"

"In this instance, yes."

Miss Van Allen was so young. Adeline hadn't realized. At one and twenty years, she was a perfectly fine age to wed. But her mother — one of those mothers — had kept her in a state of innocence. It was all there in her dress: a demure, high-necked affair in a pretty floral pattern that whispered of youth and purity and safety and made Adeline think of a lamb being led to the slaughter.

This girl had no business wearing a dress from the House of Adeline. Not with its wicked pockets and cuts that gave a sensation of freedom rather than . . . a gilded birdcage.

Or did she?

They commenced with the fitting. Adeline took note of her height and waist and all the inches she needed to know about in order to sew a gown that was more than a betrothal dress. Could she also create a gown that would create a spark in this girl and stiffen her spine? Perhaps she could even make a dress that would inspire her to refuse a duke.

"Perhaps we might also make you a day dress. For when he proposes."

"A fine idea. I'm sure my mother will be amenable."

Moments passed in agonizing silence as Adeline took her measure: the span of her waist, her bust, the distance from her shoulder to wrist. Finally she could no longer resist asking the question on her mind, if only to make conversation and even if she was afraid of the answer.

"Do you love him?"

Miss Van Allen, to her credit, answered candidly. "I love my mother. I love my father. I love everything they have done for me. He will be good to me and I do not love anyone else."

Something clenched in Adeline's chest. Was this supposed to make her feel better?

There was some comfort, she supposed, in knowing that their feelings weren't lopsided; Miss Van Allen wasn't some starry-eyed girl in love with a man who didn't return the feeling.

But did she not want *more*? Did she not want passionate kisses and true love and to move through the world with a purpose? Adeline wondered if Miss Van Allen even knew those things were options.

And what a pity it was, that a man like the duke should be wasted in a loveless marriage. All that smoldering passion of his would fade with time.

"What do you think, Miss Van Allen? Ivory or pearl?"

"I think I shouldn't know the difference. Or care. As long as my mother is happy."

"If we hang the weight of the dress from the shoulders instead of your hips, you won't feel as if you're walking around in a cage," Adeline explained. "We can keep the skirts full and use a different-style bustle instead, so you'll feel like you can move and . . . do something."

"Do what?"

"Anything. Whatever strikes your fancy."

"I like birds," she said softly. "I like the idea of birds being able to fly around freely and without worrying about being caught and kept in a cage or . . . worse. I don't care if my dress is ivory or pearl, but it mustn't have feathers or fur. I like the idea of feeling freedom, Mrs. Black. I've always imagined what it would be like, but I've never experienced it."

Adeline straightened, determined. She would not say anything to Miss Van Allen — it would be out of place to try to change her mind. She would not attempt to seduce Kingston away from what he claimed he wanted.

But she would make a dress for this girl that would give her a taste of the freedom she was about to give up. Adeline would marshal everything she knew about dress-making and womanhood to create a gown that might, just might, give Miss Van Allen the sense of strength necessary to chase her own dreams.

CHAPTER TWENTY-ONE

No one has ever spent more money on an evening's entertainment than Mrs. Carlyle has done for her masquerade ball. Thousands of flowers have been shipped from the southern states and it is rumored that thousands of bottles of champagne have been ordered. The theme is Versailles, which should tell you all you need to know.

— *The New York World*

The Masquerade Ball

Brandon Alexander Fiennes, the Duke of Kingston, Marquis of Westlake, Earl of Eastland, Viscount Blackwood, etc., etc., was nervous. He was nervous because he was about to introduce his mother to the woman to whom he intended to propose marriage.

And the whole damned thing had to be done in costume. He had dressed simply in his evening clothes and a mask. If anyone asked what his costume was, he would reply, *Englishman too embarrassed to dress up.*

On the other hand, his mother fully embraced the opportunity to appear in costume. She arrived at the masquerade dressed as a bird, head to toe, feathers and all. Or all of the feathers. In shades of deep purple, blue, and green, and accents of white, they covered her gown, her cape, and her mask. Inexplicably, she also wore a diamond tiara.

The dress had been created at the last minute — and at great expense — by a dressmaker who was not Adeline. Kingston had learned of her refusal to dress his mother — the duchess was outraged — but he understood the message. She did not want him indebted anymore, and not to her. She was trying to set him free and it only made him want her more.

The diamond tiara the duchess wore had traveled over in Her Grace's luggage.

Kingston had to introduce this woman to his fiancée, a devoted member of the Audubon Society, whose one and only passion was preserving and protecting the lives of birds.

This would not go well.

He ought to have seen this coming.

Nevertheless, Kingston performed the introductions.

Woman dressed as royal peacock, may I please present Little Bo Peep.

Miss Van Allen was dressed as Little Bo Peep. It was not a dress born in the House of Adeline.

She wore some frilly concoction of lace upon lace upon ruffles. Ye gods, the ruffles. Between the frills and the feathers, he was in some circle of fashion hell, where too much feminine adornment threatened to suffocate him.

"Your Grace, your costume is quite stunning."

"Isn't it? I have come as a bird. I don't know which one, of course. Something fabulous, though."

Mrs. Van Allen murmured her agreement because they were words from the mouth of a duchess and so one must agree with them.

Her daughter, however, turned red. Her eyes flashed. For the first time since he'd known her, Miss Van Allen displayed a temper.

"Those are feathers from a variety of birds, including peacocks and great blue herons and snowy egret," she said. "Some of these species have been hunted nearly to extinction only for the purpose of decorating women's hats and dresses."

"Extinct! Well, that should make it all the more valuable then, hmm?"

Kingston winced.

"There are campaigns underway to discourage ladies from wearing feathers. It is an important cause among many of the fine ladies in society and one that is dear to my heart."

"They're just birds, dear." Kingston's mother flashed him the *I am getting bored* look.

"Oh, but they aren't just birds!" Miss Van Allen said passionately, her voice rising to champion her cause. "They are majestic creatures who make significant contributions to nature. They are beautiful creatures — God's creatures. Why, just imagine if there were no birdsong on our walks through the park."

"There was no shortage of pigeons during our walk in Central Park today," the duchess replied. "Nasty little creatures. If they were prettier, I'd wear them."

Miss Van Allen made a garbled sound of rage.

One did not expect Little Bo Peep to make garbled sounds of rage.

It's just fashion, he had once said to Adeline. But now his future was about to be derailed by warring factions of the feathers-as-fashion debate. This collision of gowns was a collision of values and passions, just as Adeline had said.

It was a clash of identities.

It was not just a dress.

Miss Van Allen was possibly the most serene and obliging female he'd ever met, including all the demure English girls on the marriage mart. More than once, he'd had the distinct impression that she would wed whomever her parents chose, just to please them.

But birds were the hill that she would die on.

The minute she put two and two together — that her dowry would be used to pay for the duchess's collection of endangered species-themed dresses and millinery — was the minute this betrothal was over.

Miss Van Allen looked pleadingly at her mother.

Frankly, Kingston did as well.

"Now, now dear, we don't want to upset the duchess."

"On that we can all agree," he replied, trying and failing to sound jovial.

"Hear, hear," Her Grace harrumphed.

Mrs. Van Allen changed the subject. "Your Grace, isn't it wonderful that our children have taken a liking to each other. I couldn't imagine anything more wonderful."

"A prince, perhaps," his mother quipped. "But a duke will do."

And there it was: the great Aristocratic snobbery. And the great elephant in the ballroom. One might as well have asked, *how much for that duke in the window?*

Mrs. Van Allen had the decency to blush.

Kingston looked around for a passing waiter. He desperately needed a drink.

But his attention was caught by a most curious and arresting vision of six women arriving together. They appeared to be dressed as Amazons, the powerful and mythical lady warriors of Ancient Greece. They all wore matching dresses — white, silky creations that draped from their shoulders and brushed the floor. Upon first glance, they all appeared the same. But when one looked more closely — indeed, these women together were so captivating that one could not look away — it became clear that each gown was customized to its wearer, and subtly unique.

Despite the white masks covering their eyes, Kingston recognized Adeline in a heartbeat. He'd know her mouth anywhere. He recognized the curve of her shoulder, the sassy sway of her hips. He knew her handiwork, too. These dresses were Adeline creations.

She was here.

He fleetingly questioned the *how* and *why* and *what for* of her presence tonight. He decided he didn't care. His best-laid plans were blowing up all around him and she was here. He didn't believe in signs, but if he did, his heart leapt at the message this one was sending him.

Adeline is the one.

"What do you think, Duke?"

"Hmm?" He had been addressed by his mother. Who was not asking about Adeline, the recent arrival of a phalanx of ancient lady warriors, or his daring thought to cast aside his intended plans and take the risk of a lifetime.

Little Bo Peep and her mother looked up at him expectantly.

"We were just discussing a house party at Lyon House. Or perhaps Parkland," she said, mentioning their hunting box near the Scottish border. "You and your gentlemen friends could go hunt while I introduce these ladies to an exclusive mix of London society. A nice intimate launch to the haute ton, if you will."

Miss Van Allen, weary but nevertheless polite, turned to Kingston and asked: "And what do you hunt?"

Kingston hesitated. There was the right answer and then there was the truth. He could tell her what she wanted to hear, and then be the sort of man who lies to get a woman in his marital bed. Or he could tell the truth and damn himself to debtor's prison.

He tried to appear apologetic — which he was — as he answered.

"Pigeons. Grouse."

"You shoot birds? For sport?" Her voice was a strangled whisper of despair. Crushing disappointment. Heartache. And oh, the betrayal.

"By the sackful," the duchess said, utterly oblivious to Miss Van Allen's distress. "And then Cook roasts them for supper. They are delicious in a Béarnaise sauce."

And that was too much for Miss Van Allen.

She turned and fled, an angry Little Bo Peep storming off through the crowd.

Her mother patted his arm consolingly. "Don't worry, Your Grace. I'll speak to her. She'll come around."

Was it wrong that he didn't want her to?

In the crowd of guests at Mrs. Carlyle's ballroom, there were numerous Marie Antoinettes, Little Bo Peeps, and Catherine the Greats. And now, there were six women dressed as Amazons in white silk gowns, each with a unique styling to fit its wearer — a cap sleeve here, a fuller skirt there, or a more daringly cut bodice. It was Miss Harriet Burnett's idea, and she enlisted her society friends and Ladies of Liberty club members to join her in making an impression upon society. She wanted to project a different vision of womanhood than usually done, and this was an image attesting to the strength, honor, and power of women.

She thought to ask Adeline to join them, given that she was making the dresses. Adeline accepted the chance to attend such a glamorous soiree with her new friends — who wouldn't? The masquerade was the talk of the town before it even happened.

The girls at the shop were so eager for her to attend as well; they wanted stories, gossip, all the details that the newspapers would leave out. When Adeline was dressed in her costume, she slipped her hands in her pockets and laughed at what she found: some money for a hack home, a rubber shield, and even a little tin of lip paint. Little things that made her beholden to no one.

"You are all incorrigible."

"We want you to have a night to remember."

"And then tell us all about it in the morning."

Adeline was no fool — she knew that there was a chance she would see Kingston. At this, she felt a shiver of anticipation. As Harriet's guest at the ball, she wouldn't be beholden to him, as she'd been on the other occasions when they ventured out together. Tonight they might meet as something like equals. At this, she felt another shiver of anticipation.

But anticipation warred with dread. Because Adeline had fallen for the duke. She didn't know how or when or what little thing had pushed her off the fence and firmly onto the side of *I might love you* but here she was, and wearing a white dress, too.

Yet as far as she knew he had already proposed or was certainly about to.

It was a different Englishman who found her first.

Lord Hewitt. He of the unpaid bills and whose busy hands always found some uncomfortably intimate spot upon her person to rest for just a second too long.

"If it isn't Miss Black, dressmaker to the Four Hundred and enchanter of visiting dukes."

"Good evening, Lord Hewitt. It's *Mrs.*

Black, remember? What are you dressed as?"

"A rogue."

"You're supposed to come in costume, not as yourself," she said, and he laughed, thinking it was a joke.

"Will you dance with me, Mrs. Black?"

"I'm afraid that I don't know how."

"Just hold on tight and I'll guide you through the moves," he said, and she smiled weakly. He closed the distance between them and murmured in her ear. "How could I mind an innocent young miss, deferring to my wisdom and experience?"

He might not mind but *she* did.

They danced. Or rather, he danced and she managed. She only stumbled when she caught a glimpse of her duke. Correction: Miss Van Allen's duke.

He was in conversation with her and their mothers.

He did not look happy.

She knew what he looked like when he was happy: the way his blue eyes sparkled and crinkled at the corners as his lips turned up into a smile that he couldn't help. It was the way he looked at her when he realized she was teasing him about something or other.

Freddie caught her looking.

"They make an excellent-looking couple,

don' they?"

"My thoughts exactly."

And they did. He was tall, dark haired, strong. She was similarly tall, willowy, and fair. He was dark, she was light. They were beautiful and rich and proper and perfect for each other. That costume, though, did Miss Van Allen no favors.

"And now he's staring at you."

"I know." She felt his gaze before she saw it, and then the intensity of it took her breath away. His jaw tightened. He was definitely not happy now.

"We're making him jealous," Lord Hewitt said.

"There's no need for that."

"But there is," he said urgently. "It might save him from making a big mistake."

And this surprised her, coming from a man who couldn't seem to keep his hands in the proper place or his attentions exclusively upon his wife. It was no secret that Lord Hewitt had married his wife for her money; perhaps he spoke from his own experience.

"Miss Van Allen couldn't possibly be a mistake," Adeline said. The costume she wore? Unequivocally yes. The woman who wore it, no.

"Oh, she's loveliness personified. She even

charmed me into donating to her ornithological society." Adeline filed that information away — he did still owe her an enormous sum for his wife's dress order. "But she is all wrong for him. They'll make each other miserable before long."

"That is for them to decide, is it not? Not you. Certainly not me."

"He will marry her for the wrong reasons," Lord Hewitt continued. "He will grow bored and restless. His eye will wander. He is a man. He will stray. Like his father before him, or like me. But Kingston has a shred of decency and sense of honor, so the guilt will eat him alive."

"Why are you telling me this?"

"She will sense that his attentions have wandered."

"No, they won't."

"She will go to outrageous lengths to attract his attention. Run up massive dressmaker tabs."

"About that —" Adeline began.

Lord Hewitt's grip tightened on her and he pulled her closer.

"I know, Miss Black, I know."

"A gentleman settles his accounts with dressmakers," she said. "In cash," she added, in case there was any question.

"What if Kingston makes you his duchess?"

"He will not. And you will still need to pay for *your wife's* dresses."

"What you two share is the stuff love stories are made of. I might even be jealous."

"Be still my beating heart," she said sarcastically.

"No romance for you?"

"Wedding the duke would mean giving up the dream I have worked so hard for. I'm not ready to trade the title of dressmaker for duchess. One I've aspired to my whole life, the other I never even considered. I am halfway in love with him," she said pointedly to this man who held her too closely. "But I prize my independence and will not let it be compromised by *any* man."

There was one woman Kingston pursued in the ballroom that evening and she was not dressed as Little Bo Peep. He found her dancing with Freddie — Freddie! — and was nearly choking on his jealousy when he interrupted.

There was no world in which he did not interrupt them.

"May I cut in."

It was not a question. It was a statement.

Which is how dukes asked for things.

"We were quite finished," Adeline said.

"For tonight," Freddie said, then in a low murmur to Adeline he said something that sounded like, "I shall return tomorrow with the payment."

Violent. He felt violent toward his best friend because of a woman. This meant something, surely. Naturally, he assumed the worst, as his brain flashed back to all the times he'd seen Freddie and Adeline talking and laughing. He wondered if he was the mysterious benefactor who had helped her establish her shop. Marian certainly wore enough of her designs. He wondered if there was more than money exchanged. He wondered again, *why not me?*

Kingston felt his throat constrict as he thought of these things. It was best that he choked on the words rather than say them aloud.

His temper was soothed, slightly, when she slipped her hands into his. Just this simple touch was enough to have a measurable effect upon him.

"I should warn you. I'm a terrible dancer."

"I don't care."

Kingston just needed to hold her, and a dance was a socially acceptable, convenient excuse. It also gave him something to do with his hands, other than, say, start a fight or cause a scene. His cousin. Her. Payment. How could they? He shoved it to the back of his mind.

"Rough night, Duke?"

"I introduced Miss Van Allen to my mother," he said, thinking of the other horrible event of this evening.

"And how was that?"

"A disaster."

Adeline gave him a sympathetic smile. His grasp on her tightened. He did not want her sympathy. He wanted her to be happy, overjoyed, and delighted that his carefully laid plans were probably ruined. He wanted her to be eager to seize the opportunity that was presenting itself.

Because the strange thing was that he was on the verge of being happy, overjoyed, and delighted his carefully laid plans had imploded and collapsed around him.

"You were right," he said, which brought a curious smile to her lips.

"Oh?"

"It's not just a dress. It's never just a dress. If I had cared to pay more attention, I would have seen what these women — my mother, my maybe future duchess — were trying to tell me. You opened my eyes,

Adeline. You have changed the way I see the world and . . ."

He was rambling and running out of words to say that he *needed* her. Thanks to her, he saw and understood things he hadn't before. He knew that now. He needed her kiss, her wit, her perspective more than he needed money or a new roof or modern conveniences in any of his houses, plural. He needed her like he needed air moving in and out of his lungs.

"I have not proposed yet."

"Why are you telling me this?"

"I should think it's obvious."

"But you *are* going to propose."

"I might have experienced a change of heart and thus a change of plans." He watched her expression carefully, searching for a flicker of *something* that would indicate that this was wanted, welcome news. But he couldn't read her dark eyes or the way she bit her lower lip. "I don't think Miss Van Allen wants to be the next duchess of Kingston and I don't want a wife who doesn't want to wed me for me."

"Oh," she sighed. "Oh."

Kingston held her close, even though the music to one song had ended to give dancers a moment to change partners. He held her still when another song began. It was as if he could not risk letting go for even a second, lest he lose her forever.

It ought to have been better that they were out among the other dancers, where anyone could see that nothing untoward was happening.

But that was the problem: something untoward was very clearly on the verge of happening. Anyone could — and probably did — see the plain, heartfelt, potent desire for her in his eyes. Or the way he was transfixed by her lips. Or the way their bodies moved perfectly in sync to a music that had momentarily ceased playing.

A duke was about to make A Scene over a lowborn girl in an uptown ballroom.

Even more remarkable: he didn't care.

But Adeline did.

"People are watching us," she said, stepping away from him.

"So?"

"People are talking about us."

"I don't care."

"I do," she said firmly.

"Isn't it every girl's dream to be linked with a duke?"

"Not mine. I have my reputation to mind. My business depends upon it. My seamstresses rely upon it."

"If we were to marry, you would have the

protection of my name and my position."

"You forget one thing: duchesses aren't usually dressmakers."

"Change the world, Adeline."

Her eyes flashed at the challenge. "I shall. One dress at a time."

She turned and left.

He was a duke. A marquis, earl, a half dozen lesser titles. He was a wealthy, privileged male in a world made for men. He could have anything he wanted and he wanted her.

He was pretty damn sure she wanted him, too — he could feel it, see it in the flush of her cheeks and the way she bit her lip as her gaze dropped to his mouth and in the way that she did not deny it.

But she didn't want him *enough.*

She didn't want his titles, or various estates, or money or whatever worldly goods he had to offer her. She didn't want his protection, his name, the perks of his position.

He didn't know what to do with this feeling of wanting something he could not have. He was equally flummoxed by this feeling of having nothing to offer except himself — and the pleasure he could give her. If she wanted it.

Their dance came to an end and he followed her through the ballroom. This, whatever this was, was not finished yet.

It wasn't every day that a woman had a duke hot on her heels, calling out her name as she fled a fancy ball. Fridays, that's when.

Friday evenings, just shy of midnight.

That was when she refused something that sounded like an offer of marriage and something like the promise of a night of unimaginable pleasure. There was a part of her that badly wanted to accept and to indulge in the desire she felt everywhere. From her head to her toes, to her heart, and everywhere in between, every inch of her wanted him.

But did she want him enough to risk her freedom, her independence, her livelihood on one night of pleasure, on a mere suggestion of marriage? She didn't know and she couldn't *think* when all eyes were watching them and judging *her.* It almost didn't even matter if she ran out of the ballroom and straight into his bed — or not. Society would judge her based only on what they presumed.

Fleeing was the only option she could see.

But he followed.

Kingston said her name loud enough to attract attention and turn heads. How could he be so reckless? Thanks to the success of her shop, Adeline's name was now known in these rarified circles. Though she was in costume and wore a mask, the mention of her name, her gown in her signature style, and her link to the duke were enough to identify her beyond a shadow of a doubt.

Miss Adeline Black: the woman who had a duke running after her.

Miss Adeline Black: the woman who might have disrupted the wedding of the year.

Because if they were together, it would mean that he and Miss Van Allen were not.

Talk would be vicious.

Adeline feared the worst. Women refusing to wear her dresses. Husbands refusing to pay for orders already placed. She would have to fold up shop, a crushing disappointment to the Ladies of Liberty, who had taken a chance on her when no one else had, and the women she employed, who had such paltry alternative options, if any. Adeline thought of Margaret and her baby on the way, Rose and Rachel who left secure positions to take a chance with her. Mrs. Van Allen could have her blacklisted from every dressmaking establishment in the city. She'd ensure Adeline never so much as sewed a button on in this town again.

Then she might have to marry the duke out of desperation and he out of a sense of pity or obligation. It would be made worse by the knowledge that she had made her dreams come true and then ruined it all. For both of them.

She couldn't get away fast enough.

But this damned duke was such a fool, striding purposefully after her, calling her name, ruining everything. Again!

"What do you think you're doing?"

They were outside on Fifth Avenue now, under the warm glow of the gas lamps. A mass of humans, carriages, and animals — and the city itself — helped conceal them from prying eyes and gossiping tongues, to an extent — one hardly disappeared into the shadows when dressed in the bright white silk of a warrior princess.

"I should think it's perfectly clear," he said in that devastatingly swoon-worthy English accent of his. "I am making an utter fool of myself. I am ruining everything. Again. All because I fear that I cannot say goodbye to you in such a manner. Or even at all."

"What do you mean?"

"You're running away from me. Us. This *something* keeps pulling us together in spite of logic, reason, *plans* that we both have made for our futures. I fell in love with a girl and I might not be able to have her."

"I'm not something to *have.*"

"You're right. You are not something, you are Someone. You are a woman who has opened my eyes, made my heart beat harder, disturbed my equilibrium and turned my life upside down just by being *you.* And that is why I need you, Adeline. I had a very narrow view of the world before you sashayed into my life — and don't tell me you don't sashay because you do and it's mesmerizing. I would wed an heiress, fix the roof, and that would be all until death do we part. But I want you more than the roof, Adeline. I want the wide-open view of the world you have shown me. I need you to show me more. And I want you by my side for all of it. I'm hoping you'll take my hand and embark on the risk of a lifetime with me."

Heaven help her but she was moved.

He was changing because of her. He was becoming a man she could be with, if she ever allowed herself the luxury. The attraction between them was fierce and potent but these words revealed it was more, too. It was nothing less than thrilling and terrifying and wonderful all at once.

But Adeline didn't quite believe that he wouldn't wake up in the morning, more clear-headed, and proceed to Miss Van Allen and drop down on bended knee. She did know that they could not stand outside of the Carlyle mansion and bicker.

Also, she had an idea.

If he was truly tempted by her, by the idea of life with her, she had something to show him. They needed to go somewhere away from the prying eyes of society.

"Come with me," she said as she stepped into the throng along Fifth Avenue and raised her hand to hail them a hack.

"I have a carriage and —" he said.

"We're not taking your carriage."

A hired hack slowed to a stop in front of them. Kingston assisted her and all her skirts into the carriage and shut the door behind them.

"Where are you taking us?"

"You'll see," she replied. And to the driver, she requested the first address she thought of that was not at all romantic or even remotely conducive to seduction. It was a place that no one in the Four Hundred would ever go. She had to scare him off before he ruined everything for them both.

CHAPTER TWENTY-TWO

The "resorts" of the Bowery are better
described as foul dives.
— *The New York World*

The Bowery

Kingston stepped out of the carriage and
looked around. They were not on Fifth
Avenue anymore. In fact, he had no idea
which part of the city they were in. He
suspected it was the part which visiting
Dukes did not usually frequent, though it
reminded him of the places where he'd
spent a few wild and reckless nights in his
university days, when he was intent upon
nothing more than emulating and maybe
even one-upping his wastrel of a father.

Yet Adeline seemed to know precisely
where they were, and she appeared to be at
ease in these dark surroundings even though
she was dressed in a gorgeous white gown
that contrasted starkly with the surround-

ings and everyone else's attire.

"Where have you taken me?"

"McGurk's. It's a dance hall on the Bowery. This, Your Grace, is the New York to which I'm accustomed. Not quite Fifth Avenue, is it?"

It was not. The buildings were not as towering or ornate or impressive or even clean. But the energy on the street was something else entirely as men and women alike, in all shapes, sizes, colors, and hailing from different countries of origin populated the sidewalks and the streets, all carousing and (mostly) making merry together. It was crowded, loud, boisterous. There was a feeling that something was going to happen. Fun was going to be had.

In her stunning white gown, Adeline left openmouthed stares in her wake from men and women alike. While it aroused his possessiveness — how dare they gaze at her so brazenly! — Kingston understood. She and her gowns were stunning in an uptown ballroom and downright shocking here on the Bowery.

It was impossible not to stare.

Adeline led them into a particular dance hall that was dark and crowded and had an air of danger. Once they procured a corner small table and two pints of what one hoped was ale, Kingston started to feel a pressure ease in his chest. No one knew him here, certainly no one from The Four Hundred. The very air seemed imbued with a sense of devil-may-care, pleasure first, business tomorrow, and there was only tonight.

"I must confess: I do feel a bit out of place," he said.

"We are not quite dressed for the occasion."

"I don't think it's my attire alone." He eyed her gown.

"Don't tell me you're too fancy for a downtown haunt, Your Grace."

"Don't hold it against me." He paused. Sipped his ale. "On second thought. Yes, please do hold it against me."

"You are incorrigible." But she smiled and that was everything.

"What I am is out of my element. I used to frequent such establishments but it has been some time."

She reached out and clasped his hands. "I think you'll manage just fine, English. Just mind your pocket watch."

His pocket watch had belonged to his grandfather, had been a personal gift from the Prince Regent, and was worth no small sum. If he lost it tonight, he would consider it a small price to pay to spend this evening alone with Adeline in this dim, dangerous downtown spot where no one would recognize them.

That pressure in his chest eased even more.

"All right, tell me about you before you were the Duke. I want to hear stories of your wild and misspent youth."

"It's been so long."

"Has it really?"

"Not at all and I am wounded that you would think so," he said in mock horror. She laughed and he was enchanted all over again. "Once upon a time, a few years ago, I hadn't a care in the world. I wanted for nothing and was due to inherit everything — a prestigious title, vast tracts of land, houses, etc., etc. And so I did what most men in my position did. I consumed my days and nights with women, wine, and other diversions. Horse racing, boating, house parties, card games. My days and nights were very full."

"You must have been insufferable. In fact you sound awful."

He did sound awful. Because he had been awful. He wasn't mean or cruel, as some of his "friends" were. But he had no thought beyond himself and his own amusement. The death of his father and the assumption of all his responsibilities meant he no longer had time for anything other than duty. He found he liked having a clear head in the morning and a sense of purpose to propel him through the day.

"I would have kissed you already," he admitted. "More, even."

"I wouldn't have let you."

He held her gaze. "You would have wanted to."

"Or so you think," she said. She sipped her ale.

"What do you mean by that?"

"Sometimes a woman will do what she must to survive. Even if it means indulging the whims of a duke. Or some other lordly type."

"Are you saying women wouldn't have wanted me? Because I have never taken a woman against her will. There are some lines a decent man doesn't cross and that is one of them."

"What I mean is that when a man holds all the power, a *yes* may not be a yes. A woman might agree because she can't afford otherwise. Do you see, Duke?"

He was beginning to. And he was terrified to really look, for who knew what he might see? What if he discovered he wasn't the gentleman he'd prided himself on being?

He suddenly felt a deep fear of being unwanted, politely tolerated. But being with Adeline felt different. One thing was becoming clear: he needed a woman who didn't need him at all.

"What changed you?" she asked. "Something must have changed you. You pride yourself on behaving like a gentleman and supporting your family and tenants."

"My father died."

"I'm sorry." She rested her hand on his.

"Everything became my responsibility. So I decided to follow the example set by generations of Kingston dukes: wed and bed an heiress. Use her fortune to further the estate for another generation."

"You had no other example to follow, I suppose."

"Until I came to New York. Now I see that there might be another way."

What he was trying to say was that marrying Miss Van Allen was not the answer. He needed money, yes. But there were other ways to get it: this city had shown him that. Adeline was showing him that he needed a life he could commit to with his whole heart. Duty was more than providing money. Honor was more than not cheating at cards. Legacy was more than just perpetuating what came before.

The truths struck him hard and fast; he could hardly catch his breath enough to articulate them to Adeline. He could only try to explain.

"I didn't realize any of this until I met you."

"I think I understand," she said. "You are resolved to be a different man."

"I promised I would sacrifice my own pleasure to serve my family, duty, my estate." He paused, thoughtful. "I promised I would ensure my children are provided for, so that they have choices. And I promised I would not torment my wife with affairs that drive her to ridiculous lengths in trying to get my attention."

It seemed the only way to stop it all was to wed a woman he could love.

"You'd better wed a girl who entrances you then," Adeline replied. "A girl you can't take your eyes off of. A girl who you can't stop thinking about."

"In other words, I'd better wed a girl like you."

Adeline had made a grave miscalculation. McGurk's was not supposed to be conducive to romance and seduction. It was loud, dingy, dark, full of unrefined and frankly unwashed persons. But the duke didn't put on airs. No, he pulled up a chair for him, and her, and procured her a glass of ale. Then he looked into her eyes and bared his soul. To her and her alone.

That was its own kind of seduction.

The intimacy. The risks. The novelty. The surprise. The way he gazed at her, the way his firm, sensuous mouth occasionally tipped into a smile. The way his fingers entwined with hers, now delicately stroking the palms of her hands, her inner wrists. It was the littlest touch and yet she felt sparks flying. Embers started to smolder. Tonight, she was going to burn.

And damned if she wasn't falling for all of it.

And then he had to say it.

Then I'd better wed a girl like you.

"There you go with the proposals again," she teased. Deflected.

"If I ask you enough maybe you'll say yes."

She took a sip of her drink. She might be the woman he needed, but she was not the marrying kind. However, that didn't mean she didn't have wants and desires that she was more and more eager to explore with him.

"Tell me, Adeline, why you refuse to wed."

"Quite simply, I have seen that no good comes of it."

He waited for her to explain.

"My father was the first man my mama married. He went out West to seek his fortune and it was years before we learned that he had died of dysentery. Meanwhile, we subsisted on the charity of my aunt and uncle, working from dawn until dusk in our sweatshop on Norfolk Street. Everything we earned went into my uncle's pocket. He had my mother pay in other ways, too. I could hear it. I was seven."

Kingston clasped her hand and tightened his grip.

"When we learned my father had died, my mother was free to marry someone who might help provide for us. We were desperate to get out of that house, so she wed the first man who asked. He was just as bad, maybe worse. I was ten."

Kingston pressed his lips into a firm line.

"He died in the way that bad men tend to do — a stupid accident as a result of an excess of alcohol and an argument. I wasn't sad at all. I was twelve. I vowed to support us — by then I had a deft hand with a needle and thread, a rebellious streak, and *ideas*. But Mother didn't believe me that there was another way. And maybe there wasn't. So she married again. And I managed to get a job sewing in a shop —

Madame Chalfont's, in fact — so I did not have to be at home. It hurt me to see it."

Kingston just listened and held her hand.

"She didn't leave him. Because of some notion of a woman's noble duty to submit to her husband. Because of her honor. Because of me."

Kingston held her gaze. She saw the flash of understanding in his eyes.

"I saw her give and give and give until there was nothing else left of her. And I saw her husbands take and take and take." She paused, struggling to find the words. "I have something now — independence, security. I have something that is *mine*. And I have created a refuge for women who have nowhere else to go, except for marriages to men like Thomas, John, and Charles. I cannot risk giving it up. So, my dear duke, that is what I know about marriage."

"And what do you know about love?"

"The dime novels that Rose and all the seamstresses read, I suppose. And you?"

"The poets, I guess."

"What a pair we are."

What she could not say — what she dare not say — was that she suspected that this feeling was something like love.

They were both so out of place here, yet she'd never felt more at home than this:

holding his hand, confessing to the darkness of her past, her deepest fears, and her pride in the future she had fashioned for herself with nothing more than a needle, thread, gumption, and luck.

It was desire that made the heat blossom in her belly, made her achingly aware of his touch. It was desire that compelled her to press her body to his, feel the warm, firm expanse of his chest under her palms. To feel his arms around her, to feel him inside her. It was desire that inspired the wicked, sensual thoughts spiraling in her head.

But everything else might be love.

"At a moment like this, after we have bared our souls to each other, I think there is only one thing to do," she said.

"I hope it involves holding you close."

"Oh, it does," she said with a laugh as she stood and pulled him to the crowd of dancers. The hours passed in a blur of temptation. Dancing meant having him holding her close. Dancing meant feeling his body move against hers. Dancing meant breathing him in. Dancing meant forgetting everything — everything — except for the feel of their bodies intertwined and moving together. There was no risk of being seen here. As long as they were just dancing, there was no risk of anything else.

When the hour had grown impossibly late, but hearts were still pounding, they clamored into a hired carriage. Kingston told the driver an address uptown.

Adeline did not protest. She climbed into that carriage with her eyes wide open.

She loved him. She could see no future together that would make them both happy. He wanted to be a man befitting his station and that man wouldn't marry an American upstart who refused to surrender her hard-won independence.

But they had tonight.

Chapter Twenty-Three

The only thing anyone is discussing is the outrageous, ostentatious display that was Mrs. Carlyle's masquerade ball. The fact that such a gauche display of wealth even happened while people go hungry in the streets shall be the topic of conversation for weeks. Then, perhaps, society will get around to discussing what happened at the party. Or after.

— *The New York World*

The Fifth Avenue Hotel

The hour was late — that darkest hour before dawn — when the carriage rolled to a stop before the Fifth Avenue Hotel.

Like a gentleman, Kingston held out his hand and helped Adeline alight.

Everyone had long since retired and the usually busy lobby was desolate. This time there was no one present to watch them, save for a lone bellman who was barely awake. Any pesky reporters or gossipers and gawkers were all still at the Carlyle mansion, watching the guests depart. They would be able to slip through the dimly lit lobby undetected.

When Kingston reached a certain point, he stopped.

"It was here that I first saw you."

Kingston stood in the exact place. He had stopped in his tracks — then and now — at the sight of Adeline striding toward him purposefully, hips swaying. It was mesmerizing.

His heart pounded in his chest.

He knew where she was going. Where *this* was going. And it meant something to him. Tonight, he sensed, would be one of those *before* and *after* dividing lines where nothing would ever be the same again.

She gave him a playful smile and stepped into his waiting arms. Her warmth, her scent enveloped him. Then and now, he felt her breasts brush against his chest. She tipped her head up to look at him.

"It was here that I first saw you, Duke."

His hands slipped around her waist, as if to catch her, as if to hold her. He gazed down at her upturned face. Those sparkling doe eyes. That rosebud mouth. That sweet, coy smile. It undid him. Then, now.

"I wanted to hold you. Like this." He pulled her closer, tighter against his chest.

"I wasn't exactly quick to move away," she murmured, smoothing her hands along his chest possessively and he thought, *Hold on to me.*

"Then I watched you walk away," he whispered. The agonies of that moment struck him all the more intensely now.

"Like this?"

She turned and walked away now, giving an extra swing and sway to her hips and he was helpless to look away. She turned and smiled at him over her shoulder — her bare shoulder. That smile was an invitation to pleasure.

He dashed after her. Caught her up in his arms, whirled her around and set her down in front of the elevators. A little display of heroics.

"I must confess that I find you enchanting."

"Of course you do." She laughed.

The elevator attendant was ready and waiting to take them upstairs to his suite of rooms. If the elevator attendant found anything remotely interesting or remarkable about the scene, he did not reveal it. Hand in hand, they stepped into the enclosed velvet carriage that would take them to the top floor, to his rooms, to his bed.

At his floor they stepped out of the elevator.

They were alone in the dimly lit corridor.

"New York City girls are different from the ones in London," he said softly.

"Oh, you haven't seen anything yet," she murmured, twirling around him in a swirl of white silk.

"Show me." This time it was a fervent wish, a plea.

He opened the door to his suite and immediately shut it behind them.

"We talked about finding the one," he whispered between kisses. He could kiss her now, because they were alone and no one could see and because he couldn't *not* kiss her now.

Kingston pulled back to gaze down at this woman — this *one* woman who refused him. Who didn't fall for the trappings of his title or his position. Who was here because she wanted *him* and that was the most erotic thing he had ever encountered.

"And then I was enchanted. And then I wasn't thinking about talking at all."

"So let's not talk," she murmured.

And so they did not.

He claimed her mouth with his for a kiss that revealed what he didn't have the words to say. God, he wanted this. Her. To lose himself in only this moment with this woman. To forget about before and after, why he should not and all the reasons he must not. He refused to think of duty and honor and all those things. He sank into this kiss, with this girl, on this night, in this moment. He was prepared to give up everything, but the funny thing was, it felt rather a lot like finding himself. Like whole pieces of his heart coming together.

The riot of thoughts in Adeline's head disappeared the minute Kingston's mouth claimed hers. All questions of *what if* and *what next* fled. She had been thinking about what she was doing here. She hadn't forgotten all that she risked by being here with him. But she believed in him and she believed in what her body demanded: his touch, his kiss, him.

And so the only thoughts in her head now were *yes* and *please* and *don't ever stop*.

He tugged at the silk and tulle artfully arranged around her shoulders. With that out of the way, he pressed kisses along her bare skin and, *oh.*

More of that, yes, more.

He kissed her again, a deep need-you-like-air kind of kiss. He sank his fingertips into her coiffure and she didn't care at all that it was wrecked in an instant.

If dresses were a lady's armor and protection as she went out into the world, a dress was unnecessary here. Now. At this hour and with this man, there was no question about stripping it all away and laying herself bare to him. She wanted to feel like a woman — just a woman — without all the things that held her in and slowed her down.

But the thing with dresses was removing them.

"You could just rip it off," she gasped, between kisses, as he was fumbling with the buttons at the back of her gown. "I'm given to understand that men do that. Apparently women love it."

"And violate this work of art? Oh, no. Slowly and carefully removing it will be its own kind of exquisitely agonizing pleasure."

He gave her a smile that set the butterflies in her belly into flight.

The duke was right.

The anticipation of being nude before him for the duration of a slow, careful dress removal was just . . . insane. She thought she'd go mad waiting as his fingers took care of each button and lace.

Finally, the gown was slipped off and tossed aside, nothing but a heap of virginal white silk draped over the settee. But still, there were layers and layers of fabric between them. Each petticoat or chemise or scrap of silk was another chance for her to say *no.* To say *never mind.* To say *I've given the matter some consideration and. . . .*

Yes. God, yes. She had given the matter some consideration and decided to remove his jacket. She started tugging it off, and then some of Saville Row's finest tailoring fell to a heap on the floor, where it belonged. At least for tonight.

All the other pieces and underthings followed, and she felt freer and more wanton with each piece that landed on the floor.

He pulled her chemise off and cast it aside, then she made short work of the buttons on his silk vest.

They continued like that, back and forth, exchanging one layer for another until there was nothing left but him and her and the undeniable, palpable desire between them.

"You'll need to design something far more easy to remove," he murmured as his mouth found hers in the dark. She shuddered with the pleasure of it and in anticipation of the pleasure that was to come.

"I do."

"But only for me and only for you."

"I will," she whispered.

■ ■ ■ ■

I do. I will. The words aroused him like nothing else. Those were *yes* and *forever* words, which was good because Kingston knew there was no going back to his previous plans after this night. The rest of his life would be divided into *Before He Saw Adeline Naked in the Moonlight* and simply *After.*

Nothing would ever be the same for him again.

For better or for worse.

He lay her down on his bed. Dark eyes, gazing up at him. Dark hair fanned along his pillow. He gazed down at her — the smooth expanse of skin, the swells of her breasts and the dusky pink centers, down to the round of her belly, the curve of her hips, and the dark thatch at the vee of her thighs.

"You're so beautiful, Adeline. I feel lucky to look at you."

He lowered his head to kiss her again, tasting sweetness and champagne on her lips. He kissed her, skin against bare skin, until he was so hard and so ready that he could scarcely think of anything besides being inside of her. Kingston kissed her, drawing a sigh from her lips. He moaned when she threaded her fingers through his hair and kissed him deeply.

"I haven't forgotten that time with you in the carriage," she whispered between kisses.

"Yes." His palm closed around her breast and she gasped.

"I think about it every night."

"Yes." He toyed with the pink center of her breast and she moaned.

"I imagine . . . more."

"Me too."

He was hard and ready to give her everything in his power to give her. His love, his attention, the pleasure from his touch.

So he kissed her. Her lips, yes, he started there, slipping his tongue against the seam of her mouth so she opened to him and kissed him deeply.

He traveled lower tasting every inch of her skin — the column of her throat, that little hollow between her collarbone, her breasts. Oh, damn, her breasts. He tasted one, then the other, teasing her with his tongue. He licked, he sucked, he lavished his attentions on those pink buds of pleasure until she was gasping for breath and writhing beneath him.

Then he went lower.

Leaving a trail of hot kisses across her belly.

And then he went lower still.

"Adeline," he whispered. And all she said was "mmm . . ." and that was all he needed to hear. He kissed her *there.* With his tongue he licked and teased her hot center. Each moan, each *yes* drove him deeper. He made slow, determined circles around that center of her pleasure until her sighs and moans were more intense, louder. He slid in one finger, then another. She was tight around him, and so wet with wanting. Maybe even almost as much as he wanted her. Right here. Right now.

But first: her. Kingston had all night. Days. Forever. He kissed and stroked, licked and sucked and reveled with the frantic pace of her breaths, the increasing crescendo of her cries and then . . .

. . . And then Adeline couldn't take it anymore. The warmth of his body, the fire of his touch; it was all too damn much. The way his fingers stroked her to increasing heights of ecstasy. Too, too damn much.

That unbearable pleasure made her cry out as wave after wave of pleasure crashed over her. She couldn't breathe, couldn't think, couldn't control anything . . . and so she surrendered. Fully, completely, utterly surrendered. And that meant more waves of pleasure crashing and . . . *Oh.*

She had imagined this each and every night and it paled compared to the reality of his touch, his mouth, his constant, relentlessly loving attentions.

And this was only the beginning. She felt his hot, hard length against her thigh, against her belly as he dragged himself up to kiss her on the lips.

Kingston pulled back to gaze at her and was intoxicated by the way he looked at her, like bringing her such pleasure was the single greatest thing he had ever done.

"Tell me what is next, Adeline."

He hovered above her.

She felt a wicked smile on her lips.

"Everything," she whispered. "Everything."

His gaze raked over her body — her bare breasts, the curves of her belly and hips, her naked thighs — at once curious and possessive. She saw the rake and rogue that he had been and she saw the powerful man he was becoming. There was no missing the way he adored her. If there was any doubt in her mind, he soon made it very, very clear.

Kingston hovered over Adeline, enjoying the view of her bare skin in the moonlight, the tempting glimmer in her eyes, the seductive way she bit her lip.

"Everything," she whispered. "Everything."

"Let me give you everything," he whispered, after he slipped on a protective sheath and rolled above her. He lowered his lips to hers and lowered his weight upon her. His cock was hard and straining at her entrance. She felt ready — warm and wet for him — and if he had any doubt, the way she wrapped her legs around him and arched her back made it very clear.

Everything meant she wanted him inside her. Now.

A gentleman always obliged a lady.

And that was the last thought about gentlemanly behavior he had.

This was a moment — the *before* and *after* moment — that he wanted to remember forever. So he went slow, inch by tantalizing and torturous inch. Nothing would ever be the same, he knew that, but he couldn't resist the way forward. Not when she was this warm and wanting.

"Oh God, Adeline," he rasped as he sank fully inside her.

"Yes," she gasped, rocking her hips. "Yes."

And he started to move inside her. They were unsteady and uneven at first, but they slowly and surely found their rhythm together with each thrust and rock of her hips rising to meet him. Each thrust went deeper, each thrust brought them closer together, and each thrust added to that steadily increasing pressure building inside him. So. Much. Fucking. Feeling. He couldn't get enough, he couldn't catch his breath, he couldn't do anything but *this.*

He sank his fingers into her hair, she raked her fingers down his bare back.

He kissed her deeply.

She moaned in his ear.

Like that they moved, shifting positions but always tangled up in each other. He learned the little things that drove her wild — a nibble at her earlobe, a hard suck on her fingers, taking her breasts in his mouth — all the little things that made her *her,* the one and only woman he wanted to know like this. The only woman who cried out like *that* as orgasm after orgasm crashed over her.

Eventually he couldn't take it anymore. He pushed hard, he held on tight, and he surrendered. When he came, he shouted out her name. And then it ended as it began: with a kiss.

Chapter Twenty-Four

The Duke of Kingston must have a very
good reason for not having proposed to
Miss Van Allen yet. One can only imagine
what it might be.
> — *The New York World*

The next morning
Kingston awoke with Adeline in his arms.
The first light of morning drifted through
the windows, which revealed an impressive
view of the city just starting to wake. But
the scene inside the room was more captivating, more enchanting.

Adeline in his bed. Adeline in his arms.
Her body entwined with his.

The events of the previous evening,
namely the implosion of his courtship with
Miss Van Allen, seemed like a lifetime ago.
All he had done was go downtown with
Adeline. All he had done was make love to
her. But in baring his body and baring his

soul to this enchanting woman, something had happened.

His plans had irrevocably changed.

She slept on her side, her backside pressed against his manhood, which was ready for more of her. He dropped a kiss on her bare shoulder and marveled that he should be so lucky to see her in nothing but bare skin and sheets. She was a dressmaker and was always impressively turned out. Only he would get to see her thusly.

Right?

He didn't want to think about it, but once the thought occurred to him, Kingston couldn't shake it. They had exchanged all their secrets last night.

Except for one.

There was still one mystery to Adeline that he had no answer for.

How did she afford that white silk gown draped across the settee, and every other exquisitely crafted gown he'd seen her wear? How could she afford all the women who had sewn each stitch? How had she gone from penniless and unemployed seamstress to dressmaker with her own establishment in a fortnight? It was an unfortunate fact that banks were not in the habit of granting loans to working-class girls with no collateral and no one to vouch for them.

Kingston was ashamed of the thought that occurred to him next.

Instead of *how* he wondered *who.*

But if there wasn't a *who,* then there was a *how* and he wanted to know it. Now that marriage to Miss Van Allen, or any other heiress for that matter, was off the table, he needed to formulate another plan to repair the roof, rebuild the stables, provide the dowries, pay his mother's millinery bills. He had to find a way to do his duty and marry the woman he loved.

"How did you do it, Adeline?"

"Hmm," she murmured sleepily. "Do what?"

"Enchant me. Bewitch me."

She yawned and stretched against him. The friction made him want her all over again.

"It was the easiest thing in the world. It was as simple as walking away from you."

"You do have a very enchanting backside." He moved against her. She rolled over to face him. Pressed a quick kiss against his lips. Wriggled up closer to him. Her thoughts did not seem to be along the lines of conversation. Nevertheless. "How did you start your shop?"

She stilled.

"Brandon . . ."

"We've told each other all of our other secrets and that is the one of yours I don't know yet. I want to know you. All of you." He pushed a lock of hair away from her cheek.

"I'm sorry, Brandon. But that is the one thing I cannot tell you."

She tugged him closer for another kiss. But he couldn't help it; he had assumed the worst. The worst was distracting.

"I ask because I need to know how to obtain my own fortune. You seem to have made one, in a very short time."

She sat up abruptly, pulling the sheets around her.

"What happened to Miss Van Allen? Your heiress plan?"

"I'm afraid it's not going to work for me anymore. I have fallen for a different girl," he said. "It so happens that I need to marry a girl who enchants me. Who I can't take my eyes off of. No fortune required."

"It shouldn't matter. How I got it should not matter."

That she wouldn't tell him made him suspicious. It raised questions he did not want to ask. He wondered who she knew who might have the blunt. A vision of Freddie touching her arm flashed in his brain. Freddie, taking her for a turn about the ballroom. Adeline, laughing at something Freddie had said.

No.

"It doesn't matter but . . ." All of a sudden his heart clenched with jealousy. And it did matter. Because he wanted to love her with his whole heart and he could not if such a monumental secret was between them. Especially if it might involve his *cousin.*

"I cannot tell you," she said. "I am sorry, but I have given my word."

"Was it — ? No. Never mind. I will not spoil this. There is a beautiful woman in my bed." He grasped her wrist to pull her down into his embrace, but she resisted and he dropped his hold on her. Damn, he had already ruined the moment.

"I should go," she said. "Soon the city will wake up and it will be very bad if I am seen in last night's dress this morning."

"Wait, Adeline . . ."

She was busy donning various layers, which were strewn about the room. He stood to help her. She was so beautiful. She was so enchanting. She was so ambitious. *How did she do it?*

The question, now that he considered it, consumed him. One day she is penniless and alone on the street and just weeks later, she is the proprietress of her own shop. That did not just happen. Not in this world, when nearly all avenues of support that might help an enterprising man were cut off to women.

Except for one.

A benefactor. A protector. A man with money who would see her established in return for certain . . . favors. A man like Freddie, admittedly bored and unhappy in his marriage. With money to burn and a taste for young women. And the thought that she might be indebted to Freddie, his own cousin, was unbearable.

If Adeline needed a supporter, he would have wanted her to come to him.

But he was broke and she must have known it — why else would he be so doggedly hunting his heiress? He felt embarrassed. She must have concluded — perhaps correctly — that he was not in a position to make a woman's dreams come true. He felt ashamed. He couldn't provide for her, so she turned to another man who could. He felt enraged.

That — *that* — thought was the one to have sucked the air from his lungs and oxygen from his brain. The noxious feelings, that lack of air — that was the reason for what he said next.

"Tell me one thing: Was it Freddie?"

She whirled around to face him. "Freddie?"

"My cousin, Lord Hewitt. I have seen you two together. You seem very . . . friendly. He is the sort of man who . . ."

"I know who you mean," she said so coldly and instantly, he wished to take it back and never breathe a word of it again.

Freddie made no secret of the fact that he had married for money, not love, and was the sort who would pay for a mistress, whether in the form of jewels or dressmaker's establishments. It was a fair question to ask of Freddie.

But not Adeline.

"Do you really mean to ask if I slept with a married man for funds to start my shop? Do you truly mean to suggest that I traded my body for money?"

She was incredulous. Righteously furious with him. Rightfully so.

The only thing to do was quit cringing and try to back out of this hole he was digging for himself. He had not meant to insult her. But he had, deeply.

"No, I don't mean to lay such accusations at your feet. *But . . .* you have done a remarkable thing."

"Yes, I have," she said proudly.

"I have seen the way he flirts with you.

And I have seen you return his affections. And I know how the world works. I would not judge you."

"Let me tell you what you have seen," she said coldly. "You have seen the husband of one of my clients take an interest in me. An interest that I do not reciprocate, which you should know after last night. You have seen me feign delight in his attentions because I cannot afford to anger the husband of a woman who has ordered an astronomical number of dresses. Should he decide not to pay, I will be financially ruined. And until he pays, I shall laugh at his jokes and allow him to believe I might entertain his advances while at the same time doing everything to make it appear that I am an honest, virtuous woman, in case I scare off the rest of my clientele. Shall I tell you more about the impossible position in which I find myself?"

Kingston was speechless.

Freddie. Harmless old Freddie. Good old Freddie. Just having a spot of fun and oh, just keeping a hardworking woman suspended between a rock and a hard place. He could not quite wrap his brain around it.

"I shouldn't even be here with you," she said, storming about the room collecting bits of her attire. A stocking, underthings.

"You do not deserve me."

He could not disagree.

"I cannot tell you how I came to open my establishment — and now I most certainly will not — but I hope I have sufficiently explained Lord Hewitt to you."

"You should have a word with him. Explain your position. Tell him to stop."

She laughed.

"Too many people depend upon me for their livelihood. I'll sacrifice myself before I ruin everything for them. You should understand that, Duke. Isn't that the same reason you will marry an heiress you don't love?"

"I'll have a word with him." Kingston said this in his most ducal, lord-of-the-manor voice. His *I will solve all known problems of the universe* voice.

"Will you, though?" Her voice was weary. "Will you really stand up to your fellow peers, your own family, your good friend on behalf of some working-class girl?"

"You're not just some working-class girl to me."

"But to the rest of the world, I'm nothing. A nobody. Are you willing to risk your reputation to go protect mine?"

"Yes," he said. "Yes, I will. Yes."

She tilted her chin up stubbornly.

"And what if I don't want you to fight my

battles for me?"

He had been to Eton. Had the best tutors. Taken a first at Oxford. He had done a tour of the Continent, passably spoke a few languages, had a seat in the House of Lords. He was an educated man who knew things. He did not know what to say to Adeline in this moment.

"I want to be a man worthy of you."

"You can start by not accusing me of trading my body for money in order to get ahead. And so what if I have? Why should I be faulted for seizing one of the only ways of advancement the world allows a woman?"

Kingston was still, silent, rocked to his core.

His jealousy had gotten the better of him. His determination to step in and be the hero had gotten the better of him. He had gotten in his own damn way. Once again, Adeline opened his eyes and set him straight.

"Where are you going?" he asked. She was struggling to get into her gown, and he moved to help her.

"I am going home. I am going to my shop. Some of us have work to do."

Later that evening
The Metropolitan Club
Kingston had come to Manhattan to find

an heiress and a fortune. Instead he had fallen in love with a dressmaker. Now he had neither fortune nor dressmaker. There were some decisions he needed to make about how to save his dukedom and if — no, how — to woo an angry woman.

And then there was his cousin Freddie, the devil himself, strolling toward him as if nothing had changed at all.

"There you are! Where did you disappear to last night?" He dropped into a chair opposite and signaled to a waiter for a drink. Of course he assumed that Kingston was in the mood for his company.

Kingston thought of all the times they'd done exactly this: secluded themselves in their clubs and traded stories of wild and reckless nights the next day. Ever since they were schoolboys, during university, and through the early years of their London seasons. And, to Kingston's everlasting shame, even after Freddie had married Marian, though Freddie never spoke intimately of her.

"I finally discovered some haunts downtown," he said by way of explanation. He found that he did not want to discuss the details of his time with Adeline with his cousin, friend, partner-in-crime. For all sorts of reasons.

Not that any of this was apparent to Freddie.

"Finally." His cousin grinned. "Finally you've had enough of your respectable engagements and we can now have some real fun. Just don't tell the missus."

"How is Marian?"

"Running up quite a bill at the dressmaker's but, you know, it keeps her out of my hair."

It was the little thing, a throwaway line that until last night, Kingston wouldn't have given much thought to. Of course a person of their position often had an outstanding amount due to a tradesperson. Frankly he did as well, on behalf of his mother.

But Kingston never flirted with the milliner.

He never made his presence known or felt at the modiste his female relations frequented.

He never slid his arm around the waist of a barmaid.

He never told maids bad jokes that required feigned laughs, right?

"So I've heard," Kingston remarked dryly. He felt a constriction in his chest as Adeline's words clanged in his head: *Will you really stand up to your fellow peer, your own family, your good friend on behalf of some*

355

working-class girl? She had been asking if he would really stand up for *her.*

If he would burn bridges for the love between them.

If he would simply respect a woman of her position.

This morning, he hadn't quite believed that his cousin was the man she accused him of being. But tonight, now that his eyes had been opened, Kingston could see that Freddie would take a flirtation too far, intentionally or not, and would think nothing of it. After all, no one had ever asked him to consider anyone else's position.

The question was now whether Kingston should *say* something. Here. Now. To Freddie. It would be easier to laugh the whole thing off or to make his excuses and leave. But that would not stop Freddie from pressing his advantage with Adeline or any other girl.

He was a duke. A member of Parliament. He was born to lead. Yet these words — defending a woman against his fellow peer — were not ones that had been handed down to him, generation to generation. They were not readily available but Kingston started searching for them.

"Your seamstress *is* quite fetching," Freddie went on, either oblivious to Kingston's inner turmoil or intent upon being deliberately provocative. "Say, did you finally run off with her last night?"

"Dressmaker," he corrected. Kingston was determined to prove — if only to himself — that he was a changed man. "She's not a seamstress, she is a dressmaker. A proprietress of her own shop. As you are well aware."

"Oh come on." Freddie laughed. "She's just a girl, and she's not even duchess material!"

"You should probably quit with that line of thinking," Kingston said hotly. His hands flexed and clinched around the arms of the chair. It was either that or start throwing punches.

"Are you honestly considering wedding her?" Freddie asked. "Or is she just a girl for a bit of fun before settling down with someone else? Or, in my case, just a girl you flirt with when you are trapped in a loveless marriage. But all in a day's — or night's — work for us lordly types. Give it a year or two with Miss Van Allen and you'll see what I mean." Freddie sullenly sipped his drink.

It was almost as if Freddie were deliberately taunting him with this dismal vision of the future.

"You give Miss Black too much of your attention. It's improper. Unacceptable." He stopped short of saying *unwanted,* remembering what Adeline had said about her difficult position.

"She's a pretty girl." Freddie shrugged as if to say, *why does it matter so much?*

Kingston felt the pressure inside him start to build as his heart pumped harder. He leaned forward, barely containing his fury.

"Just a pretty girl? That's the only reason you touch her arm, make her laugh, make insinuations of *more* with her?"

Freddie was now taken aback. "Christ, it's simply flirtation, Kingston. She likes it. She flirts back. What does it matter to you? Especially if you aren't even going to marry her?"

Kingston had never quite recovered his equilibrium since the words of this morning. Hell, ever since Adeline had crashed into him. Because of her, things had been churning around, breaking down, and building up into something new. Because of her, his placid and perfectly planned existence was simply no longer an option. Because of her, the little fissures that had appeared in his relationship with Freddie were starting to crack wide open.

He wanted, more than anything, to be

with her.

To do that, he had to become a man worthy of her.

If he married her, or not.

She wasn't here to see or hear him champion her, but he was going to do it anyway.

"You're wrong. She doesn't flirt back. She politely tolerates your attentions. You should stop."

"Well, no need to spoil a man's fun."

Fun. He thought it was fun. It was Adeline's whole life on the line and for Freddie it was just a bit of amusement. But Kingston had a glimpse at Adeline's outrage and frustration. He had bemoaned the constraints of his position, but now he was aware of hers.

"Did you ever consider that she didn't genuinely return the sentiment?" Kingston asked.

"Are you saying I'm not the charming lord about town I think I am?" Freddie replied hotly.

Kingston knew his friend; he always *meant* well but he was spoiled by his position. As he was a decent-looking, wealthy peer, most people were forever obliging to him if they meant it or not. The time had passed for making excuses for him.

"Yes. I am saying that. You should settle

your bill with her, then leave her alone."

"Are you her lord and protector now?" Freddie retorted. "I know you'd like to be, but I doubt you'll step up to the job. I'm not sure she'll even have you if you do."

"I would like to be her protector. Starting yesterday."

"What about Miss Van Allen?"

"We will not suit."

Freddie leaned forward, a gleam in his eye that Kingston could not read.

"The duke I used to know would have his cake and eat it, too. All the Kingston dukes wouldn't have thought twice about a dalliance with a dressmaker on the side. What happened to you to turn your back on tradition?"

"What happened was that I fell in love."

"What about your family, your tenants, your servants? What about the goddamned roof?"

It had come down to this: choosing between his best friend and the woman he loved, choosing between tradition and some uncertain future.

"I will find another way. But I won't compromise when it comes to the woman I love."

CHAPTER TWENTY-FIVE

His Grace has still not proposed to
Miss Van Allen. Inquiring minds want to
know why not, and more than a few
women — marriage-minded mothers,
particularly — want to know if the duke
is still up for grabs.
— *The New York World*

The next day
The Fifth Avenue Hotel

It had been little more than forty-eight
hours since Adeline had stormed out of his
room. Hours had passed in which his written apologies were returned unopened.
Hours had passed in which he considered
what to do about the pressing matter of his
future happiness and the rest of his life.

He decided to take a risk. Gamble everything on a long shot. New York City seemed
to have gotten to him after all.

When one decided on a course of action,

one did not waste time in making it happen.

"Are you certain about this?" his mother asked nervously while Kingston's valet finished brushing off his jacket. A man of his position, *in* his position, did not make a call looking anything less than perfectly and impressively attired.

His mother did not so much as travel from one hotel suite to another without a full ensemble. She completed the look with a feathered fascinator. Her days with those were numbered, though she didn't know it yet.

"To be honest, I have never been more certain," Kingston said.

"The gossip will be rampant," his mother said. *"Rampant."*

"It always is." A man of his position was always subject to scrutiny. He couldn't accidentally walk into a woman in a hotel lobby without it being written up in at least three different newspapers.

"Your sisters —"

"Will thank me later."

"And what about me, your dear mother?"

"Will buy another hat. Only this one I shall be able to pay for."

The duchess harrumphed, which was to say that her chief concern had been addressed.

She picked up the box with the ring, flipped the lid, and eyed the piece of jewelry. "I have always loved this one. Your father gave it to me when he proposed."

He turned to his mother and looked at her, really looked at her. She was a handsome, rather than pretty, woman. She'd been a good mother to him and his sisters, always fiercely championing them and ensuring that they didn't witness the worst of their father's excess. For the first time he wondered at the personal cost to her. His father hadn't realized what a good woman he'd made his duchess.

Adeline was right; no wonder his mother wanted vibrant-colored dresses and outrageous millinery, all so someone might notice her, a woman of a certain age who had been overlooked by her husband, deemed frivolous by her son, and dismissed as just a nagging mama by her daughters.

"You deserved better than him. You're a good mother," he said. "Thank you."

"I am speechless."

"You are not. You have been questioning me all morning."

"What you are about to do is irreparable. Permanent. Life altering. I want you to be certain."

"Mother, I came to New York to seek my fortune. I shan't leave without one."

For some, heartache and rejection was a gray, foggy morass one could not see or move through. But after his fight with Adeline, after that conversation with Freddie, after all those unopened letters, Kingston knew what he had to do. He saw everything now with a sharpened, heightened clarity.

Change the world, Duke, she had said to him once. Well, that was too much to ask of one man.

Take the risk. He knew what he had to do.

And so, he went to call on Mr. Van Allen with a diamond ring in his pocket.

177 Fifth Avenue

Mr. Van Allen, a short but distinguished man of advancing years, stood when Kingston entered his library, a wood-paneled situation with soaring ceilings, designed to look like the studies in English country houses like his own. The difference was that everything here was new and lacked the patina of dust and the air of centuries of intimidating people.

"Your Grace."

"I've come to discuss something with you, sir. A proposal, in a manner of speaking,"

Kingston said, lowering himself into one of the chairs in front of his desk.

"It's about time. My wife has already started planning the wedding, according to these bills here. But I don't see a ring on my daughter's finger."

Kingston removed the velvet box from his pocket, opened it, and set it down on Van Allen's desk. The diamonds and sapphires sparkled brilliantly. The stones alone made a valuable piece. That it had been in the possession of dukes and duchesses for generations conferred even more value upon it.

"A Kingston family heirloom. Dating back hundreds of years. All the duchesses ever since then have worn it."

"Your intentions are quite . . . clear."

"My intentions in coming to Manhattan have always been clear: I need a fortune. I had thought to obtain it in the traditional way, by marriage. But I have been made aware of other ways of doing so."

"Interesting. Keep talking."

"I could give this ring to your daughter. I could wed her and I would be a kind, respectful husband to her. But I do not love her." Kingston paused. Because one paused at the moment their life was about to take an unexpected turn. "Or, I could sell this ring and invest the proceeds in your newest real-estate project. I've heard it said that Manhattan real estate is a sound investment."

Van Allen's eyes flashed.

As a rule, a member of the aristocracy did not engage in trade.

A man of his position did not sully his hands or leisure time with matters of money, unless it was to spend it. One could argue that this did indeed count as merely spending money in his leisure time. One could twist and fashion the facts to fit the very narrowly defined existence he had been raised to expect and perpetuate.

Or . . .

Change the world, Duke.

The world was changing with or without him. Kingston could stubbornly cling to the old way of doing things, calling it tradition, calling it noble, calling it his sacred, honorable duty. But if he took his duty to steward the dukedom for another generation seriously, he would have to change how he would do it.

One could not expect old methods to work in a new world.

Kingston leaned back in his chair, his pose deliberately one of ease, which was highly at odds with the internal turmoil he was experiencing. Risking your past and future all at once, for the love of a woman who refused you, would make a man's heart beat a little faster.

Mr. Van Allen leaned back in his chair, a thoughtful expression on his face but a note of challenge in his voice. "The question is, which one will give you a better return on your investment? My daughter's dowry is significant. My own wealth is astronomical. I have no other children. Apparently, I will not live forever."

"And tell me, Mr. Van Allen, how do you value happiness?"

"Money makes me happy."

"But in your calculations, do you not account for the quality of one's company at the breakfast table, the pleasures of the marriage bed, the joys of mutual respect, admiration, and love of one's spouse?"

Van Allen's eyes narrowed. "I thought we were talking about business."

"We are talking about the return on investment. I wager that if I invest the value of this ring in your real-estate venture, I will be rich and happy. As opposed to marriage to your daughter, in which I will be rich and content. Surely happiness is worth more than mere contentment."

"The venture could fail."

"You could die penniless."

"You could have it all," Mr. Van Allen said.

"That depends on your definition of *all*."

"This is not what I had expected from a man of your position."

"I could say the same. I had thought you and the other robber barons cared about money above all else. Not something as old-fashioned as a title in the family. Are bragging rights that your grandson will be a duke worth more to you than the profits you would earn from the success of your new building projects? Or what of your own daughter's happiness?"

Kingston now knew that he could not respect himself if he did not take seriously his duty to care and provide for those who depended upon him. But perhaps he did not have to sacrifice the love of his life to do so.

CHAPTER TWENTY-SIX

The Dress to Ditch a Duke?

Anyone who is anyone in New York City now orders her gowns from the House of Adeline, dressmaker of the moment. Those pockets! Even the Duke of Kingston cannot resist the stylings of his longtime friend. He was seen calling after her as she fled the Carlyle Masquerade. Imagine that! Fleeing a duke! It is one thing to design a gown to snare the town's most eligible bachelor, quite another to design the dress to wear when ditching the duke.

— *The New York World*

It was the question mark that made her nervous. If the paper had printed *The Dress to Ditch a Duke!* she would be safe. That exclamation point would emphatically deny any connection with His Grace. But that

369

question mark lingered and made improper suggestions that Adeline did not care for.

Mrs. Van Allen did not care for them either.

She arrived at the shop with fire in her eyes and purpose in her step.

"Mrs. Black."

"Mrs. Van Allen. How may I assist you today?"

Adeline was not precisely in the mood to design a gown for her to wear to the betrothal ball or the wedding itself. One was never quite in the mood for that.

"I am not here for a dress. I would like a word."

"Is something wrong with the gown for Miss Van Allen?"

"The gown is fine. It is the occasion to wear the gown that is proving to be problematic."

The bell on the shop door rang softly and two women entered the shop. It was all the reason Adeline needed to escort Mrs. Van Allen into a fitting room, where they might have some privacy to speak freely.

"My daughter was going to be a duchess. Until you intervened."

"I'm sorry, Mrs. Van Allen, but I don't understand."

"He will not be proposing after all."

It was difficult to form words when one could not even manage a coherent thought. *What the devil was he doing?* He needed Miss Van Allen. Adeline couldn't give him what he needed and would not, especially after he had questioned her integrity.

He was a duke both in want of a fortune *and* a wife, and so to let it be known that he would not be proposing made no sense at all.

"I'm so sorry, Mrs. Van Allen, but I have no idea what this is about."

Mrs. Van Allen narrowed her eyes. "But I think you do."

She was definitely not here for a dress. This would not be a fitting, it would be a dressing-down of possibly epic proportions.

"My daughter's future was secured until you seduced him and bewitched him."

"Enchanted him," Adeline whispered under her breath, so quietly that no one could hear. But she had left. Returned his letters unopened. They had no future together.

"Do you know what it is like to want security for your daughter? Mothers will do anything to ensure their daughters are secure."

"I know," Adeline whispered, thinking of her own mother and all the men she endured for the sake of her daughter. All so that Adeline might have a roof over her head and food in her belly. She had sacrificed herself for her little girl. Adeline understood all that now.

"Between her father's fortune and the duke's social standing, my daughter would never have wanted for anything. She would always move in the best circles and live in the best circumstances. I did that when I married her father instead of . . . never mind. And when I encouraged her and the duke, I — we — were close to success. Security. And now, we are not."

"I'm sorry, but I don't understand. I thought he was going to propose."

"So did I. And then he was seen running after you."

That damned newspaper. That damned question mark!

"Do you see a ring on my finger?" Adeline held out her hands: her working-girl hands, no matter how successful her dressmaking enterprise became.

"Oh, he sold the ring," Mrs. Van Allen said with a bitter laugh that seemed to say *foolish girl*. "He has some notion of investing the proceeds. He's going to take his chance on investments."

Oh? *He wouldn't be proposing.*

Oh! *He would be investing!*

Oh . . . Adeline understood perfectly. He was risking his past for his future, in a thoroughly modern way.

He was taking a chance so that he could marry for love.

He was taking this risk for her.

"Oh my goodness," she whispered.

"Do you know how that looks for my daughter? They were practically betrothed and suddenly he's risking his family legacy on some real-estate ventures rather than wed my beautiful girl. She'll never find another match now."

"Your daughter is loveliness personified. I'm certain she'll find someone. Perhaps it may even be a love match, with someone who shares her passions for the birds."

Mrs. Van Allen was not interested in that possibility. "Oh no, you have ruined everything for her with your beguiling gowns and your seduction of the duke. Do not deny it, Mrs. Black. I have seen the way he looks at you. And I have spoken to Madame Chalfont, my preferred dressmaker. Apparently you and the duke have been carrying on for some time."

"It's not what you think —"

"Oh, it doesn't matter what I think or what it actually is. But Madame Chalfont and I will ensure that every society woman considers you a risk to their marriages or to their suitors. And who wishes to have their dressmaker steal their spouse or suitor? No one. No woman you care to dress. And so I will see that you pay for this."

And with that, she was gone.

Adeline sank to the floor.

All it would take were a few well-placed rumors making suggestions about the nature of her relationship with the duke and a few questions about her character. It would make her seem unsavory, unseemly — all noxious qualities which would transfer to the distinctive designs of her dresses. Her gowns would not be worn. Her business would fail. She would go back to simply cutting and sewing for someone else, all the while muttering, *And to think, I could have been a duchess!*

Adeline had to do something. She had fought too hard, overcome too much, and come too far to let her dreams be wrecked with a few well-placed rumors. Too many good women relied upon her now and too many daring women had gone out on a limb for her. She would sacrifice everything before she ruined things for her sisterhood.

She could not burden her seamstresses with matters like this. She could not destroy

Rose's faith in love, confirm Rachel's worst suspicions, or leave Margaret and her baby at the mercy of bad men.

When another letter from the duke arrived, she knew exactly what to do.

To my enchanting New York City girl,

I have seen all the sights Manhattan has to offer and the only one I want to see again is you. Would you do me the honor of joining me for a walk in Central Park?

— Kingston

CHAPTER TWENTY-SEVEN

One knows not what to make of
the new trend of marriage proposals
in Central Park.
— *The New York World*

A short while later
Central Park

Kingston waited at the entrance to the park, the one on Fifty-ninth Street and Fifth Avenue where he had previously waited on Adeline once upon a time. He felt the same nervous energy coursing through him; it was the way one felt when they knew their life was about to change. Forever.

He had written her letters that at first had returned unopened. When she finally replied agreeing to see him, hope sparked. This was his chance to make a grand demonstration of his love, to humble himself before her, to grovel, to sweep her off her feet, all at once. It was his chance to prove that he was the man for her, that she was the woman for him, and that they could be happy together. Forever.

He looked up, and there she was, strolling purposely toward him in another one of her stunning creations — a deep blue dress, simple, elegant, fitted to perfection. He dared to think, *My future duchess.*

If he was lucky.

If his groveling apology was sufficient to make her forgive him for the grievous insult to her integrity and ingenuity. If love was enough, she would be his wife. She was here and that gave him hope.

"Hello, Duke."

"You're here. I'm glad. I didn't think we were finished," he said. She gave him a weak smile that made him nervous but he ignored the feeling. This was right. She was here — why would she have come if not to say yes?

So he took her hand in his and they walked into the park, favoring one of the shaded paths, until they came to a particularly picturesque spot. People relaxed on benches, children played games on the grass, and a string quartet he'd hired played enchanting songs, just to make the moment more romantic.

He turned to face her and gazed down at her upturned face. Yes, hers was definitely the face he wanted to see each night before sleep and each morning at the breakfast table. Forever.

His heart was pounding as he held her hands and hoped he spoke the right words.

"Adeline, I owe you an apology. I am sorry for insulting your honor and your ingenuity when what I truly feel is admiration for you and your accomplishments. I want to know you, Adeline. If I want to know all your secrets, it is because you are endlessly fascinating and enchanting to me. But I can live with mystery; it's you that I cannot live without."

"Oh, Kingston . . ."

"There is something else I must ask you."

Kingston was aware of people watching them; a young couple holding hands, attentions fixed on each other could only mean one thing. A public proposal.

"Kingston, I have something to ask you as well."

"Will you marry" — he started.

"Will you marry" — she started at the same time.

"Me," he said.

"Miss Van Allen," she said in a rush. "Will you marry Miss Van Allen? It's the only way to fix everything."

"I beg your pardon?"

"Will you marry Miss Van Allen?"

Would he marry Miss Van Allen?

Kingston rubbed his jaw. Pushed his fingers through his hair. He was a bloody duke. One who was easy on the eyes and who knew how to bring her to dizzying heights of pleasure. He was a man who examined his entire life's plans and centuries of tradition, because a woman challenged him to be better. Any woman should want to wed him. Or at the very least entertain his proposal.

Not request that he marry someone else entirely.

Why was this so damned hard?!

"Adeline —"

"Mrs. Van Allen and Madame Chalfont will ruin me otherwise," she said, her voice cracking. He tried to make his heart start beating again, make his lungs draw breath, make his brain work. *She was asking him to marry a woman he didn't love.* "Mrs. Van Allen is determined to ruin me; she believes I have ruined her daughter's prospects with you."

It was not entirely untrue.

"She has a willing ally in Madame Chalfont."

Who previously fired Adeline because of him.

"Ladies and their dressmakers . . . talk."

This was also true. They had capitalized upon it.

"Women will not wish to frequent my establishment if there is unsavory gossip about me and you. And especially if it suggests that I would steal their intended."

This was, unfortunately, the way of the world.

Change the world, Duke.

Everything she said made painfully perfect sense. His urge to protect her, to save her, warred with his desire to be with her. Either way they won. Either way they lost.

"I need you to believe me, Kingston. I obtained the money for my shop by honorable means, but I have been sworn to secrecy. Even if I hadn't, what does it matter? The lives of good women whom I employ depend upon the shop's success. They are women who would have no other opportunities for an honorable and dignified life. And I *like* them. I am ready to sacrifice my happiness for theirs. If you care for me at all, you will do this for me."

Kingston did believe her. Adeline had never disassembled and had never given him reason to doubt her word. He also loved her wholly and completely. As such, he knew that, had she entered into a liaison with Freddie or any man to achieve her dreams, he could not stop loving her. It would be a part of her and he loved all of her.

It was that simple.

And yet . . .

"Adeline. You do realize that you are asking me to sacrifice my happiness as well. I cannot help but think that if you loved me, you would never ask this of me."

"What do you mean?"

He sighed and pulled the ring box out of his jacket pocket, opened it and presented her with an empty box. It was all part of the romantic proposal that was going horribly, horribly wrong. The musicians were still playing. People were watching them, murmuring as they anxiously awaited a kiss or some other signal that she had said *yes.*

Adeline looked up at him with her dark eyes full of questions.

"The ring in this box has been worn by generations of Kingston duchesses. I have sold it. I have taken the proceeds and invested it in Mr. Van Allen's real-estate project. I am making arrangements to sell other things of value — smaller estates, works of art — so that I can invest them in other businesses. This is me symbolically trading the traditions of my past for the opportunities of the future. One that I had hoped we would share. I love you, Adeline. You have opened my eyes to a love and life that I have never thought possible. I may not be able to change the world, but with this ring I had hoped I could change the course of our lives so that we can marry for love. At least, that was the speech I was going to make. That was the question I was going to ask. But you wish otherwise."

You don't love me. She didn't need to tell him in words, he understood.

She pulled a delicately embroidered lace handkerchief out of her pocket and dabbed at the tears welling up in her eyes. *What does a woman need pockets for?* For when they needed handkerchiefs because men made them cry, obviously.

He had imagined her saying *yes.*

He had not imagined this painful, extended silence. When she didn't speak for the longest time — a painfully long time — he closed the box. A stupid, empty box for a stupid, empty gesture that was too little, too late.

He put it back in his pocket.

"I have booked passage back to England. My ship leaves on Tuesday. If you change your mind. If not . . ." Kingston did not have the words for a moment like this. A moment when he dared to say *something* of his feelings, when he dared to be something of the man he thought she wanted him to be. He was too aware of people watching them. He was too aware of the seconds and minutes passing. He was painfully aware that she didn't say yes. She didn't even say anything at all.

Eventually, he had to walk away. The musicians still played.

Just once he turned around and saw — in Central Park she sat down and cried.

CHAPTER TWENTY-EIGHT

No one saw this coming: that a
handsome, charming duke would
fail to make a match with one of
New York's dollar princesses. Or,
indeed, any woman, if his failed
proposal in Central Park is any indication.
His ship departs this afternoon.
— *The New York World*

Tuesday afternoon
The Fifth Avenue Hotel

His ship was leaving at four o'clock this
afternoon. His valet had already boarded,
along with the duchess, his sisters, and all
of their luggage. Dozens upon dozens of
trunks stuffed with gowns, hats, trinkets,
and the finest Saville Row tailoring had all
been carefully packed up and transported
from the hotel to the docks to their suite of
rooms on the ship.

Kingston had declined Mrs. Whitney's

invitation to a ball and refused Freddie's invitation for goodbye drinks at the club. They would be partners in crime no more. Instead, Kingston spent the previous evening walking aimlessly through the streets of New York, drinking in the sights, sounds, and lamentable smells; half hoping that he might turn a corner and run into Adeline. He spent the night alone. It was not how he ever imagined his last night in New York.

Now he was taking tea with Miss Harriet Burnett, the actual girl next door to his suite at the Fifth Avenue Hotel. It was the last thing he would do in New York. She was the last person he would see.

She had issued the invitation.

He had no reason to refuse.

And so they took tea in the restaurant adjacent to the lobby.

"Isn't it interesting how in some circumstances, being seen with a man can wreck a woman's reputation but in other circumstances, it can only enhance it?" Miss Burnett remarked, apropos of nothing, as she sipped her tea. "For example, if we were waltzing, I would be deemed more desirable because you took an interest in me. But if I were seen leaving your hotel rooms . . ."

She did not need to finish the sentence.

"Circumstances."

"If I am seen taking tea with you, people will think I am vying for your hand in marriage. When in fact, I have no such intentions. If anything, I am trying to get you to wed another."

He'd really had enough of women trying to marry him off to other women.

"Isn't it a tad late for matchmaking? My ship leaves in a little over an hour."

"Oh, it's never too late for matchmaking," Miss Burnett replied, as if they had all the time in the world together, when in fact, he urgently needed to get down to the docks.

"I have decided that I will marry only for love," he said.

"What about your needs for an heiress and a fortune?"

"I am taking my chances with investments."

She lifted her brow. "Is that so? How modern of you. Did you know that I also make investments?"

He raised one eyebrow, curious in spite of himself. "I'm not the only one. Hetty Green, for example, has made a veritable fortune on the stock market. I have taken a different track. For example, I invested some of my money in a dressmaking operation."

Kingston straightened. Suddenly, Miss Burnett had his full, undivided attention. She knew it, judging by the smile on her lips and the sparkle in her gray eyes. She continued.

"Isn't it such a sad commentary on the world that no one would think a woman had the funds, or interest or simple wherewithal to support her fellow womankind?"

"It is positively tragic," he said, finally understanding fully. Why had he not seen this sooner? Why had not it occurred to him that a woman might have the means and inclination to help her fellow womankind? For whatever reasons, Adeline hadn't been able to tell him this. But she shouldn't have had to.

"It is sad and stupid and leads to hideous misunderstandings," he said. "But what is a man to do?"

"One would think an apology is a good start."

"At length. Repeatedly. I have tried that course of action."

Miss Burnett pursed her lips. "My investment will soon be for naught, given some gossip that is about to spread like wildfire. All because a woman was seen with a duke in the wrong circumstances."

"Are you going to ask me to wed Miss Van

Allen as well? I thought I was clear that I shall marry only for love, or not at all."

Miss Burnett dismissed him with a wave of her hand.

"I am suggesting that you wed Miss Black."

"I proposed. She refused. My ship leaves in an hour."

"Well, no wonder. If that is the extent of your love, then I shall have to proceed with my secondary plan."

"And what is that?"

"I should hate for you to find out. It would mean you do not marry the woman you love."

"Do I not get a say in the matter?"

"You can have all the 'say' you want, but I think it's a conversation best had with Miss Black, don't you think? I would think a dramatic declaration of your undying love would be the thing to do. Which you would know if you read dime novels."

He glanced at the clock. He would have to leave shortly — within the next few seconds — if he had a prayer of getting to his ship before it sailed without him. If he took the time to propose *again* he could very well find himself refused, *again,* and stranded on this island while a ship with all his luggage was out on the Atlantic, enroute to England.

"If you'll excuse me, I have a meeting to attend." Miss Burnett dabbed her lips with a napkin. She stood and smoothed her skirts. "I suppose you must go as well, if you are going to catch your ship."

And like that, she was gone.

Kingston remained seated with his gaze fixed firmly on the clock. It was a quarter of an hour before three o'clock.

If he left now . . .

He could catch his ship. He could sail back to England with his family and proceed with the plan he had concocted that involved sales and investments and business plans. He would have made some point about being the master of his own fate. He would have allowed Adeline and himself to sacrifice their happiness for others, without ever considering a secondary plan.

If he left now, he would have left the woman he loved to fend for herself against the gossips of the world. He would be leaving her to fight her battles alone, which she was fully capable of doing, but she shouldn't have to. She should fight her battles with true love on her side.

Chapter Twenty-Nine

At a recent meeting of the Audubon
Society in Central Park, Miss Van Allen
made a great show of releasing birds
from gilded cages. She kept the key to
their cages in the pocket of her dress.
— *The New York World*

The Ladies of Liberty Club
25 West Tenth Street
The duke would be leaving Manhattan at
four o'clock this afternoon and returning to
England. This was quite possibly one of the
least important things that was happening
today; nevertheless, it was the thing that occupied Adeline's thoughts the most. It was
not every day that a dashing duke sailed out
of one's life, bound for another continent.

Tuesday, that's when.

Tuesday was also the day that the Ladies
of Liberty club took their callers and today
Adeline had NEWS. Such good news that it

merited all capital letters. News that she was eager to share.

It was just such a pity that her day of triumph should be marred by the agonies of heartache and quite possibly regret. Seated among her fellow members of the Ladies of Liberty club, she sipped her tea and allowed one small sigh.

"How fares our favorite dressmaker's establishment?" Miss Burnett inquired.

Adeline took a deep breath. "I have all sorts of good news to share. To start, I shall be able to return *all* the funds invested in me and the shop."

The ladies burst into applause and good wishes and Adeline felt her cheeks flush with pride.

Lord Hewitt had come through to pay his outstanding bill for Lady Marian's extensive wardrobe and that — along with all her other clients — had meant she'd earned enough to repay the club's loan, with interest. It meant that everything she earned now was hers. It gave her a bone-deep satisfaction that she had never imagined.

But it brought another feeling, too: an awareness that it was *hers* and it was her honor and duty to nurture and protect it at all costs. She imagined this might be how Kingston felt about his dukedom, and this made her acutely aware of what he had risked to propose to her.

"There is more," Adeline continued. "Margaret has had her baby, a healthy girl. Both mother and child are doing well. We are holding a position for Margaret, but even so I still have more positions to fill if we should learn of any young ladies in distress."

"That is so good to hear, as unfortunately there are always more women who need the help and the opportunity of a decent position."

It was her duty and honor to help whatever young women she could. Especially when she might soon be one of those ladies in distress, if Mrs. Van Allen and Madame Chalfont had their way.

"That is all splendid news! Congratulations to you, Miss Black."

"I must thank you all for the opportunity."

The ladies applauded again and that only made it more difficult for her to share the rest of the news.

The BAD NEWS.

So bad that it merited all capital letters. Adeline glanced nervously at Miss Burnett; they had spoken privately about this yesterday. It only seemed fair that her benefactor, fairy godmother, guardian angel — whatever one might call her — knew the desperate situation in which Adeline found herself.

She was on the verge of utter ruin.

And in the depths of utter despair.

"There is just one pesky matter," Adeline said. "And by pesky I mean completely and utterly catastrophic. I fear it shall destroy everything."

The ladies of the club erupted in murmurs.

"How dreadfully intriguing!"

"Do tell!"

"Mrs. Van Allen feels that I have ruined her daughter's prospects with the Duke of Kingston." There was no need to explain more; these women all read the newspapers and were well informed. "My former employer feels I have wronged her by leaving to establish my own shop and by taking her clients."

Miss Burnett frowned and sipped her tea and glanced at the clock on the mantel.

"They are conspiring to ruin my reputation. I fear women will not want to be attired by a dressmaker of ill repute. I have done my best to stop the gossip, but I'm afraid my initial plan failed and I am at a loss as to how to save my shop."

"What did you do?"

"Something very reasonable. I asked the

duke to marry Miss Van Allen. It was the perfect plan. We all know that he had intended to wed her anyway. The marriage would please Mrs. Van Allen, which would prevent her from attempting to destroy my shop — and ruining the livelihoods of the women I employ."

"That *is* a perfect plan —"

"If one isn't in love with him herself."

"And how would that have addressed the concerns of your former employer?"

"I had hoped that she would have less cause for anger or at the very least that she would not have Mrs. Van Allen fueling it," Adeline explained.

"The plan does make sense."

"What went wrong?"

"What went wrong? The duke has a mind of his own and a notion of following his heart," Adeline said. Her voice cracked. How embarrassing. "Just as I asked him to marry Miss Van Allen, he proposed to me instead."

Adeline could almost still feel the warmth of the sunshine on her shoulders, could almost still hear the sweet song of the string quartet, though it was growing faint in her memory. What she remembered with heart-stopping clarity was the look of crushing disappointment on Kingston's face. She had hurt him. She had made a mistake. Her best intentions were wrong.

"The duke proposed to you?" Miss Parks asked.

"In Central Park. Musicians were playing, people were picnicking and watching us." Adeline confirmed. Her heart sank a little more at the memory. How humiliating it must have been for him. Yet, he had known she was not inclined to marriage and arranged the proposal anyway, which again demonstrated how much he was willing to risk for her. For their love. For their everlasting happiness.

Someone in the room sighed.

Adeline glanced at the clock. The minute hand continued with its steady march around, making reliable progress toward four o'clock. His ship might not yet have sailed, but her opportunity to tell him *yes* was long gone.

"It doesn't matter. I have refused his proposal."

"You refused the duke?"

Someone in the room took a sip of tea and sputtered and another woman choked on a crumpet.

"The tall, dark, handsome duke prone to displays of heroics who also staged a romantic public proposal in Central Park?"

"I cannot even believe it."

"Pity that gossip doesn't quite stick to a duchess in quite the same way," Miss Parks replied breezily and Adeline thought . . . *Wait.*

"But duchesses aren't dressmakers," another woman replied. And Adeline thought, *Yes, that!*

"Yes, and women aren't usually doctors, but times are changing," said Phoebe Jane Babcock, a doctor. Then, with a pointed look at each woman in the room, she said, "All it takes is one brave woman to set a precedent and to open people's eyes to the possibilities."

"But people, good people, are counting on him to marry an heiress," Adeline explained. "He is indebted. There is some problem with the roof."

"People are counting on him to provide, yes," Miss Burnett said. "But there are other ways than marriage. Your duke is — or was, until very, very recently — extremely old-fashioned. One might invest in businesses or start one's own. One might economize. My point is that he has options, whether he chooses to see them or not."

"Besides, you might soon have a fortune of your own, Adeline," Miss Lumley pointed out. "If your shop continues its current trajectory of success. Dare to consider that *you* might save *him.*"

The thought had never even crossed Adeline's mind. For, as Dr. Babcock said, who had gone before her to set the precedent and open her eyes to the opportunities? What seamstress had ever saved a duke before? Not one she knew.

"But I'm just some girl from the tenements . . ."

"You are not *just some girl* from the tenements," Miss Burnett said sharply. "You are a woman with admirable ambition who dares to follow her dreams and supports her fellow womankind while doing so. You might be a woman from the tenements, Adeline, but you are not just some girl."

Handkerchiefs. Pockets were excellent for keeping handkerchiefs on hand, which was proving to be very necessary lately.

One by one, the ladies of the club punctured Adeline's reasons for refusing the duke and exposed them as the excuses that they were.

"What are you afraid of, Adeline?" It was Miss Lumley who gently asked the question that got to the heart of the matter.

"I am afraid of losing my independence. I am afraid of disappointing everyone who is counting on me. I am afraid of giving up my dreams."

It occurred to Adeline as she spoke, that she and the duke were not in very different positions at all. But he had sought and found a way that allowed them to be together without requiring him to sacrifice what mattered to him. It just may have looked a little different from how he had imagined it.

But Adeline was still struggling with the weight of her past, the things she had seen her mother endure, the things she was determined to avoid at all costs.

"It's like Miss Goldman said at that speech," Adeline said. "Marriage and love are incompatible. She said marriage makes a woman a parasite and absolutely dependent. I have seen my mother —"

"Miss Goldman says that is true when a woman marries *only* for financial support, as the world so often compels women to do," Miss Burnett answered. "But a woman like you, with means of her own, has the liberty to marry for love. So the only question to consider is this: Do you love the duke?"

That was the question.

Did she love him? Yes, of course. Completely, wholly. That was never in question.

Could she believe that a man like him

loved a girl like her — just some girl from the tenements? Whether mere seamstress or esteemed dressmaker, she had seen the way he looked at her with love and lust shining in his eyes. She knew the way he spoke to her, the way he touched her. Yes, he loved the girl she was and the woman she was becoming.

Now that she thought about it, the question was not if she loved him, but if she was willing to take the greatest risk of her life on love. Would she let her fears hold her back from a lifetime of happiness?

Was she a coward?

She had never thought of herself as a coward.

She was just a girl from the tenements who had gotten herself *here,* taking tea with the finest, most powerful ladies she'd ever known. All because she had courage, seized opportunities, and took the risk every time. So why on earth would she not reach out for this dream — of a life full of love — with both hands?

Just as Adeline was ready to leap to her feet and dash out the door — she had to find him! Stop him from leaving! — the clock struck four o'clock.

Four aching blows to her heart.

It had been widely reported that his ship

would be leaving at four o'clock.

Today. Tuesday.

"It doesn't matter now. It is too late. His ship is departing now," Adeline said numbly. Glumly. Dumbly. Gone.

She pictured him standing on deck, the wind tousling his hair as he watched the Manhattan skyline get smaller and smaller until the ship sailed well out of view and true love sailed out of her life forever, because of the one time she had doubted herself and questioned love.

"Pity that. I would have enjoyed a romantic scene."

"Oh yes," another woman gushed. "Where he strides in, sweeps her off her feet . . ."

"And a good, groveling speech. Anything can be forgiven with a good grovel," Miss Neville said.

"I thought this was a business club," Adeline said, perplexed at all this talk of love and romance. "A placement agency, of sorts."

"It is, of course. But why should a woman have to choose between love and professional success?" Miss Lumley said. "Between marriage and work. Business and pleasure. Why can a woman not have both?"

"Have we not told you our motto?" Miss Burnett asked, smiling. "Love, liberty and happily ever after."

Meanwhile . . .

Kingston dashed out of the hotel. There was no time to lose. He sprinted down Fifth Avenue, not caring at all about the scene he was inevitably causing as he twisted and turned around slow-moving pedestrians and leapt out of the way of oncoming carriages.

His heart was pounding hard in his chest. It was not merely because of the exertions.

It was something a man's heart did when he was about to take the risk of a lifetime. Again.

Kingston burst through the shop doors.

"Where is she?" he asked, out of breath. A few well-dressed women stared at him and began whispering. A shop girl he did not recognize came forward and meekly asked how she might assist him.

He strolled to the back of the shop, to the workroom.

"Where is she?" he asked again, to Adeline's entire staff. "And do not get cheeky and ask which 'she' I'm asking about."

"We wouldn't dream of it," Rachel replied.

"How can we help you?" Rose asked.

"Where is Adeline? I need to speak with Adeline."

"She just left."

"You just missed her."

He swore. "Where did she go?"

They, the lot of them, hesitated. Hesitated!

"Rose," he said, turning to the one he knew to be the most inclined in his favor. "You are an avid reader of dime novels and true love conquering all. You wouldn't deny a dashing hero an opportunity for a dramatic, romantic scene, will you?"

"Oh you think you're dashing, do you?" Rachel scoffed.

"There's no time to argue the point," he replied.

"We could put it to a vote," volunteered a woman he didn't recognize.

"Based on looks alone, or should we request a romantic speech?"

While the women were debating, a squawk emerged from a corner of the room. Kingston watched as a woman set aside her embroidery work to tend to a newborn baby. Nearby an older woman with old hands and stiff fingers turned to help the new mother.

He thought she couldn't possibly do much sewing work with hands like that and yet Adeline employed her anyway. It was then that Kingston took a moment to look around the shop and see, really see: the women all wore a similar uniform of dark gray skirt and crisp white shirtwaist but beyond that were all so different — different colors of their skin, ages, backgrounds. He detected different accents as they debated whether or not to enlighten him as to Adeline's whereabouts.

He had no basis of comparison, but Kingston suspected that it was these women — these unlikely to be otherwise employed women — that she was protecting as much as her own dreams.

"She wants me to marry Miss Van Allen because she has some notion of protecting you all. Not because she is selfish." He said this aloud for the first time and truly understood it. "She refused me not because she doesn't love me."

"Not just a pretty face, are you?" the old woman said with a grin. "You have the right of it."

Kingston began to pace about the bemused women, the tables covered with patterns and expensive fabrics and the mannequins draped in muslin.

"There must be a way so that we can marry for love without sacrificing our duties to those who rely upon us."

"If there is, you should probably discuss it with Adeline first," Rose said.

"I would like to. I would very, very much like to."

It was Rachel who finally gave him the address.

25 West Tenth Street

Adeline was ready to rush to the docks and book passage to England when any thought or action was interrupted by a heavy and incessant pounding at the front door.

"That doesn't sound like one of our usual lady callers."

"Has anyone misplaced an angry husband?"

"Open up!" a male voice called out. A British male voice. There were murmurs among the ladies until Adeline said, "I think he might be here for me."

"I don't suppose that is the lovelorn and jilted duke."

"Most likely," Adeline whispered. She couldn't manage more than that. He was here. Here!

"I nearby declare that this meeting of the Ladies of Liberty club is adjourned," Miss Burnett announced. "And the meeting of the Charitable Ladies Auxiliary Club shall commence."

With that, all the women wordlessly reached under their sofas, settees, and chairs to withdraw bibles and half-done samplers. Someone even pressed a sampler into Adeline's hands. It was a stroke of genius — any man who walked in and saw a coven of women stitching and embroidering and bible reading would think nothing of it, would ask no questions, and would take his leave as quickly as possible.

Except one.

The butler opened the doors and announced, "The Duke of Kingston would like an audience."

The duke strode into the room like every second counted and came to an abrupt stop when he saw the gathering of nearly twenty women seated in a makeshift circle, sipping tea and idly leafing through bibles. It was the very picture of simple, traditional domesticity.

Yet Adeline's heart was pounding.

"Good afternoon, Your Grace," Miss Burnett said, rising to greet him. His eyes narrowed. "I thought you had a ship to catch."

"My plans changed. And I thought you had a meeting."

"You are now present for it." She gestured to the women.

He nodded his head. He was confused, but still polite. "Good afternoon, ladies."

"To what do we owe the pleasure of your visit?" Miss Burnett asked. He scanned the room and finally, his gaze landed on her. Adeline's heart continued its heavy pounding in her breast. She was nervous. She was in love. She was curious and optimistic but also utterly terrified. She felt all these things intensely, and all at once.

"I'm here to see Miss Black," he said in that low voice of his that sent shivers up her spine.

"I'm here." She stood, in a rustle of silk and satin.

"We didn't have *romantic scene* on the list of topics for today's meeting, did we?" one woman murmured to another.

"I daresay we're about to witness one anyway."

Adeline watched as his attentions shifted from her to the rest of the women and back to her again. Perhaps he suspected something. He would certainly ask questions later. If they should be so lucky as to have a later. She glanced at Miss Burnett; she smiled and nodded *yes*. She had their blessing to pursue her love and to live honestly with the duke and perhaps one day she would tell him all about the secret ladies' society that made all her dreams come true.

Kingston stood before her, not saying a

word, leaving her on tenterhooks.

"What a small world," he said finally.

"How did you find me here?"

"It so happens that seamstresses are privy to ladies' secrets and occasionally prone to gossip."

And Adeline simply said, "Rose." Of course it was Rose, that eternally hopeful romantic, who would have directed him here.

"It was Rachel, actually," Kingston said, to the surprise of them both. If Rachel had been the one to direct him here, he must have given a very persuasive speech indeed. And that was another blessing of this match that Adeline had badly wanted. She had never wanted to marry and never wanted to sacrifice her independence. She was *terrified* to risk it. But she rather thought that she could take the risk with Kingston.

"What brings you here?"

He smiled like he smiled at her that first day. A rakish smile, his blue eyes sparkling.

"I must confess that I find you enchanting."

Someone in the room sighed. It wasn't her. But her breath definitely caught. She tilted her head and gave him a coy smile in return.

"Of course you do."

"I see that New York City girls are different from the ones in London."

"Oh, you haven't seen anything yet," more than one woman murmured. And more than one woman agreed.

Adeline knew her next line. Every moment of their first meeting written in her heart and permanently etched in her memory. Daydreaming about it endlessly will do that. She also knew that as soon as she said it, the course of her life would alter forever, in ways she had never imagined and probably could not even fathom. But she had the support of her friends and the love of a good man and she had faced more daunting challenges with less.

She took a deep breath.

"Well, I suppose I should ask, what brings you to New York?"

"I am here to get married," he told her.

"Congratulations," she said. "Well, I *suppose* congratulations are in order. Does your bride know that you are storming into women's groups unannounced to make dramatic and romantic scenes to a girl you find enchanting?"

Kingston took a step toward her. It was time to start closing the distance between them.

"Oh, it's too soon for felicitations," Kingston said.

"Have you not yet proposed?"

"Not exactly. Not properly. Not as befitting my future duchess."

"I suppose it's too soon for you to have met the right woman."

"I don't know that I'd say that . . ." Somewhere in the room a woman sighed. Or maybe it was Adeline. It was definitely a swoon-worthy moment. She wanted to leap into his arms and declare her undying love for him forever but she equally wanted to savor every second of this moment. It wasn't every day that the man she loved strolled into one's life and made devastatingly romantic speeches and proposals.

Tuesdays. That's when. Tuesdays.

"You might have to stay a little longer to meet someone," she told him.

"And what if I have met her already?" He lifted one brow in that dashing way that only dukes in novels seemed to do.

"There you go with the marriage proposals again," she said with a little laugh and quiver in her voice. She so meant to be teasing but was also just so happy.

"This time I mean it, Adeline." He dropped to one knee before her and clasped her hands with his. "Will you marry me?"

"This time, I'm saying yes."

Epilogue

The Duke of Kingston and his designing duchess are returning to New York City, where their love affair began, to celebrate the opening of her impressive new dressmaking establishment on Fifth Avenue.
> — *The New York World*

Ten years later

Adeline had discovered that all the best things came in threes. For example, there were all sorts of magical strings of just three words. To start: *I love you.* Adeline woke up to the duke murmuring these three words to her each day and they were the last three words she heard before drifting off to sleep beside him. She said those three words — *I love you* — constantly to their three children, two boys and a girl.

The duke had a different three-word phrase that he derived immense satisfaction from: *Return on Investment*. His bet on Mr. Van Allen's Manhattan real-estate project had proven to be a lucrative one, and his investments in those newfangled telephones and electric companies granted excellent returns as well. They even provided enough for the duke to buy back the duchess's ring, where it now graced her fourth finger, like all the duchesses of Kingston before her.

The various houses were sold or converted into new things — a hotel, a museum, a home for unwed mothers. There were moments when Kingston felt anguish over the changes he — and time — had wrought, such as when he stood in the library at Lyon House and looked out the window, as his father had loved to do, but instead of a pristine and unspoiled spread of nature, he saw railway tracks leading toward the station. But that change had provided generous dowries so that his sisters could marry for love, which they did. And so his mother could have all the dresses she wished for. She especially delighted in having a dressmaker for a daughter-in-law.

Another trio of words Adeline found particularly delicious were these: *London. Paris. New York*. Especially when they applied to her dressmaking establishments, one in each of the three great cities. It was a feat that she managed thanks to Rose and Rachel and other talented young women she trained to oversee the shops, where teams of misfit seamstresses crafted gorgeous gowns with pockets and beautiful dresses in which women felt they could go forth and conquer the world in pursuit of love, liberty, and happily ever after.

New York City. Those were another three words that never failed to thrill Adeline and the duke, as much as they enjoyed life in London and the English countryside.

So, when their ship was sailing into New York Harbor, Adeline was on deck to watch the impressive skyline rise up out of the mist. It was different, bigger, grander every time she saw it.

"It's your favorite sight in the world, isn't it?" Kingston murmured in her ear, closing his arms around her. She leaned back against his still firm, well-muscled chest clad in the finest cashmere wool, expertly tailored.

"My second favorite. Perhaps even my third favorite."

"What could possibly be more enchanting?"

"The sight of our children sleeping," she said and he laughed. They were tucked in their beds now. "And the sight of you."

She turned to face him and her beloved husband lowered his mouth to hers for a kiss, with New York City in the distance. When did a girl experience pure bliss and happily ever after? Tuesdays, that's when. And all the other days, too.

AUTHOR'S NOTE

My guiding principle as a novelist has always been to write the books that I want to read, and *Duchess by Design* is no exception. As someone who adores historical romance and my hometown of Manhattan, it was inevitable that I write a romance set in historical New York. I chose the Gilded Age because it had the glittering parties, pretty dresses, outrageous fortunes, and high society that so many of us love in a classic Regency romance. But it was also a time when so many people were fighting for things we have long taken for granted — the right to vote, the right to an eight-hour workday, and the protection of the environment, among other important causes. It's also the perfect time period for the heroines and heroes with fierce activist spirits that I want to write happy ever afters for.

Some notes on the history in this novel . . .

The Ladies of Liberty club is modeled on

The Sorosis Society, a women's club founded in 1868 by Jane Cunningham Croly after women were barred from a New York Press Club dinner. According to *The New York Times* this club "inaugurated and epitomized the women's club movement and was itself one of the most influential organizations for women in late nineteenth-century America." Their purpose was to further the educational and social opportunities of women. The members included activists, writers, female physicians and ministers, a fashion magazine editor, businesswomen, and even Emily Warren Roebling, the woman who oversaw the construction of the Brooklyn Bridge. While Sorosis membership tended to be upper-class white women, I have made the choice to diversify my fictional ladies club with the inclusion of the real-life African-American millionaire businesswoman, Madam C. J. Walker (she has an amazing story — look it up!).

On Dukes and dollar princesses: This was a real trend. The most notable example is the Duke of Marlborough's marriage to Consuelo Vanderbilt in 1895 (it was definitely *not* a love match). But there were many, many others. For further reading, I suggest *To Marry An English Lord: Tales of*

Wealth and Marriage, Sex and Snobbery, by Gail MacColl and Carol McD. Wallace.

On pockets: I did not entirely fabricate the drama around pockets in a woman's dress. Of course pockets, or something like it, had long existed. There was definitely discussion around the inclusion of them in women's dress — the chapter epigraph about pockets from *The New York Times* is real and dates from 1899. The rational dress movement was real, as progressive women recognized that respectable female attire physically limited their ability to move around the world. Interestingly, it was the bicycle that really changed women's fashions (but that's another story for another day!).

Miss Van Allen's advocacy for birds and feather-free fashion was inspired by the real-life women who were outraged by the slaughter of birds for the millinery trade and who campaigned to end the use of feathers in fashion in order to protect dwindling bird species. The first such organization, The Massachusetts Audubon Society, was formed in 1896, so I have taken a slight liberty with the dates. Many other Audubon Societies followed, and together they achieved passage of the 1918 Migratory Bird Treaty Act. Interestingly, some scholars have noted that the trend toward short hair for women did more to end the trend of large feathered hats than anything else.

On Free Love: The speech Adeline attends in Union Square draws directly from the work and words of real-life activist Emma Goldman. As a young woman, Emma reportedly left home with her sewing machine in one hand and five dollars in the other and made her way to New York City. (As one does.) In the 1890s, this anarchist, activist, speaker, and champion of women's economic freedom was living and working on New York City's Lower East Side as a nurse and midwife. In the speech she delivers in my novel, I took the liberty of quoting from her essay "Marriage and Love," even though it was published in 1914, since it is likely she spoke about these ideas earlier. The radical notion of "free love" (essentially that relationships should be based on love, not on economic or legal reasons) dates back to a particularly scandalous 1871 speech by Victoria Woodhull, so the concept would have been known in 1895. I should also note that the epigraph that starts that chapter is taken from real-life daring girl reporter Nelly Bly's interview with Emma Goldman for the *The New York World*.

All other *New York World* snippets I made up.

For more on my research, inspiration, and further reading, visit me online at www.mayarodale.com

ACKNOWLEDGMENTS

This book would not be possible without my personal village: Tony, Mom, Eve, Lucia, Lou, Helen, Jonathan, Gigi, Sarah, Nathaly, and Antonia. And my professional village: Tessa, Jessica, Pam, and the team at Avon Books. Special shout-out to Rose L for her advice. And especially my Lady Authors, Caroline and Katherine, who answered my panicked phone call and plotted this novel with me. Thank you all!

ABOUT THE AUTHOR

Maya Rodale began reading romance novels in college at her mother's insistence. She is now the bestselling and award-winning author of smart and sassy romances. She lives in New York City with her darling dog and a rogue of her own.